MANNEQUIN
GIRL

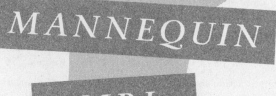

MANNEQUIN

GIRL

A Novel

Ellen Litman

W. W. NORTON & COMPANY

NEW YORK   LONDON

This is a work of fiction. Names, characters, places, and incidents either are the product of the author's imagination or are used fictitiously. Any resemblance to actual persons or business establishments is entirely coincidental.

The play in Part II of the novel is inspired by *The Last Days* by Mikhail Bulgakov. The play in Part III is adapted from a short story: "The Same Old Dream..." by Dina Rubina.

For information about permission to reproduce selections from this book, write to Permissions, W. W. Norton & Company, Inc., 500 Fifth Avenue, New York, NY 10110

For information about special discounts for bulk purchases, please contact W. W. Norton Special Sales at specialsales@wwnorton.com or 800-233-4830

Manufacturing by Courier Westford
Book design by Lovedog Studio
Production manager: Louise Parasmo

Library of Congress Cataloging-in-Publication Data
Litman, Ellen.
Mannequin girl : a novel / Ellen Litman.—First Edition.
pages cm
ISBN 978-0-393-06928-0 (hardcover)
1. Young women—Moscow (Russia)—Fiction. 2. Jews, Russian—Moscow (Russia)—Fiction. 3. Parent and child—Moscow (Russia)—Fiction.
4. Scoliosis in adolecen—Moscow (Russia)—Fiction
5. Successful—Fiction. 6. Psychological fiction. I. Title.
PS3612.I866M36 2014
813'.6—dc23
2013041207

W. W. Norton & Company, Inc.
500 Fifth Avenue, New York, N.Y. 10110
www.wwnorton.com

W. W. Norton & Company Ltd.
Castle House, 75/76 Wells Street, London W1T 3QT

2 4 6 8 9 7 5 3 1

For Ian

PART I

1980

1

In July she becomes an anomaly, a glitch in a plan, a malfunction in an otherwise perfect mechanism. There is no pain, no warning signs, and no heredity issues, contrary to what the doctors imply. Her mother says Kat's diagnosis is a slap in the face and a curse and the blackest day of their lives. "You should've seen us," she says. "We were black when we came from the doctors." Her mother's face is white, her hair short and dark. She resembles the champion figure skater Irina Rodnina, and everyone knows she is prone to verbal extravagance.

The day Kat will remember is hot and bright. The queues at the children's policlinic, the smell of iodine, the hard cardboard cover of the novel she's reading: *The Wonderful Adventures of Nils*. Her mother, too, is reading. They've come for Kat's physical, which she needs for school.

She is starting first grade in September. All the school forms have been assembled and nearly all the shopping is done. For the Knopman–Roshdal household, this in itself is atypical.

Kat's parents are bohemians, fantastically disorganized. But in this instance they surpass themselves. The school is their milieu, their pride. They teach Russian and literature, and run a drama club, and whatever might be said of their slip-shod ways at home, at school they are unrivaled, they are loved. As T. N. Zolotareva, who teaches grades one through three, puts it, they are the school's last hope.

Naturally Kat has to ask what is wrong with the rest of the school, and T. N. gets flustered for a moment. The school, after all, is like any Soviet school—politically savvy, ideologically grounded, its teachers 60 percent Party members, two exemplary educators, one educator-methodologist. As for Kat's parents, they are still too young to have any distinctions, and also they happen to be Jews.

Kat already has a bit of reputation at the school. She is known as a local wunderkind: she reads on the par with fifth-graders, spews quotes from memory, soaks up everything—epigrams, quips, staircase conversations, the merciless assessments her parents bestow on their associates and friends. She plays a page in her parents' school productions; at holiday parties she and her father enact short comic sketches.

At home, her parents call her "our little bureaucrat," which doesn't upset her, not in the least. She's organized, responsible. Somebody has to be, with parents like these. Though of course, she adores them. They are brilliant, daring, the kind of parents who'd risk anything for truth. The least she can do is remind them when they are out of milk, or when their apartment payment is due.

This summer they need few reminders. They spend money with abandon on pencils, pens, counting sticks, stacks of thin notebooks, extra sets of penmanship exercises. They travel by subway to Children's World to buy Kat her first uniform, an itchy brown dress with two pinafores, one white and one black.

At home, each item is stashed in the three-door wardrobe in Kat's room, and every afternoon she inspects her new riches: the dress with its snowy accents of lace, a satchel and a silky bag for shoes, new ribbons. She is growing out her hair. By the end of the summer it will be down to her shoulders. She'll have braids on her first day of school. For now, she fixes it up in two sickly pretzels, and when no one is looking she puts on her new dress, too. She loves how it slims her into a whole new person, all grown up and tidy. The skirt flares slightly, and whenever she has the dress on, she wants to twirl, twirl, until the world spins around and gravity loosens its hold on her.

Later she takes the dress off, puts it back on its hanger, makes sure there's not a speck of lint on it, not a wrinkle on the seat of the skirt. She is ready. She's been ready since the start of summer—except for the physical, which her parents have been calling a stupid formality. This flippancy alone should have tipped her off. Formalities, she is to learn, have a way of wreaking havoc on your life.

THE QUEUES are enormous at the district policlinic. They have to see a battery of doctors—an oculist, a dermatologist, an ear-nose-and-throat specialist, a neurologist, and many more. They do what any sane person would: secure their spot in several queues (with the standby excuse of "I'll just step away for a moment"), and every ten minutes Kat goes to check on their progress in each queue.

It doesn't look good. The hallways are chock-full of sniveling babies; they spill and holler everywhere. Their mothers—crude shapes in flowery summer patterns—try in vain to keep hold of them. The mothers glower at Kat, and their looks promise nothing positive. They don't care that she's a child herself. You want your turn, they say, you wait like everybody else.

"I can't do this," Kat whimpers, returning to her mother, who has planted herself on a low red banquette by the blood lab. "I can't deal with these people."

"Then don't," Anechka says, and stretches slowly. She looks sleepy and gorgeous in her T-shirt and knee-length pants with cuffs and buttons, like the actress N. Varley from *Kidnapping, Caucasian Style*. A beauty, a Komsomol member, an athlete! "Don't fuss, don't fret, and people will flock toward you."

"I don't want them to flock," Kat says.

"It's an expression, baby. They're just cattle, you have to understand. You can't waste your intellect on cattle."

"At least you could have helped," says Kat. But she knows it's useless: Anechka doesn't help. She doesn't quarrel with the masses, doesn't demean herself in daily skirmishes, doesn't squabble over a vacant seat on the bus or lose face over some bread or cabbage. If she needs bread and cabbage, she'll send Kat's father to the shops.

"Baby, calm down. You're fraying your nerves."

Kat's nerves are already in a shambles.

Her eyes, on the other hand, turn out to be perfect. In the oculist's office, she is told to shield one eye with a small plastic paddle. There's a poster filled with round shapes and another one with the alphabet. Kat says she prefers the alphabet, but the oculist woman says she might mistake a letter. "I don't make mistakes," Kat says.

"You're a disgrace," Anechka grumbles, as they wait outside the orthopedics office, their last appointment.

"Because I can read?" Kat says.

"Don't play daft like you don't understand me." Reading isn't the problem. Reading is great. The problem is *behaving*, being a decent girl, not arguing with adults, not talking back. "You'll be at *our* school next year. If we can't discipline our own daughter—"

"When did you ever need to discipline me?"

"Plenty of times."

"Like when?"

"Don't be a nudnik," Anechka says, which is what she says when she runs out of arguments—which, truth be told, doesn't happen very often. The problem is, she has no patience. One moment she's all smiles, and the next, seemingly with no provocation, she's spinning herself into one of her snits. "A rein's got under her tail" is how Kat's father sometimes puts it, though never within Anechka's earshot.

———

THE ORTHOPEDICS doctor, a big flabby blonde, has a voice like the folk singer L. Zykina, unwavering and droning. Any moment now she'll burst into a song: "Orenburg Downy Shawl." She tells Kat to undress; she tells her to bend forward. "Lower," she says. With her blunt stubby finger, she pokes her below her right shoulder blade. "There!" Another poke, now in the lower back, on the left.

"It's like you parents don't have eyes," she says. "Don't you look at your daughter? In the shower? When she undresses for bed?"

"Of course we look at her."

The doctor tells Kat to get dressed.

"First they neglect their children, and then it's up to us—*and the government*—to bear the consequences."

"What consequences?" Anechka says, quietly, gravely, as if making a threat. "What on earth are you ranting about?"

"Me ranting?" The doctor goes all aflutter. "You've got yourself a girl with an ailment. Third-degree scoliosis. That, *mamasha*, is a sign of neglect. You should be deprived of your parental rights. You've crippled your daughter."

When they come out of the office, Anechka's eyes are pitching lightning bolts. She crumples the referral papers, shoving them in clumps into her bag. "Swine," she is muttering to herself rather than Kat. "Insolent piece of garbage. Fat, uncultured, ballooning on bribes."

"What about school?"

"I don't know," snaps Anechka.

In the days to come, Kat will rehash it many times—"crippled, ailment, scoliosis"—and it will dawn on her eventually, the full extent of her misfortune. She'll learn that scoliosis is a curvature of the spine; that in the best-case scenario its progress can be halted; that it can only be diminished with surgery, but even then the damage can never be fully undone.

Her father meets them by the door of their apartment—barefoot, warm and rumpled, bleary from an afternoon nap. He squints nearsightedly and clears his glasses, a look of surprise on his face. Life to Misha is a series of pleasant surprises. "Button!" he says, which is his pet name for her. "How's my Button?"

If only he'd gone with her that day. It is a whim, a superstition; scientifically it doesn't make sense, but Kat will never shake the conviction that her whole life might have turned out differently had she gone to the doctor with Misha.

It's been a long, plodding summer. The asphalt streets are hot and cracked; the air quivers like the meat jelly Kat's grandmother makes for holidays. The hot water has been turned off for its annual summer repairs. The Department of Residential Affairs has posted notices: "No hot water!" Outside, men in hard hats have begun drilling a trench. Moscow in the summer is no place for children. Children need nature: dachas, summer camps, the whispering of pine needles, the gurgling of a river or a lake. Or else they need a good Black Sea resort, with sand and a tan and turquoise waves and shish kebab in cafeterias—something Kat's parents can never afford.

Anechka and Misha finished teaching back in May, but they still dart to school every day, first to supervise the summer practicum for the eighth-graders, and later, as far as Kat can tell, for no ostensible reason. They won't take her with them. "Dust, Button!" Misha explains. Too much dust in there. Repairs, and so on. Meanwhile, the weather is marvelous.

"Marvelous, sure," Kat grumbles. She waits for them at the playground, which isn't even a playground but an empty, unpaved space with a couple of benches along the perimeter and a sandbox that smells so bad no one will touch it. Boys use the playground for soccer, while girls prefer the smooth, bouncy surfaces of sidewalks for hopscotch, jump rope, and elastics. Every game this year seems to involve classes, grades, advancing to the next level. Their world is normal, orderly, like a sheet of ruled paper, like hopscotch squares. They live in apartment blocks with identical floor plans.

The girls are the first to leave. Then the boys. For a week in late May Kat gets herself adopted by a group of older kids who drift in from neighboring streets. They play "The Sea is Roaring" and "I Know Five Names." She is the youngest and the best at word games. "I know five titles of novels." A bounce of the ball for every name. "One: *War and Peace*. Two: *Vanity Fair*. Three: *Don Quixote*." Of course, she hasn't read these books. Not yet. They are waiting for her, crammed into shelves, piled on the floor by her parents' sofa, on the desk, in the corners. Still, her new friends are impressed. But after a week, they too disappear.

Kat stalks the playground alone save for a group of neighborhood grandmothers, who scrutinize her every step and question aloud what her parents are up to. It is the summer of the Moscow Olympic Games, and directives have been issued to remove from the city all children between the ages of eight and fifteen, lest they be exposed to foreign germs or capitalist provocations.

In the past, Kat's parents took her to her grandfather's dacha for the summer. At the end of May, the three of them would make their pilgrimage to Kratovo. A station-wagon taxi would be reserved in advance. The journey took two hours, and inevitably Kat got carsick after the meat-processing plant. The driver would be asked to pull over, and Anechka would get out some spare plastic bags. She'd call Kat her misfortune.

Their misfortunes didn't end there.

At last, the taxi would pull into the shadowy yard of the dacha, and moments later, the craggy figure of Alexander Roshdal would stagger heavily onto the wooded path that led up to the two-story house at the back of the property, the house he occupied year-round with his second wife.

"Anya?" he'd say, as if his daughter's arrival hadn't been expected for weeks, but was instead a complete surprise.

For a minute, he and Anechka would study each other, their eyes meeting and making a pact—a pact, everyone knew, that Anechka would break by the end of the afternoon—and then, his knuckles whitening over the handle of his cane, he'd give her a one-armed hug.

ANYA, ANECHKA, Anna Alexandrovna Roshdal. Even after she married she didn't give up her last name, making their family a hybrid, a two-headed dragon. Her father, Alexander Roshdal, had been a translator. Once upon a time he'd corresponded with the writer V. A. Kaverin, and had known others from the famed Serapion Brothers group. His wife, Anechka's mother, wrote poetry—exquisite, mystical, and, according to her husband, utterly unpublishable in their days of fast tempos and five-year plans. He was a cautious man, he'd seen what had happened to the Serapion Brothers, and to others like them.

His wife was a beauty—a frail, fiery woman with a pale smile, feverish cheeks, hair like a dandelion about to be blown away. She died of a heart condition when Anechka was fifteen, leaving father and daughter alone and reeling, their grief so acute they knew not what to do with themselves.

They pulled through, of course—people recovered from worse blows than theirs—and scrambled out from under the wreckage. They lived idyllically in the one room of their communal apartment that was assigned to them, looking after each other, studying, translating, reading aloud in the evenings, cooking simple suppers of sausage and buckwheat kasha. Neither could do much in the kitchen. Foolish, impractical, they were a solace to each other, and it didn't matter that their good silver disappeared gradually, their clothes needed darning, the floor hadn't been waxed in years, the dust on the dresser was two fingers thick. But maybe it did matter. Because one day, Alexander Roshdal brought home Valentina, a woman of no literary inclinations.

Now there were three of them sharing the room, the new couple sleeping on the little sofa in the corner, where Anechka's parents had once slept, and Anechka on her folding bed behind a thin partition. She was painstakingly polite to Valentina. She expressed her dislike in a language so circuitous, so elevated, that it was bound to go over Valentina's head. Who was Valentina? A glorified washerwoman. The ancient chandelier was polished with tooth powder, the parquet floor now sparkled, and dinner became a regular three-course affair, with soup to begin and sweet compote at the end. Wasn't Valentina fantastic? Wasn't she talented?

Anechka's compliments were duplicitous, laced with puns and contempt. If Alexander Roshdal saw through his daughter's antics, he said nothing. And what could he say? He was the guilty party. He'd sprung his new lover on Anechka like a sudden snow on her head. The girl had been completely unprepared. He'd been caught by surprise himself.

Now, thirteen years later, relations remain strained. A mother, a teacher, thirty years of age, Anechka Roshdal reverts to her teenage self the moment she steps onto the grounds of the Kratovo dacha. The food is too salty or else too bland, the house is too damp, and all the fresh air in the world can't make up for the fact that she still has to share her father. Every day after breakfast she tries to commandeer his attention, taking him away from Valentina, inventing an errand for just the two of them—the department store in Udelnaya, the big outdoor market in Malakhovka. Misha and Kat are left to nap in hammocks while Valentina, always light on her feet, hums and spins, chops and sautés, weeds the garden, cans fruit for the winter, scuttles back and forth with her wicker shopping bag. All of it done gamely, with a smile and a wink, a treat for Kat, a joke for Misha.

Kat secretly likes Valentina, her perky face, flaxen perm, carrot lipstick. She even tried to defend her to Anechka once, which didn't go down very well. Whatever Valentina had done in the past, surely she'd earned Anechka's forgiveness since then?

"She made me an orphan," said Anechka, and that, as far as she was concerned, was the end of *that* conversation. Kat never dared broach the subject again.

IT MUST have been that orphaned feeling that brought Anechka and Misha together. He too had lost a parent. His father, an officer, died in a botched surgery when Misha was three. His mother, Zoya Moiseevna, never remarried. She worked as a secretary at the Institute of Steel and Alloys and hoped her son would wind up a student there. Instead, her gentle Misha, in a rare display of bullheadedness, applied to the Lenin Pedagogical Institute. "Have you gone mad?" said Zoya Moiseevna. "You'll crash and burn and end up in the army for the next two years." When that didn't work, she tried another tack: "Teaching is for girls, not for a boy."

She was desperate; they had no connections at the Pedagogical Institute. He applied and got in anyway, got in based on his own sheer brilliance, and fell in love with Anechka Roshdal before the winter exams—the two events Zoya Moiseevna later conflated in her memory, and never forgave either of them.

It is, therefore, absurd and unnatural that Kat is forced to spend most of her days in the company of Zoya Moiseevna: Zoya Moiseevna who, according to Anechka, is nothing but a vengeful, dried-up bone; Zoya Moiseevna who calls at odd hours, cleans incessantly, rearranges the kitchen cabinets, and grumbles all day long that she hasn't raised her darling Misha to live in such a hovel.

"Is that so?" Anechka asked dryly the first time Zoya Moiseevna volleyed this idea at her.

"Look at him, skin and bones. He's lost ten kilos and his socks are full of holes."

"Take him back if he's so unhappy," said Anechka.

But of course, Misha wasn't unhappy, nor would he ever leave Anechka, who at that point was already three months pregnant with Kat. He hadn't lost any kilos. He'd darn his own socks. Misha? Socks? It was laughable.

Except Anechka wasn't laughing. She perched on the windowsill and lit a cigarette. "You decide," she said to Misha. "It's me or her."

And what could he possibly decide, with her pregnant and already showing a little? March was raging outside—wind, snow, sleet, rain—and Anechka was hunched in her serpent-like way underneath an open ventilation window.

Tapered pants, bare ankles, her striped shirt paper thin. And smoking. Smoking was bad for the baby. She'd quit the day she learned she was pregnant, quit easily, with no ill effects, and hadn't slipped up once until then.

Zoya Moiseevna was a shrewd enough woman to recognize a losing battle. She collected her parcels and flounced off before her Misha could renounce her. "You idiots, live any way you want."

"Thank you!" Anechka called after her, in the voice of a diligent schoolgirl. She'd always been a perfect actress.

Kat was born six month later, on September 1.

When Anechka's maternity leave ended and she went back to work, Zoya Moiseevna made her triumphant, if cautious, return. Anechka had been against it, but they were against the wall: it was either that or put little Kat in a state nursery.

Installed back in the apartment, Zoya Moiseevna cleaned. She scoured the cutlery, scrubbed the refrigerator inside and outside. Every morning she trekked from her place in Kuzminki to find—what exactly? Dark spots of gravy on the counter, floors sticky with spilled compote, Anechka's feminine things left in the bathroom. She had a theory that her daughter-in-law, the stinker, dirtied the place on purpose just to spite her.

As Kat grew from a toddler into a little girl, her grandmother managed to effect in her a certain taste for tidiness: all those *mishkas* and *matryoshkas* were brushed and polished to perfection, picture books alphabetized on their shelves. But Kat, at her core, was her parents' girl: weaned on classical poetry, precocious, moody, passionate. She'd learned to read early. At five years old, she could recite Tatiana's letter to Onegin—not mindlessly, either, but with the right emotions and inflections.

She had inherited her parents' teaching bug. Her favorite toy was a blackboard. She made up her own class registers, pinned back her hair ineptly, dressed up in Anechka's old shawls. A scarecrow, her grandmother called her. "Boys tease girls like you."

Kat said, "No they don't. They tease dotty old grandmothers."

"Let's make a bet," said Zoya Moiseevna. "We'll see what will become of you." And as she withdrew to the kitchen to make her most prosaic chicken soup, Kat was left with a lost, queasy feeling, an infant Sleeping Beauty, forever cursed. What would, indeed, become of her?

HER PARENTS are two self-absorbed, beautiful rebels. They leave for school in the morning, always together, always in a hurry, always forgetting something—a book, a dry-cleaning ticket, a key. They come back in the late afternoon, often accompanied by a group of older pupils—adorable, disheveled louts. "How are you, Zoya Moiseevna? How's Kat?" "Hooligans," Zoya Moiseevna whispers, fastening her coat on the way out. "By the way, I just washed these floors!" "No problem, Zoya Moiseevna." They will leave their muddy boots by the door, and Kat will extricate some old slippers from the back of the closet. Those who get no slippers pad around in socks.

They huddle in the kitchen, and a couple of girls—there's always a couple, industrious, domestically inclined—rinse the dishes, fry potatoes, put the kettle on. Misha gets out the reel-to-reel tape deck. Anechka's guitar is tuned and passed around.

They speak of famous dissidents, the Prague Spring, someone called Andrei Sakharov. Kat doesn't know who dissidents are, but she loves the songs—the gruff voices on the tapes, the hindrances in the background. She loves the keen, anxious faces of the students, contained as they are in the six square meters of the Knopman–Roshdal kitchen. She understands, even now, that what they are doing is illicit, possibly anti-Soviet, a secret she has to protect. The same way Misha's wireless is a secret, with its BBC call signals in the morning. Or Anechka's typewriter, which she uses to copy stacks of thin, crinkly papers. Later she stashes the copies in the plaid grocery bag. She puts on her oldest, most dilapidated coat, a shrunken knitted cap, and sometimes she and Misha argue whether she should go or he should go. Go where, Kat wants to ask, but she knows they won't tell her. Not because they don't trust her, but because knowledge can be dangerous. Some people get arrested, detained. It almost happened to Anechka once, and since then she's done no more typing jobs, and the old coat and hat have been stowed in the topmost cabinet. They never talk about that. Instead, there are these gatherings with students, forbidden books, guitar songs.

How bitter it feels the next morning, when the magic vanishes, her parents go away, and she is left again with

Zoya Moiseevna. The humdrum of their uninspired days: the grumbling and the cleaning, the radio station Mayak— "Moscow speaking. Moscow time is ten o'clock"—day in and day out, from the morning calisthenics to the music program based on the workers' requests. "Today we're reading your mail."

Summers are Zoya Moiseevna's reprieve; this year she's gone to Estonia, to celebrate the end of her "imprisonment" with Kat. She's made a big production out of it: Oh, the years she's wasted! The days she could have spent shopping at GUM, or going to the movies, or taking a cruise on the Volga river. And what did she get in return? Did she ever get a thank-you from Kat? Nope, not once, no ma'am. Nothing but spite and mess and tattling to her parents. Well, let her go off to school then. Good luck with that! Good luck and a road like a tablecloth.

"Same to you," said Kat.

THEY DON'T miss her. She is still in Estonia when Kat's affliction becomes known. They don't bother to send her a telegram. Everything's gone topsy-turvy since the diagnosis: the phone book is scrounged for useful contacts, important phone calls are made. "Hello? Mariya Andreevna? I'm sorry, you don't know me . . ." Anechka, coiled up with the phone in her lap. Misha, straining over anatomy diagrams.

Kat is like a finely calibrated device, a needle trembling, attuned to the tiniest deviations in their family life. She frets a lot. She listens. She arrives in the doorway and they halt their conversations and put their books away. "What about school?" she keeps asking. They feign innocence: "What about it?"

Meanwhile, they've scheduled appointments at the Institute of Trauma and arranged for a physical therapist, Maria, a dusky beauty with a birthmark on her neck, to come twice a week from Medvedkovo to give Kat massages. "How bad is it?" they whisper to her in the bathroom, where Maria is washing her hands. She seems to think not so bad. Not third-degree, that's for sure. The policlinic doctor was probably trying to frighten them.

Alexander Roshdal and Valentina arrive from Kratovo to help. The summer gets even more chaotic: suitcases, folding beds, buckets of water being boiled every few hours, for bathing, dishes, laundry. And of course, all attention is focused on Kat. "Kat, eat your veggies. Have you done your exercises, Kat?" Even watching TV becomes impossible. "Kat, sit up straight! You're slumping!"

The TV is Kat's distraction. The Olympic Games are starting, and the programs teem with athletes, singers, actors. They speak of competitive spirit in the arts and in sports. Stress, obstacles, persistence, and, inevitably, the triumph of the human will. "You've got it too, Button," says Misha. "All it takes is hard work. We'll conquer this thing of yours."

The thing, the bump, the curse. In the face of Kat's scoliosis, the family has united, gone into fighting mode. To win, you have to think like an athlete; you need discipline and practice, like in sports. They hunker down, become Kat's very own national team. Valentina's job is nutrition, Misha's research. Alexander Roshdal takes Kat on long walks, recites Robert Browning to her. Anechka, of course, is head coach. They seem to think that Kat's illness, with all its subsequent appointments, is something you can train or cram for.

It almost works at first. Kat is tickled by her family's attention, the extra walks, the tiny bright boxes of juice and sweet cream released for the Olympics, which her team now procures for her on a regular basis. She'd like to see the Olympics—the athletes, the stadiums, the giant wooden mascot bear on Michurinskiy Avenue. Can't they at least see the bear? Her team tells her no, they cannot.

"Security, Button," says her father.

"Yes," agrees Valentina, "and also the germs."

The germs, the viruses, the danger of foreign people (especially those from Africa), not to mention the American boycott. They talk of it at night, when they think Kat can't hear them. "A disgrace," says Valentina, and Anechka says no, the disgrace is sending our boys to Afghanistan. They play cards, as they do every evening, their conversations interspersed with pauses and cryptic remarks: Seven. Misère. Pass.

"For God's sake, Anya," says Alexander Roshdal. "You don't need to climb up on a gun port. Wasn't the last time enough? You want to end up in *psikhushka* this time? The Kashchenko loony bin, like your hero Brodsky? Or go straight to a labor camp?"

The tension is rising, and it's different from previous summers. Misha and Anechka bicker. Alexander Roshdal complains. Anechka screams at Valentina for giving Kat some candy. ("It's diabetic," Valentina mutters.) They seem to teeter on the verge of total collapse. Kat's gone in for two X-rays and one appointment with a specialist. A big consultation at the Institute of Trauma is scheduled for August 1.

She's been having nightmares. Bandaged bodies, the noise of ambulances. She wakes up in the night, and her only relief is Valentina, who's sleeping on a mattress on the floor. She's so close, Kat can reach for her. She smells of lavender. She snores a little, though it's more like whistling, a soft and peaceful sound. If the nightmares get bad, Kat can wake her. In the dark Valentina tells her stories: how she married her first husband, the captain, and what a birdie of a girl she was back then, with nothing to her name but two dresses and the four years of the war, during which she was a radio operator. After the war, she and her captain met again. "Like in the movies," she says. She hums a pretty melody, a song called "Sevastopol Waltz," and as Kat falls asleep she imagines her and the captain dancing.

ON JULY 25, Vladimir Vysotsky, the beloved and censored songwriter and actor, dies in his sleep from something like asphyxiation. No one's exactly sure of the cause. He's forty-two. There are no big announcements in the newspapers, just a brief obituary in *Evening Moscow*. But the news spreads anyway, by word of mouth or BBC broadcasts.

On July 28, Kat's parents go out in the morning. They don't tell Kat where they're going and she, at first, isn't par-

ticularly worried. They always disappear. To the department store Yadran to look for table lamps. To the market
in Khimki for cherries. But when there's no sign of them by
lunchtime, she starts to get concerned. Why now? Where
are they?

She goes to the local grocery with Valentina. When they
return, her grandfather is pacing in the hallway.

"Was it really necessary? I ask you. Today of all days."

"Don't wind yourself up. They'll be back," says Valentina.

"And what if they won't? What then?"

"Didn't they say it's just a service for some actor?"

"Not just any actor, Valya. It's all political. They're playing
with fire again. Can you imagine if this place gets searched?
It's full of samizdat and God knows what else. Do you know
what you get these days for anti-Soviet agitation? Seven
years, if you're lucky."

"Are they in trouble?" Kat asks him, and he says, "No
darling, your parents are okay. Why don't you be a good girl
and go to your room for a bit now?"

She has no choice but to obey.

She sits in her room on the bed. Let's sum up, shall we? A
famous actor/singer turns up dead. On TV, Soviet athletes
are winning all the medals, but no one's watching TV. Her
parents are missing, possibly getting arrested. Her big consultation is on Friday, in three days.

Kat opens her wardrobe. There are her clothes, folded
neatly on the shelves, and there, on a hanger, is her school
dress. Not a speck, not a wrinkle on it yet.

She puts it on and stands before the wardrobe mirror,

waiting for it to reveal the dainty, nimble girl she is. But the dress doesn't fit like it used to. It's awkward, too tight in the shoulders.

She adds the white pinafore and white knee socks. She finds her new shoes, tan with black patent-leather tops. But the girl in the mirror still looks lopsided.

She tries to put her hair in braids. She is not very good at it, doesn't know how to thread the ribbons properly or the best way to tie them at the ends.

The last thing is the satchel. It's beige, with a giant appliqué of a ladybug. She stuffs it full of children's books, so full she barely can close it, and heaves it, with some effort, onto her back.

What she sees in the mirror is an odd little person. Disheveled, hunched over, and lurching to the left. A gnome. A scarecrow.

Step by step, she erases the damage. She empties the satchel and puts away the shoes. The ribbons are straightened and rolled up. The knee socks disappear into the sock compartment.

Slowly, lovingly, she takes off her dress, makes sure there's not a speck of lint on it, returns it to the hanger. Farewell, my friend. She'll never wear it again. Tired, very tired now, she climbs into her bed, and there she will remain until her parents return in the evening, alive and quite intact—three days before the final consultation.

2

S HE ARRIVES AT THE SPECIAL SCHOOL ON SEPTEM-
ber 2, having missed by one day the official start of the
school year. She is dressed, confusingly, in a boy's uniform:
blue trousers, a matching jacket, and a flared rain slicker,
meant to protect her from bad weather as well as inquisitive
stares. Her hair is snipped into a cap of floppy curls.

As of yesterday, she is seven. Girls her age don't look like
her, don't miss the first bell, don't lie to their parents. Her
parents are with her. She is safe and hemmed in by them,
shielded by their shoulders and elbows. Anechka carries her
book bag—not the beige leather satchel with a ladybug they
returned a week ago, but an ugly canvas thing that looks
like a shopping tote. Misha carries her suitcase, her name
pasted near the lock. Her name is everywhere, the name tags
ordered hastily and sewn inside her panties and her shirts.

The school is on the outskirts. But they also live on the
outskirts, so it only takes them half an hour to get there.

They board the number 90 bus by the fruit and vegetable shop, and twenty minutes later they get off at a desolate spot by a House of Culture and an adjacent textile factory. Kat's parents consult their notes, while she holds their umbrellas. It's been raining all morning, on and off, whereas the previous day was sunlit and golden as the city celebrated the Day of Knowledge—songs dribbling from loudspeakers, balloons, bouquets—and Anechka and Misha came home with armfuls of gladioli. Kat herself spent the day on the green nubbly sofa in the living room, trying to read *Without a Family* by H. Malot and watching a rerun of a World War II movie.

The school, Anechka says, must be at the back of the park, and indeed, there is a park stretching off behind them, dark, moribund, like the grounds of a deserted hospital. It's humid inside the park, the air reeking of decay and rotting timber. A playground with a seesaw, a heap of bricks, a crumpled hut.

This is not what Kat's been promised, not the huge leafy campus with multiple blocks and immaculate alleys, flourishing poplars and alders, a swimming pool like a giant aquarium. The paved road ends and now they are in a field of tall, yellow grass. A pond looms ahead of them. They follow a muddy path. Her parents are looking uncertain and a little distressed, and she knows they are thinking that if she hadn't pulled the vomiting stunt the morning before, they wouldn't be wandering alone here like idiots today. Or maybe they're wondering whether the whole thing is a mistake, and wouldn't it be better to just turn around and take Kat home? Because when she keeps her back straight and pays attention to her posture, you can't see any deformity there.

"It's just a boarding school," Anechka says. "Like in *Jane Eyre*, except you get to go home on weekends."

"Didn't she almost starve there?" Misha checks.

"Hardships build character. Besides, it ended well."

Kat tells them she doesn't remember.

"Your grandfather *read* it to you," Anechka says. She glares at Misha—a plea or a command: Kat's being difficult.

Misha moves closer, puts a hand on Kat's shoulder. "What's happening, Button?"

"I just don't remember the book," she says. "Is that a problem?"

"No," he says, stepping back.

She won't make it easier for them. She's been stoic and brave since the first mention of a special school. It has limited spaces. It is known as one of a kind, innovative, with its complex approach to muscular-skeletal ailments: bracing, swimming, daily medical gymnastics, injections, massages, and more. Children are referred to it from all over the country.

Kat cried when she was told. She refused to believe it, pleaded with her parents to not send her away. It was all wrong, this school, she told them. Couldn't they see how wrong it was for her? She was supposed to be at *their* school, the three of them finally together, putting on plays, winning awards, sitting next to one another at lunchtime.

She has been hoping for a miracle, a pardon. There was some talk of it at first, some alternatives offered and bandied about: she could do half-days at her parents' school, physical therapy at home. They'd find a policlinic with a swimming pool. But in the final weeks of August it all came to naught; a space at the special school had been secured, and Anechka and Misha spent the last days of summer hassling with alterations and returns.

Now they eye Kat with caution, as if she were a ticking bomb, or as if she'd gotten sick on purpose. And that is the worst part: she did, in fact, fake her little sickness the morning before. She'd stayed awake all night, thinking of the special school, of what a travesty her first day of school— not to mention her birthday—would become. By morning, stricken with grief and insomnia, she already looked green around the eyes. All it took was a couple of hard coughs and the shove of a toothbrush deep against her tongue. Voilà! Afterward, as she was resting on the sofa with a glass of cold water, she wasn't sure if the vomiting had been entirely an act.

The truth is, she hates deformities. She's always been weirdly sensitive to trauma. A pair of crutches, an empty sleeve, a prosthesis (crude, wooden or metal, ending in a sickeningly narrow peg)—a glimpse of any of these guarantees her a night of fitful vomiting, a week of nightmares. There are certain streets she avoids, certain shops she won't go near. Anechka tries to shame her. Her fears, she says, are plebeian, banal. The legless man by the grocery, who sits on a low dolly cart, was probably injured in the war. Same with the drunk who has a leather bulb for a hand. These men are heroes!

Heroes or not, it doesn't matter anymore. There won't be any heroes here. Just children. Deformed, freakish children.

THE SCHOOL grounds, it turns out, lie outside the park. You have to climb through a hole in a low concrete fence with pieces of iron sticking out. You wonder what sort of desperate force it took to break through these concrete planks, what insane yearning to escape could have been driving the people who did it, and then you have to ask how bad it must be inside.

The sight of the campus is dispiriting. The low-slung boxes of the buildings, unadorned, identically drab. The medical block. The dorms. The school block. Perhaps it's the drizzle that makes the campus so featureless. They dither in between these buildings—which one is block seven?—their feet sinking into the soggy gravel paths. "Use your imagination," says Misha. He points to the flowerbeds, which must be bright with pansies in the summer, but now are dark squares of mud.

Kat tries. There are walkways connecting the blocks, seemingly suspended in the air, and there's the swimming pool—not quite like an aquarium, no, but it does have one wall that's a giant green panel of glass, and it's not unthinkable that on a good day it might look as if it housed exquisite sea life. Still, no matter how hard she tries, all she sees is how bleak the campus is, sealed off, and, above all, hospital-like.

THE DOOR to the principal's office, upholstered in leather
and studded with impressive metal bolts, is guarded by a
secretary. She is a youngish woman, thin and sallow, with
a drippy, malnourished sort of face. You take one look at
her and imagine all her troubles: a slogger husband, sickly
kids, limited salary, early pain in the joints, the long wait at
the laundry, the sales clerk at the milk store who called her
an imbecile, the shoes that pinch her toes. Add to that the
total chaos of the special kiddies the day before, reams of
new paperwork, and the last thing she needs today is these
stragglers, this pair of milksops.

"Our girl was indisposed," says Kat's mother.

"She was *what*?"

"Ill. Ailing. Unwell. Laid up." Anechka abhors all manner of crudeness. Also, she has a great vocabulary.

"And now she's suddenly healthy?" The secretary nar-
rows her eyes. She flips through a sheaf of papers to verify
Kat's name. "You must take her to block five."

"And where is that?" says Kat's father, advancing, making
it clear he isn't impressed with the way she is doing her job.
Misha, for all his gentleness, can be a daunting presence—
tall, curly-haired like the poet A. S. Pushkin, and decked
out in a suit and tie. He looks like someone who can make a
few phone calls and get this woman fired, though of course
in reality he's just a teacher and has neither an office nor
a phone.

Faced with such a surprising burst of power, the secretary yields. "Fine, I'll take you," she says unhappily, because frankly it's not part of her job.

They follow her: up and down the stairs, through a series of French doors, in and out of hallways—an unsettling sequence of turns, a whiff of something meaty from the canteen, a dip into a tunnel of bedrooms, the vomity linoleum of long, connecting corridors. There have been no deformities so far. They've seen no one at all. Still, whenever they pass a wall display with pictures, Kat lowers her eyes.

They are moving along the cold yellow walkway when at last they hear voices in the distance. Kids' voices. Two girls, singing. The melody leaps wildly inside the hollow walkway. It's a popular song from two summers ago: "Kings can do anything. Kings can do anything except marry for love."

The girls look tiny. There's something odd in their appearance, something unyielding and stiff, and it takes Kat a moment to take in the contraptions they are in. Their heads are held up by white plastic collars; thin metal slats run alongside their necks; and beyond that, she can see the shape of something cumbersome, like armor, gripping them under their blue uniform jackets and pants. When they turn, it is with their whole bodies.

The secretary asks, what's with the ruckus? "Why are you here? What's going on?" The girls try to explain: they've misplaced their school diaries, and now they must find them, because . . . because . . .

"Go back to your class."

"But the diaries?"

"Out! Now!"

The girls seem untroubled by this harshness. They do a comical about-face and scurry off in the direction they came from.

"How can you speak to them like that?" says Anechka. "Is it not enough that they're physically damaged? You have to maim them on the inside?"

"We *treat* these children," says the secretary. "We *educate* them. You don't like our methods, you can take back your girl's paperwork. We have a waiting list full of very grateful people."

"Grateful for what?"

But the secretary won't engage in the fine nuances of Anechka's argument. "You want out?"

Kat's heart nearly stops. It is her chance, her miracle, her pardon. Anechka is a hothead when it comes to the injustices of school life. She takes up the flimsiest of causes, writes letters, makes phone calls, or, as Alexander Roshdal says, blows things out of proportion. Last year, when a few boys in Lithuania got expelled for not informing on their teacher, she and Misha joined a protest, which nearly cost them their jobs. Poor judgment, Roshdal calls it, and though Kat disagrees, right now this so-called poor judgment is a gift. All it will take is one word: Yes! Yes, we want out.

"No," says Misha. "We don't."

The four of them pause, and in the momentary quiet there's a faint giggle from the far end of the walkway, then a few tentative notes. The girls, emboldened by the distance they have covered, start again with their ludicrous song. "Kings can do anything. Kings can do anything."

"We maim them here, don't we?"

ON THE INSIDE, the school is a spidery organism. You follow the web of its walkways, and you barely notice as one building ends, another one begins. Soon you don't notice at all. Borders become blurry, indistinct. There are several dorm floors, two classroom blocks, two separate canteens.

Block five is where the lower grades attend their daily classes, where they keep their belongings, where after evening walks they return to do their homework. It has an ordinary school layout: rows of doors, parquet floors in the hallways, all the usual displays on the walls: Milestones of Our History. Nothing's Forgotten; No One's Forgotten. At the end of the hallway on the second floor is a faculty lounge with an adjoining bathroom.

"I'd like to meet the teacher," says Anechka.

"You can do it on Saturday, when you pick up your girl."

"I'd like to do it now," insists Anechka.

"Have I been unclear?" says the secretary. "Have I been speaking to a wall? No outside people during regular school hours."

"Let's go," Misha begs under his breath, taking Anechka gently by the elbow. They are already desperately late.

"I'll write a letter of complaint," says Anechka.

"Knock yourself out," the secretary says. She moves to the

side, her arms folded, her foot tapping ostentatiously. She stands there and waits.

Before they leave, Anechka gives Kat some two-kopek coins in a cellophane baggie. "You call us if anything happens. You hear me? Anything! If anyone dares to touch you—"

"They won't," Misha jumps in to say, and his words are like a soft splash of water against Anechka's mounting excitement.

"She'll be fine," he says, and Kat agrees: "Of course!" She'll be fine, she'll be great, she has been born and bred for greatness; she knows they are expecting nothing less. And now they are leaving, so at last it's done, it's finished. There's no more hope for her, no time for the last lucky break. Her lovable, fumbling Misha. Her Anechka, the queen. Her pals. Her accomplices. How glad, how eager they are to leave. Every step fills their bodies with confidence. Their tired shoulders straighten. Their proud backs expand. She's never noticed until now what beautiful backs they have. They have their work ahead of them, the work they love and are good at. And she? Trained under their command, she turned out imperfect. Deficient.

The secretary shifts, becomes apparent again, like a transfer picture on a kitchen tile, or rather, like a water stain. It is only then, minutes away from the life so alien she can't begin to comprehend it, that Kat remembers that, sheltered as she's been, she's never learned to use a pay phone. And if that's the case, what else has she failed to prepare for?

———

AN UGLY troll lives in your spinal column, coiling itself among the nerve endings, scaling the rickety knobs of your vertebrae. When you get well, he will come out and we'll catch him. Catch who? The troll, of course! Who else? Keep him under glass, in a cage, in the museum of scoliotic trolls and other medical curiosities. Bet you didn't know there was such a museum.

Kat thinks this is incredible. Her first lesson is a fairy tale. Has she fallen into a rabbit hole or drunk from a forbidden bottle? Hands, feet—no, she is still the same. It is her new teacher, Olga Ivanovna Fromkina, who seems to belong elsewhere—small, androgynous, with muted blue eyes and short hair. She has a slender body, an elongated face. An elf. A Thumbelina. Dressed in a denim skirt and white turtleneck, she flits across the classroom in her stocking feet, her shoes shoved into the corner by the rubbish bin, abandoned like an afterthought.

Kat is an afterthought herself.

"Oh yes, the new girl."

She is only a day late. Aren't they all new, this being first grade? All of her classmates look the same in their blue trousers and jackets, a plastic emblem on their sleeves—an open book, a flame. Their hair is shorn, just like Kat's, for some implausible reason that has to do with swimming.

The classroom has no desks. Instead there are rows of cots, each with a matching triangular prop and Plexiglas writing tray. They study while sprawled on their bellies, because their bones, the story goes, are too frail to withstand a full day at a desk. Which also explains the uniforms.

Can you imagine lying down in a dress? Awkward, not to mention unseemly.

"Children, this is Katya Knopman."

"Kat," she corrects, and sees a quick exchange of glances in the back row. A smirk elsewhere, as if to say, What a poser!

A cot in the center of the second row has been reserved for her. Ugly, cream-colored, its ink-spotted vinyl smelling like stale noodles on a plate. Kat stalls a little at the sight of it, then lowers herself gingerly. She's not completely flat, she's leaning on her elbows—anything but to touch the filthy vinyl.

But that's wrong—can't she see?—and Thumbelina is quick to point it out. "Darling, put your elbows down. Rest your chin on the prop."

"It's dirty," Kat says.

"Is it? Well, do you have a handkerchief?"

She does, a clean one in the breast pocket of her jacket. It's small, but it will have to do for now.

"You must be patient, doves," says Thumbelina, and Kat understands that others have also been unsettled by the cots. "Soon we'll have brand-new cot wrapping. Warm and soft. We'll do money collection at our next parent assembly."

Parent assembly. How wrong, how utterly out of place are these two words. They belong to her parents. They are a part of their vocabulary, along with pedagogic councils, methodology tutorials, Marxist–Leninist studies. Something mentioned at breakfast, a scheduling nuisance remembered with a groan. She used to loathe the sound of these words. They took her parents away from her, carried their work late into

evening hours. But now . . . Sadness has stung her. She sees
her parents as they were this morning, lofty, lovely, Anechka
fiddling with the camera, Misha in his one spiffy suit which
he has worn just for her.

Kat drops her face down and in the process discovers that
the prop she is lying on is hollow and that inside is a bit of
eraser and a broken pencil stub.

No one is immune to sadness. The classroom gets quiet,
and the two littlest girls in the front row start crying. A
girl to Kat's left makes a snorting sound, and for a moment
Kat thinks she's also in distress. Her cot is pushed against
Kat's cot. The girl is dark-haired and bulky, with sour
dairy breath. The primer in front of her is wrapped in green
paper and already splattered with something. The scribble
of her name, *Sonya Bronfman*, is like a squished bug on
the cover.

Kat's about to speak to her, but Sonya Bronfman looks
away and quickly pops a candy in her mouth.

"Cow," someone whispers, and Kat whips around to see
a boy on the cot to the right of her. He is watching her with
interest. "Not you," he says. "Your neighbor. She's been eating those Little Cow candies since she got here."

The boy is green-eyed and attractive. He has the haughty
manner of a movie spy. There's an aisle between their cots,
but it is narrow. His name is Igor Zotov. "At your service,"
he says. Were they both standing, he'd probably click his
heels and bow, and ridiculous as it seems, she might even
curtsy in response; but as they are horizontal for now, they
simply shake hands across the aisle.

So taken is she with this strange boy that she forgets she's supposed to stay down. The moment she props herself up on her cot, Thumbelina says, "Is something wrong?"

Stupid Thumbelina. She is in the middle of her nonsense troll story, trying to soothe the two weeping girls up front. As a teacher, she has zero personality, none of Anechka's brilliance or Misha's charm. But maybe you don't need those qualities, as long as you don't plan to teach past the third grade. If you never aspire to be anything of worth, maybe all you need to be is kind and docile.

AT RECESS, Kat finds herself surrounded, encircled by a small posse of girls. The most insistent of them, the two little weepers from the front row, are practically leaping in her face. Are you foreign? they want to know. Are you from another country?

"You've got a weird name," says the girl Kat remembers as Kira Mikadze. She read from the primer at the end of class, read briskly, offhandedly, the way Kat herself would have read if she'd been asked.

The name, Kat begins to explain, is indeed short for Katya. She is about to tell them about her translator grandfather, but Kira Mikadze interrupts: "I mean, your last name."

"Knopman. Knopka. Button," someone promptly recites in the back.

"A doorbell," offers someone else.

"It's weird," says Kira Mikadze. "I'd rather die than have a name like that." She flips back her stringy blonde hair and saunters away. It's like she fancies herself something incredible, whereas in reality she is thick as a sausage, speaks with a burr, and has a weird name herself. What sort of last name is Mikadze?

As if on cue, the other girls disperse as well. Kat is left with the weepers. They alone still find her fascinating. The wispy, sharp-nosed redhead is Nina Petrenko. Her blonde, cherubic counterpart is Vika Litvinova.

"We won't let them tease you," says Nina.

"The *boys*," Vika explains.

But the boys don't seem to be a problem. There are so few of them anyway—they must be less susceptible to scoliosis—and she's already made friends with one of them. She looks for Igor Zotov, but by now the hallway has become one swirling, sweaty mass: girls strolling in pairs, boys racing along the perimeter and sliding on the sleek parquet.

Their class is 1A, and Kat is glad, because A implies excellence, whereas B or C can't help but be hopelessly mediocre. In the canteen, 1A sits closest to the entrance, which also pleases Kat. The whole canteen is in a state of chaos: there's pushing, and rushing, and banging of trays. She is overwhelmed and impressed.

She's sitting next to Igor Zotov. They bonded in math, which they are equally good at. In penmanship, they shared a laugh over Kat's atrocious chicken scratch. Igor's own cursive is impeccable. His mother, he said, is an industrial artist. He has inherited from her his steady hand.

"Are you homesick yet?" he asks Kat.

She shakes her head, though it's a lie. Not homesick, she thinks, but apprehensive.

Igor tells her he's not homesick either. It's just that this whole place is stupid. He's already phoned home, and he's absolutely sure he'll be out of here by the end of the week. His father has access to a government policlinic.

They both stare off into the depths of the canteen. Only now is Kat starting to glimpse what the rest of the students (or patients) here look like. There's an occasional club foot or hip anomaly, marked by a special boot, a lopsided walk. A case or two of stunted growth. The rest are spinal ailments, and most kids are in braces, the kind she saw that morning on the two singing girls.

"No braces for us, pal," Igor Zotov assures her. Which for him is probably true—he only has first-degree scoliosis.

Kat tells him hers is first-to-second.

"That's nothing," Igor says. "At least we're not like him," and he nods almost imperceptibly at a boy not far from them, seated across the table. "His must be fifth degree."

The boy is Seryozha Mironov. He is pale and freckly, his overgrown hair a shock of tarnished gold, and if you don't look too closely—or if, like Kat, you only focus on the freckles and thin lips that curve in an impertinent smirk—you might think him just another little hoodlum, the sort who breaks windows and trips up the neighborhood girls. Then you take a better glance, and—dear God, so this is what scoliosis looks like. It's not just that he's huddled, neckless, collapsed into himself. His whole body is wrong, a nightmare of bad bones. There's no way around it: Seryozha Mironov is a hunchback.

Kat knows she is staring. It is her most loathsome habit, the one that drives Anechka mad, because for the life of her she can't understand why Kat would just seize up, become fixated like that. It's inconsiderate, offensive. But Kat can't help herself. It is as if her brain is waiting for the impression to take hold, so that later, at night, it can assail her.

She knows she mustn't, and yet she stares anyway. And then it's too late: Seryozha Mironov has felt it. He flinches, his eyes turn hateful, and it's that hate that finally snaps Kat out of her idiotic trance. She looks away, and almost instantly an apple core flies at her forehead. She knows where it came from.

"Are you nuts, Mironov?" says Igor. "Are you out-of-your-mind mad?"

Mironov grins and gives no answer.

"You don't treat girls like that."

"You gonna stop me, Zotov?"

"Suppose I am?"

"Suppose your nose. You're a weakling, Zotov." And as if to prove it, Mironov spits, the spittle landing millimeters from Kat's hand.

"You're such a pig, Mironov," says Kira Mikadze. "We as a class won't tolerate your behavior."

"Tolerate this," says Mironov, and he spits at her too, this time his aim more accurate. The spittle settles on the lace-trimmed collar of Kira's jacket.

"I'll kill you, you freak," Kira roars, forgetting her good manners. She lunges across the table, grabbing a handful of his hair, and he, in turn, catches a few of her own limp strands. The girls on either side of them shriek, and then in a flash it's over and Thumbelina's leaning over them, consoling hysterical Kira.

She asks who started it, and they all point to Mironov.

It's not true, not exactly. Some of the blame is Kat's. She knows she ought to say something. But maybe not? Probably not. There's a difference, Misha often says, between standing up for your principles and showing off. Kat doesn't want to be showing off, especially not on her first day.

She stays seated and lets the events take their course.

"Mironov was spitting."

"And swearing."

"And throwing apple cores."

"Zotov tried to stop him."

Not a gasp, not a whisper concerning Kat. Can it be they haven't noticed?

Later, at the disciplinary meeting, Mironov has to stand before the class.

"He's a coward," says Kira Mikadze. "Only a coward would attack girls."

Thumbelina kneels in front of him. "What made you do it, Seryozha?" She is trying to glimpse something in his eyes, because she's the sort who believes in the goodness of all girls and boys, no matter how rotten. But Mironov won't tell her his reasons, and his eyes are fixed stubbornly on the most mundane spot on the floor. And if the eyes are the mirror of the soul, then Mironov's soul looks like a steel door bolted closed.

THE LAST bell explodes in the hallway, splitting the day down the middle. Upstairs, Thumbelina is tying her trench coat, her desk already occupied by someone new.

"Rosa Dmitrievna!" yelp the weepers, flinging themselves at the woman who must be 1Λ's evening matron.

"You'd think she's their favorite aunt," says Igor Zotov. "Never mind they only met her yesterday."

He's been like this all day, drawing near Kat then drifting away, as if unsure whether his link to her might be a gain or liability.

They watch a group of eager girls gather around Rosa. She tells one to sweep the chalk beneath the blackboard, sends another one to wipe the windowsills with a rag. There's something glacial about her. She is a large, imposing woman, her dark, frowsy hair held back with a silvery barrette. Her skin is faintly yellow. Her black eyes were probably once beautiful—huge, fiery, and even full of dangerous allure—but now they are flat and heavy.

Where Thumbelina was lax and gentle, Rosa is systematic, her mind a collection of lists and seating charts. At dinner she sends Kat to the far end of the table, to sit with the dregs of the class. By contrast, Igor Zotov is somewhere in the middle and Kira Mikadze sits right beside Rosa.

In the dorms at naptime, Kat is assigned to room eleven. Six beds, a wardrobe with a broken door. Next to her are the

weepers, and on the other side are Sonya Bronfman, sickly
Masha Sivova, and Vera Dinnershtein with her mucusy
voice. All the worthwhile girls are elsewhere, and what's
more, they apparently have much better bedrooms. "Night-
stands!" says Nina Petrenko, and that alone seems like an
advantage. Kat wouldn't mind a nightstand, too.

Rosa walks in at three o'clock and stands in the doorway
to survey them. The nap, she says, is mandatory, an essen-
tial part of their treatment, and she'd better not hear a peep
from their dorm.

"Knopman, did you finish your dinner?"

Kat says yes, though it's not true. She found the dinner
inedible. Barley soup. Rice and meat with fatty, untrimmed
edges. She fiddled with her dishes until nearly everyone left,
then stashed them at the busy serving station.

Now her stomach growls; she is ravenous. Per Rosa's
instructions, she keeps her eyes shut. But the noises in the
room are irresistible: the rustle of butcher paper, the crackle
of aluminum foil. She has to look. The girls, every one of
them awake, are snacking on cookies and fruit, unwrapping
buttery sandwiches.

"Rise and shine," Nina Petrenko greets her. "Don't let
our Rosa scare you. She can't do anything to us."

"And if she tries, I'll tell my daddy," says Vera Dinnershtein. Her parents are in cybernetics, which sounds impressive and strange.

Nina says her mother is a nurse, and her mother's friend,
Uncle Vitya, is a militia man. She doesn't have a daddy.

Masha Sivova's father is a pilot, and her mother is also a nurse.

"My mama's in the hospital," whispers Vika Litvinova. "If she dies, I'm gonna kill myself with gas."

"Young people don't just die for no reason," says Nina.

"It's not for no reason. She's sick with cancer."

"Wasn't she with you at the assembly?" Sonya Bronfman asks.

"That was my aunt, you idiot."

"Well then," Sonya says, "same difference. If she dies, you can live with your aunt."

Vika starts sobbing. She flops face down on the bed, and her whole little body begins trembling. She makes the thick keening noise old peasant women make.

"You're such a cow, Bronfman," says Nina Petrenko.

The girls close around Vika, hushing, consoling her, rubbing her shoulders, tenderly patting her head, until the wailing lessens to small pitiful hiccups and she is sitting up again, helpless as a baby chick and pink all over.

After that, they return to their beds. For the last twenty minutes their dorm is noiseless, save for the crackle of Sonya Bronfman's packages. Kat thinks she can smell the contents: mayonnaise sandwiches, soft-spread Viola on white bread.

"You got any treats?" whispers Vika.

Kat says maybe. Some apples in her suitcase, some honey cakes.

"Will you share with me while my mama's sick?"

Kat says all right.

"I'll share with you, too," Vika says. "When my mama gets better."

YOUR MOTHER'S waiting downstairs, someone says, and Kat thinks it must be a mistake. But when after the evening snack she comes down to the coatroom, Anechka is indeed outside. She is slumped in the chair in her old Bologna trench coat, her hair flat, her lipstick flaking. Her plaid grocery bag sits at her feet. Inside are bread, butter, kefir, three sets of copybooks for grading.

Kat can never decide whether Anechka is truly beautiful. She has a strange, off-kilter face. Some days, when she's well-rested and the light falls at a favorable angle, the answer is yes. Her gypsy eyes glow, her skin looks smooth and luminous. Other days, she is at best a plain Jane. Today is a bad day. She looks like she needs a good meal and a nap. Kat offers her a cookie she saved from snack.

"You eat it," says Anechka.

"You don't look too good. What are you doing?"

She shrugs, as if to say she herself isn't sure. "Just thought I'd check on you, that's all."

They sit side by side in the chairs, their shoulders touching, their fingers interlaced. Kat's classmates, en route to their walk, keep glancing at them jealously. Anechka closes her eyes, her face hollow, pale, and for a moment it looks like she's stopped breathing altogether. It worries Kat that she's not sensible. She can go all day without eating, for example. She just forgets. One time she fainted outside her classroom.

"You better go home, Mom."

"What will you do?"

"My homework," Kat says.

"You have homework? Already?"

"It's not a hospital, Mom. It's a school."

Anechka nods. "Sure, sure. You want to come home with me, baby? Just for one night?" She's not herself today: hasty, impulsive, tipsy with some inexplicable sadness.

Kat thinks of home: the sizzle of potatoes on the stove, the sofa piled with soft pillows, the three of them snuggled together, reading or grading papers, while on TV the news program ends and the weather forecast scrolls across the screen. But then tomorrow they'll have to reenact this morning's wrenching business. The tense, hurried breakfast. The impasse at the bus stop (Anechka insisting they must take a cab and Misha, predictably, resisting). The trudge through the park and the rushed farewell in the hallway on the second floor. But worst of all would be watching them leave again, their easy carriage as they descend the stairs, their perfect, splendid backs.

"What do you say?" Anechka nudges. "You want to do it? Should I speak to that matron of yours?"

Kat tells her not to. She says, "I like it here."

3

THE SCHOOL OPERATES MONDAY THROUGH SAT-
urday, each day regimented, sliced into intervals,
controlled by the jangle of electric bells. The occupants
arrive Monday morning, their suitcases bursting with fresh
laundry and replenished snacks. Inside, their routine never
wavers, from the wake-up call at 7 a.m. to lights-out at 9:30
p.m. Morning calisthenics are held outside, whatever the
weather. Lunch comes after third period. Dinner, at half
past two, is always followed by nap.

By week two, Kat decides that she does indeed like it here,
or that at least she's not unhappy. She falls gratefully into
her new communal schedule. She loves the consistency, loves
that they always return to the same well-lit classroom. She
loves the compartment in the base of her cot; the stacks of
newly wrapped textbooks; the plants in their birch-colored
holders, which need watering every afternoon. Above all,
she loves the soft clucking call of Thumbelina: "Come
along, my chickens. Hurry up, my doves." They gather up

under her wing and there's safety there, and certainty to every undertaking.

There's much she doesn't know: how to get to the gym or the music room; how to make her bed so the quilt looks flat. In medical gymnastics, she puts her leotard on inside out. In art, she fills her jar with scalding water. No big deal, Thumbelina tells her, when the jar cracks in half.

The school is just like any other school. They follow the same curriculum. The treatments haven't started; they haven't been evaluated or even cleared for swimming lessons yet. The only things different are the cots and medical gymnastics.

She does well enough in her classes, though she's not exceptional. Her penmanship is poor; she sometimes gets distracted in math, her mind drifting off to her parents' school. She wonders what they might be doing at that moment. If it's third period on Tuesday, Misha's got his rowdy fifth-graders, or if it's after lunch on Wednesday, Anechka's got her 8B. Galochka P. is in 8B; she's always been Kat's favorite, saving for her the cheese rolls in chocolate that the school serves for lunch once a week.

Thumbelina calls out Kat's name, and it takes Kat a minute to remember where she is. And to think that at home Anechka and Misha must be thinking she is conquering the world with her intelligence. She'll have to tell them otherwise.

Something else is required to conquer the world, something more than declaiming nineteenth-century poetry from memory. She found "Winter! The countryman enchanted" in her primer, but what does it matter if she is the only one who knows where it comes from? Does it matter that she can recite pages from *Eugene Onegin*, and not just the nature bits? Not unless you're also in possession of a twenty-two-piece marker set, pink and green scented erasers, a pack of foreign bubble gum, a luminous pencil case made in Romania or the GDR. Kat's pencil case is wooden with a plain squeaky cover and a pokerwork squirrel on the top. No one's ever been impressed by a pokerwork squirrel.

It's worse in the evenings, when Rosa comes in. She never praises Kat for anything, never forgives her blunders. Whenever she addresses her, she uses only her last name. You can always tell who Rosa likes, because she calls them by their first names. There's Kira Mikadze, Rosa's deputy, ready to apprise her of everyone's transgressions and mishaps. There's pretty, pony-tailed Alina Nesterenko; Tanya Kushina, quiet and responsible; Lida Kravchenko, with her chiseled Mongoloid face; Inna Smirnova, whose father is a Party functionary. These are Rosa's homing pigeons. During homework hours they carry little missives from her to other matrons, and when Rosa herself must step out, she tells one of them to watch the class.

On their evening walks, a retinue of girls follows Rosa. Her favorites cling to her arms. They are trailed closely by other hopefuls, the girls from the middle rungs. Even the weepers, who in the dorm at night say nasty things about Rosa, all but sprawl at her feet.

"Slave mentality," Igor Zotov calls it. Like Kat, he keeps away from this circus, and Kat suspects that his arrogance is why he's not one of Rosa's pets. Slave mentality, his father told him, is a uniquely Russian quality. Igor says people in Russia are like dogs. The worse you treat them, the more they adore you. "That's why Stalin was so popular."

Kat knows a bit about Stalin. From the kitchen gatherings at home, she's already figured that he wasn't a good person. She knows about the cult of personality. She knows about the big mosaic portrait that used to grace Arbat subway station a long time ago, and how it was destroyed one night by a group of strange men in civilian clothes. There's also a song her parents play sometimes: "And on the left side of my chest, Stalin's profile. And on the right side, Marinka full-face." If only she had listened harder, she could remember the rest of the song. Igor, it turns out, knows lots of songs. Banned songs, he says. *Blatnie* songs. Made up by criminals, in labor camps. His favorite one is about the Bermuda Triangle and an insane asylum.

Though maybe it's good that she doesn't remember the words to "Marinka full-face." What if it's also banned? She might even embarrass herself; her grandmother says she has a voice like a crow. It's best to just stroll next to Igor and listen to him murmur *his* songs. Sometimes he puts his arm around her waist, the way adults do. At night, the weepers ask if she is going to marry Igor Zotov.

But not all attention is welcome. There's the curse of Seryozha Mironov, who stalks them, pelts them with sticks and rocks. "Bride and groom," he chants. "Bride and groom. No brain and no room." There's nowhere they can hide from him. They are restricted to the small paved square where they do morning calisthenics—that, and the rough empty lot at the back of the block. The rest of the campus is off-limits.

They are, however, allowed to walk the short distance to the entrance gates and watch the arrival of visiting parents. Unlike Kat's parents, these parents don't arrive through the hole in the back fence. They come by a different bus, which takes them from the subway to the campus. The more lavish of them show up in cars and cabs. Or, in the case of Igor Zotov's mother, in a black government Volga.

She comes to visit him on Wednesday. In the semicircle just outside the gates, the Volga swings sideways. A woman emerges from the back, as dazzling as a TV variety performer. A tall, pouty beauty with long blonde hair and pearly eyelids and lips—though up close you notice that her nose is a touch too broad, her lower lip too thick, and there's something else marring her face, a hint of unhappiness or boredom. She toddles up to Kat and Igor on her incredible hairpin heels, and Igor doesn't introduce them.

A boy like Igor Zotov! Rosa gets a puzzled expression whenever she spots him with Kat. What does he see in her? Kat's sure it's her intellect. She may not have the right kind of school supplies, but her parents have taken her to all the major art museums. She's read *The Three Musketeers* and seen films with Fernandel and de Funès. No wonder Igor, himself a cultured person, appreciates her company.

But Igor's attention is inconstant. It flickers into being and fades again, and each time she wonders if she's somehow disappointed him.

"Your mom is really beautiful," she tells him. They are

walking back from supper, and though she's not totally sincere, she *is* intrigued by this strange sparkly creature, so unlike the tired parents that come for everybody else.

"She's not my mother," Igor says.

He avoids Kat for the next two days, and when at last they speak again, neither of them mentions the woman.

ANECHKA TURNS up Friday evening. She sweeps in all breathless, pops up out of nowhere in her typical illogical Anechka fashion, without warning or excuse. It's useless to remind her that the next day is Saturday, that Kat will be going home after school.

"Everyone's parents came yesterday," Kat whines. "Either yesterday or on Wednesday."

She should know better, of course. This line of logic never works with Anechka. "Since when are we comparing ourselves to 'everyone'?"

She's brought Kat a jar of grated carrots mixed with sugar, and her rabbit baby spoon. Kat's poor appetite is legendary.

Kat tightens the lid on the jar after only a couple of spoonfuls.

"I'm not taking it home," protests Anechka.

"You eat it then. You need it more than I do."

They sit side by side on the curvy park bench by the entrance. Kat studies her surreptitiously. Anechka does look better than she did last week. The blue hollows under her eyes have nearly vanished. She's put on a tight-fitting turtleneck and a pretty nephrite necklace. She's reapplied her cherry lipstick, which brightens up her face, makes it appear almost restful. Anechka's beauty is a secret: it teases you, it peeks and retreats, shimmering mischievously in the corners of her eyes and lips.

"Let's take a walk," Kat says to her.

With a parent in tow, you can walk anywhere on campus. Every path is open to them to roam and explore. You can slip out the back into the park. You can leave through the front gates, go as far as the bus stop. Or go home altogether.

Kat's desires are modest. She knows there's a swing behind the swimming pool, so she leads Anechka that way, down the central alley. She asks her what's new at her and Misha's school. Has anybody asked about Kat? Have there been new gatherings at home, with manuscript copies read aloud, dissident talk, songs on tapes?

Anechka snaps, "Are you crazy? What gatherings?" Then she softens and says they've had no energy for anything like that. Not to mention that it's gotten too dangerous, and now with Kat's serious illness they can't take any risks.

As they pass the big canteen, they are walloped by the heavy smell of food: warm cocoa and baked pudding. Anechka stops and holds a handkerchief against her mouth.

Kat says, "What's the matter?"

Anechka doesn't answer. After a moment she runs behind the garbage cans, and there she is sick, sick in the most overt and vile way, in full view of anyone who might happen by. Rosa and her girls, for instance. It wouldn't be unthinkable. Kat can see Rosa's squeamish expression: Who is this inappropriate person? Is she drunk? And the girls will make the same prissy faces as Rosa.

When Anechka returns, her makeup is all smeared and there's a bit of vomit on her shoe. She tries to clean herself with her soiled handkerchief, which doesn't really help. After a while she gives up and tells Kat, "Come with me."

Together they sneak into the nearest block.

"Are we allowed?"

"Be quiet, Kat. Be quiet."

Inside, the corridor is dim. The floors are covered in chipped institutional tile. They find a dank bathroom with a sink. It smells bad, the mirror is painted over, and Kat feels that she herself might throw up. Anechka sends her to wait outside.

In the corridor, white boat-like objects are placed against the walls. Kat leans in to examine them. She touches their plaster-cast surfaces, hard and grainy against her fingertips. No, not boats. There's something unnervingly human about the shapes of these things. They're like molds of real people. A last name is scribbled on the back of each one, blue letters where the shoulder blades would be.

"What are they?" Kat asks Anechka.

"Beds," she says. "Special beds. You probably won't need one."

In the secluded corner behind the swimming pool, Anechka sits on the swing. She studies her face in a tiny hand mirror, applying powder to her nose and her cheeks. "Do I smell bad?" she worries.

Kat says, "Are you sick?"

"I'm just too wound up lately, baby."

"Because of me?"

"Because of everything." Anechka fumbles in her coat pocket and draws out a pack of cigarettes. "It's constant stress and hurry-scurry. At work, at home. Everyone wants a piece of me. Get the dry cleaning, do the laundry, buy and prepare goulash, and while you're at it, be so kind as to organize a museum excursion."

"You're smoking?"

"It helps with the nausea."

In Anechka's slender fingers the cigarette signals a threat. Kat knows that she used to smoke in college. She and Misha spent all their free time in the smoking room of the Lenin Library, mingling with dissidents and sympathizers like themselves. Those were different times, though, exciting times, long before Kat was born, when her parents could rush on a whim to a Fellini retrospective or Okudzhava concert at the Central House of Art Workers. Sometimes, at a party, Anechka might still sneak a quick cigarette or two, but never like this, never in the open.

"Throw away that poison. You need water and some decent food." Kat searches through Anechka's plaid bag, but all she comes up with is the unfinished jar of grated carrots. "Some vitamins at least?"

Anechka wrinkles her nose.

"I need you to do something special, baby. Can you do something special for me?"

Kat nods eagerly. "What?"

Anechka gives her a look like she's the last friend she has in the whole world. Her eyes are enormous, imploring; her voice, barely audible, is soft. She's so impetuous, so rash, always speaking too soon, plunging headlong into every project and often getting hurt. You wish you could shield her somehow.

"Don't tell your father what happened."

"The cigarette?"

"The cigarette and the vomiting."

"That's it?" Kat's disappointed. She wanted something grander: a sacrifice, a task. Maybe she could sneak into the infirmary and make off with some medicine.

"It doesn't seem like much, but it's important. Changes are coming, baby. I can't explain it now, but later I might ask you to do more."

Kat wants to ask, What sort of changes? But she knows Anechka won't tell her. Later means later. The thing is, she's scared of changes. In Kat's experience, they're almost never good. They start with this thinly veiled secrecy—a dismissal, a smile, a cryptic hint—only to explode in your face, breaking your life into bits, scattering them without a second thought.

THEIR APARTMENT seems different now that Kat's at school most of the week. It is as if in her absence it has morphed into an utterly new entity—echoing, mysterious, bigger than it used to be. In reality, it's not a very big apartment. Two rooms, furnished with sparse, disparate furniture: her parents' sleeper sofa, the old desk in the corner, the thin-legged coffee table, as rickety as it can be. The armoire. The bookcase. The ancient mahogany dresser which holds their television set. The only ornament is an odd figurine made of tree snags and branches; it sits on the top bookshelf next to Cervantes and Rabelais.

Kat's own room is just as spartan: bookcase, wardrobe, bed. Her toys are packed away in boxes, because she has no more need for them. Her desk is always organized, her clothes neatly folded.

Her parents are the opposite. They leave behind trails of their clothes and random scraps of paper. Crumpled notes and receipts, discarded ticket stubs, theater programs, telephone numbers jotted on newspaper margins, which later no one can identify. Kat thinks of their slovenly ways as a sign of their genius, though the chaos upsets her sometimes.

Home from school, Kat pads between the rooms of their apartment. She tries to sniff out the changes Anechka warned her about, the telltale messages and signs. In the hallway, she checks the built-in closet. In the kitchen she studies the Moscow Circus calendar, which has all their upcoming appointments. In the end, she finds nothing and only makes Anechka annoyed.

Anechka hates their apartment. She calls it a rat cage, a low-clearance death trap, and sometimes, when she thinks Kat can't hear her, simply a piece of crap. The ceilings are too low. There's no decent sound insulation. Not to mention the overall shoddy craftsmanship and the never-ending winter drafts. It's not her fault, she says, that she was raised to appreciate quality.

That mythical apartment of Anechka's childhood and youth! How it haunts them, with its cavernous hallways and three-meter ceilings. How often it is invoked, bemoaned, and pined for, and even thrown down as a trump card in family spats.

Anechka took Kat to see it one time. On the way from a matinee, they stopped in a small cul-de-sac. It was winter. The building had a shabby old façade and looked dilapidated. Anechka said, "Let's go inside." She had this loopy idea that they could actually visit the apartment, that its current residents would greet the two of them with open arms. Insane, to be sure. But Anechka had this mad glow about her: you wanted to be on her side, you wanted to believe in her. She had the magic, the gumption, the world at her feet. All you had to do was grab her hand and leap . . . Still, Kat balked and pulled back, suddenly stiff with fear.

Anechka called her a coward and marched in by herself. She came back not five minutes later and wouldn't admit that she'd failed. Best-case scenario, no one answered the door. Or maybe the residents thought she was a gypsy. There had been stories of gypsies ringing the bells of random apartments, forcing their way in, robbing innocent citizens.

Kat dislikes old apartments, with their yellowish murkiness, the waxy smell of age. She prefers the simplicity of their little place, so light, and neat, and compact. In the morning, sun skims the pink wallpaper in her bedroom, blurring the discolored pattern, warming up the space. She loves waking up in her bed, breathing in the dusty scent of home.

On Sunday morning, she wakes to the sunlight playing on her eyelids. From the kitchen comes the banging of the frying pan, the quiet murmur of her parents. She keeps her eyes closed, chasing the tail end of a dream. Mornings at school are too abrupt and early. They arrive unceremoniously, with a burst of energetic stomping, the thud of opened doors, the intrusion of bright electric lights.

In the kitchen the voices grow strident, and now it sounds as though her parents are quarreling.

"Let's not make me into a tyrant!" says her father, just as she enters the kitchen.

"Who's being a tyrant?" Kat says.

Anechka, at the stove, is boiling laundry in a pail.

"Ah, Button!" Misha says. He seems absurdly thrilled to see her. He will do anything to circumvent an argument. Right now, he is finishing a plate of eggs and sausage, which on Sundays he makes for himself.

"You want some eggs?"

Anechka says, "She's having oatmeal."

Kat scrunches her nose, makes gagging noises, gestures like she's being strangled by the oatmeal. She means it as a joke.

"Stop it," Anechka says. "Stop at once this inappropriate performance." Wrapped in her bathrobe with the buttons askew, she is looking bedraggled this morning. "I've gone to the trouble of making it for you—"

"Darling," Misha says.

She ignores him. "The least you can do is have the decency—"

"Darling, oatmeal is not a problem."

"I hate that you're always encouraging her."

But what is there to encourage? Kat picks at the oatmeal that's by now gone tepid, while Misha hurries her along. They are supposed to visit Zoya Moiseevna this morning.

"Do we have to?" Kat groans, and Misha says, "We do!"

"Just you and me? How come Mom doesn't have to go?"

"Oh Button, come on. You know how she and Grandma get. It's a small apartment. Things can get awkward."

"You're joking," Kat says. "You're always joking."

From her post by the laundry pail, Anechka says she'd be happy to go, but who will finish the laundry? Grind meat for the cutlets, cook soup for the next couple of days, peel potatoes, darn Kat's tights and underthings, scrub the floors, clean the stove?

"I'll stay and help," Kat offers.

"You're more hindrance than help."

"Button, don't look for excuses. You haven't seen your grandma since July. She loves you, you know."

"Sure," mutters Anechka. "Let's pretend she's capable of loving *anybody*."

Love or no love, they're going. With Misha you can snivel and moan all you want. He never gets annoyed. He keeps kidding around with you in his involved, kindly way, and in the meantime, you put on your warm socks and boots and wind a scarf around your neck. The next thing you know he's holding up your coat and the whole errand is a foregone conclusion.

Kat doesn't like to visit Zoya Moiseevna. First, it takes them forever to get to Kuzminki, and once you're there, there's nothing to do. Her grandmother lives in a five-story Khrushchev building. Her apartment is one of those nine-square-meters-per-person deals: it consists of a single room, no hallway, a midget-sized kitchen.

Zoya Moiseevna's skin is tawny from her vacation in Estonia. As far as Kat's concerned, they are still feuding. Her grandmother appears to concur. "That's quite a hack job," she says, examining Kat's hair. "You look like a boy."

Kat tells her the tan makes her wrinkly and stupid.

"Girls," Misha begs them. "Don't quarrel, girls."

In her grandmother's single room, a sewing machine is perched atop a wobbly table. She's always fiddling with it, making curtains, pot holders, or plain canvas bags—though never anything attractive. Still, it's a beautiful sewing machine. Black and shiny, with a golden harpy on it. Misha's father brought it back from Germany in 1945.

"I could teach you to sew," Zoya Moiseevna says out of the blue.

Kat begs off, because a) she doesn't want to, and b) she knows her grandmother's just showing off. Kat's brought along her book, *Timm Thaler, The Boy Who Lost His Laughter*. She points to it now.

"Reading," grumbles Zoya Moiseevna. "Always reading. You should be moving, running. Your back's already crooked; next you'll need glasses like your dad."

"God forbid," Misha says.

They are seated across from her in matching armchairs; Kat's book, closed for now, is in her lap. She knows there's a copy of *Literaturka* in Misha's coat pocket, and she suspects he'd rather be reading as well. He yawns. He is tired. But he doesn't tell Zoya Moiseevna about the nights he and Anechka spend crafting articles for small samizdat rags, the articles they publish under pseudonyms. His mother knows nothing, and apparently it's always been like that. She doesn't know, for example, that Misha, while still in high school, spent three winter days outside the courthouse where the dissident writers Sinyavsky and Daniel were tried for their anti-Soviet activities. She doesn't know that on the third day the KGB swooped down on the crowds and Misha was just lucky that, having gotten too cold, he happened to be at a *pelmeny* joint around the corner. Later he'd discover that Anechka was there too, though at the time they didn't know each other.

Zoya Moiseevna, of course, has no inkling. To her, Misha is a hardworking, straitlaced boy, and he makes sure to foster this illusion. He gripes to her about school matters: his workload this term is absurd, truancy is rampant, and the principal is clamoring for more ideological outreach—more pageants, rallies, marches.

"And your wife?" says Zoya Moiseevna. "She's healthy, I assume? Running around as always and squandering your money?"

"It's her money, too."

"You're hungry?" she changes the subject, and when he

grunts something uncertain in response, she tells him to come help her in the kitchen. "I don't have much," she warns him. "Tea, biscuits, that's all. Some of us have only our pension to count on. Some of us know enough to live within our means."

"Miss prudence!" Misha laughs at her. "Living like a monk in a cell."

"I fail to see the humor."

Left alone, Kat reaches for the stack of her grandmother's magazines. They are called *Working Woman*. She flips through the pages of fashion advice, food recipes, lurid relationship letters from a waitress at the restaurant Sunrise. She finds a profile of an actor she likes, with a daughter her age, a pretty wife, a miniature poodle. But her attention drifts. Almost despite herself, she listens to the conversation in the kitchen. How can she resist? Misha has a lovely booming voice, and the walls in Zoya Moiseevna's apartment are so very thin.

"She's eating poorly," says Misha. Everyone's always talking about Kat's eating, her pickiness, her lack of appetite. They seem to treat it as a neutral topic, like weather or food shortages.

"I told your wife to stop indulging her."

"She's been sick, throwing up a little."

"Who?" says Zoya Moiseevna. "The little one's sick?"

No, Misha tells her. *Not* the little one.

The kettle blasts its ear-splitting whistle, and for a while no one speaks.

"You're joking," says Zoya Moiseevna. "It's the *last* thing you need."

"Please stay out of it, Mom."

"I'm warning you, Misha. I'm absolutely serious."

"It's our decision."

"Sure it is. But who's going to raise your decision? Go ahead, breed more cripples. Just don't come to me—"

Whatever else she means to say is drowned by a din of many plates plunging to their death. A cupboard full of plates, plus something else, solid and rattling. Kat jumps in her armchair. Her grandmother shrieks in a strange, strangled way, and then it's so quiet that Kat wonders if she's been crushed to death.

"You're inhuman," Misha says to this invisible, silent, possibly dead grandmother. "I never want to speak to you again."

And this is what Kat sees as they are leaving: An overturned chair. A kitchen table resting on its side. On the floor, a river of tea, shards of red polka-dot cups and saucers.

Her grandmother, though, seems unharmed. She stands upright and unrepentant, staring out the window, her shoulders raised, her back straight as a plank. "Get out," she says, not bothering to face them.

IT IS UNTHINKABLE. Kat can hardly believe it, though she's seen it with her own eyes: Misha—her dear gentle Misha, who under normal circumstances won't even raise his voice, who only has to look a bit perplexed in order to subdue the most unruly of his students—her Misha, her idol, her dad, has just destroyed his mother's kitchen.

"What did she mean—" she begins.

But he shrinks from her question, and later he says nothing as they ride the subway home. He has this darting, lost expression. She rests her cheek against his sleeve. Cripples, she thinks. That word again. Her grandmother called her a cripple, but why did Misha have to get so angry? Maybe because it's true. Except she's not a cripple—is she? She's got her limbs; she doesn't hobble when she walks. Unless something has marked her already. She thinks of all the times in recent weeks she has stood before the mirror. Some days she sees nothing; her body looks perfectly symmetrical, or maybe she's convinced herself it is. Other days it's there from the start, the damage lurid, unmistakable. Her parents told her that no one could see it, not when she has her clothes on, but now she knows: she's faulty and the world can sense it.

A few blocks before they reach their building, Misha clears his throat. "Can you do me a favor?"

"What is it?" she says, though she's already guessed it, both the question and her eventual response. She won't mention the incident to Anechka, not under any circumstances.

4

PROFESSOR FABRI HAS DRY, ELDERLY HANDS. HE taps Kat's shoulder blades, tugs at the band of her panties. He tells her to bend. She is standing barefoot in front of him, on a soft, silvery carpet, in a room slick and modern, full of big geometrical paintings and polished Italian furniture. Is it really Italian? She doesn't know. What she knows is that Professor Fabri lives in Italy and also in Moscow sometimes. He is a famous specialist, he travels constantly. The school is his pride and his special project. He founded it, but he's only around for a few weeks at a time.

Dressed in a smart three-piece suit, he doesn't look like other doctors. His hands smell delicious, like good foreign soap. He wraps them around her waist. She's a ceramic pot, a sculpture he is molding. "A perfect little figure," he says. "Our mannequin girl." She knows who mannequin girls are. They are in her grandmother's *Working Woman* magazines, modeling flouncy dresses and berets. "Bend," he tells her, and she does, so pliant, so obedient. "Bend and touch the

floor. Keep your knees straight." She tries, but she can't. She
is sorry to disappoint him. "Just as well," he says. "Just as
well. Limited range of motion, but the curvatures are small.
I see no significant problems." And then he says, "Let's take
a look at her X-rays."

It started last week. The first nurse showed up on Wednesday. Short and thick, with great bluffs of shoulders, she
called the names of a few kids and made them leave with her.
You could tell they didn't want to. Don't worry, Thumbelina
told them. It's only Professor Fabri. He's in town. He's doing
consultations.

The nurses have been coming ever since. They vary in
age and appearance, and Kat has a distaste for all of them,
their sharp medical smell, their stiff and officious demeanor.
They take a few kids away with them, and those they pick
now leave unafraid. The consultations aren't painful, and
nobody minds a short trip to the medical block. Nobody
except Kat, that is. She's been dreading this new consultation that's supposed to confirm just how bad her scoliosis is
and recommend a course of treatment. She still sometimes
thinks it's a mistake, this sickness. She feels fine. She can't
be sick.

The last few weeks were almost blissful as she focused
on mastering her penmanship, collecting dry leaves for a
herbarium, learning about the nature of the rain, snow, and
wind. Regular schoolgirl activities, typical of first grade.
Until the nurses came, she could almost forget why she was
here. She could pretend that medical gymnastics was no different from gym. She could simply not look at the hunch-

back Seryozha Mironov, ignore the braced and stumbling figures of the older kids.

Now, at the consultation, a small group of doctors crowd around her X-rays. There's the head of orthopedics, Doctor Razumovskaya, pretty with pinned-up orange curls; and there's the cruddy-looking Doctor Bobrova, who is 1A's attending doctor.

Professor Fabri takes a pencil and traces a long letter S. Lumbar fifteen, he says. Thoracic twenty. Now ladies, be so kind to direct your attention to the widening of the gaps between Ms. Knopman's vertebras. What does it tell us, Dr. Razumovskaya? Yes, that's correct: the disease will develop aggressively. Bracing is imperative; surgery, not out of the question for this patient. We'd like to avoid it, naturally. For now we'll call it a wait-and-see phase. A pity, such a pretty little figure. She'll be our mannequin girl yet. Don't you agree, Dr. Bobrova? Dr. Razumovskaya?

THE FIRST floor of the medical block looks deserted and smells, inexplicably, like a shoe repair shop. On the walls are dour portraits in oil, medical drawings. Children in strange contraptions. A crooked sapling tied to a pole.

She isn't sure how it happened: for a moment she was almost perfect, but then the good doctor changed his mind, spoke of numbers and vertebras and called her something else. Not a mannequin girl, but a "patient." She's probably supposed to call her parents. She's supposed to get back to her class. But the nurse who brought her here must have left,

and Kat, too nauseated to think straight, keeps trying random passages. Another corridor, another door, its handle
wrapped in gauze. She steps across the threshold, and everything becomes bright and distorted. She's in a large room
filled with body parts. Throat molds, pelvic enclosures,
shelves of plaster torsos.

A man in a black smock approaches her. "You've come
for a fitting?" he asks. His left thumb is missing, his middle
finger's cut in half. With the remaining fingers he's holding
an odd metal device.

"What's wrong? Have you swallowed your tongue?"

He follows her eyes, fixed on that horrible, misshapen
hand of his. He thinks she's looking at the clumsy appara-
tus, which he's holding by its horizontal plank. So he gives
it a shake, this thing, this *brace*, and asks Kat if she likes it.
"Clunk, clunk," he says at the metallic sound, and laughs—
as if it's a funny joke to make the brace jerk like a puppet.
"You like it? I'll make you one, girlie. You *are* a girlie, aren't
you? Hard to tell with these damn haircuts."

"I'm sorry," she says, backing out, her legs like cotton
wool. "It's just a mistake. I'm sorry."

IN HER dreams there's water. A smooth expanse of glit-
tering azure. It's surprisingly firm, firm like a bed, and can
easily hold her small body. It's warm, and the lights at the
swimming pool are always on.

The real swimming lessons are in the afternoon. No one
bothers to turn the lights on, and because of this the water

looks not welcoming but turbid. They do exercises at first, breathing and dribbling, but after that Kat can't let go of the low tiled wall or the metal handrails. "Trust the water," the trainer tells her. Next to her, the weepers are flopping on their bellies, gliding a couple of meters to the nearest rope, stretching out in a "starfish," gathering themselves into a "cork." They are fearless, the weepers. A few lanes over, some older girls are doing laps, so fluid and fast, just like Kat in her dreams, their graceful arms cleaving the water.

Back in the changing room, the weepers leapfrog from bench to bench, celebrate their terrific weightlessness. Kat watches the older girls get dressed. They must be in ninth or tenth grade. They have womanly breasts, shapely hips. They goose one another and sing, apply their mascara and lotions, shuffle back and forth in their towels and underthings. Their braces rest atop the dressing cabinets.

Kat can't recall how she escaped the brace shop, how she made it back to class. Someone must have found her and led her back to Thumbelina. She got ill that evening, running a fever and throwing up. The night nurse had to take her to the infirmary, and in the morning Anechka came in a cab to pick her up.

"I don't want a brace," Kat said, when they got home.

"You want to be an invalid instead?" Anechka gave her some water and aspirin. Then she gave her the usual spiel about perseverance and heroism. Life's not a holiday, she told her, with trumpery and prizes and cream puffs. Then she went to the toilet, because she had to throw up.

Kat knows all about life. She also knows that she's got

company. Most of her classmates are about to be braced; only a few remain unscathed (Alina Nesterenko, Igor Zotov). Some have already gone to their brace moldings, and their reports set Kat on edge. Nina Petrenko says you are "immured." Mironov insists there are knives and hooks. He says that the molding people hang you by your throat. One wrong move and you're strangled or your throat's cut. He stares at Kat as he says it. Sometimes he laughs. He can't wait for her to get accidentally murdered.

She's learned by now what the braces look like. She eyes them each time after swimming, studies the lattice of their metal planks and clamps. Each brace is like the carcass of a prehistoric animal. There is a wide band of plastic to catch one's hips and bottom; a swath of corset; an awful circular head-holder. She watches the older girls put their braces on. Step by step, they tighten the laces and belts, lock up their chests, anchor their heads. They allow these monstrous things to swallow their bodies, and when at last they rise they're not the same. Brittle and halting and strange. All of the liveliness is gone from them.

KAT'S MOLDING is scheduled for first thing Friday morning, and announced three days in advance. Anechka takes the morning off. She arrives, as directed, with a fresh towel and an old swimming cap that she won't be sorry to have spoiled. She is not happy about this whole setup, keeps talking about her 8B, how they might flunk their regional exams next month.

Kat is undressing in a narrow shower room. It has a boarded-up window, a brown cot, a bathtub. In the next room, she has glimpsed two giantesses in heavy-duty aprons. She's taking her time: folding and refolding her uniform, fiddling with her hair, pushing the ends under the swimming cap.

Anechka's face is queasy as she watches her. After a while she drops her head, covers her eyes. "I can't stand the smell in here, baby. Gypsum, or whatever. You mind if I wait outside?"

"But Mom," Kat begins, then grits her teeth and says it's fine. She's ready to cry with disappointment. She is frightened, so frightened. And the smell, the sickly gypsum smell, it turns her stomach too.

The giantesses have crude but kindly faces, and when Kat at last appears, swathed in a white sheet like some Greek goddess and naked underneath, they don't scold her for tardiness, but smile at her gently and slowly. Soft-hearted rogues, they tell her not to be afraid.

A tall wooden construction resembling a gallows stands in the center of the room. They help her to this scaffolding. They strap her in. Hard wooden planks rest firm against her buttocks; a rubber harness is looped around her chin. The screws are tightened to the maximum, the harness cranked up so high she can't even glance at her feet. You must be absolutely still to get a perfect mold.

The women slather her in Vaseline. They start with her hips and pelvic area, wrapping her in warm, moist bandages. They wait until the bandages congeal. Now it's a shell, tough and sticky. They wait some more, then label it and cut it in the back with a pair of blunt, crooked scissors, the blades rasping with effort, the cold metal tickling Kat's skin.

Next they do her upper torso, a process that follows the same precise steps.

Then it's her head and neck: the wet swish of bandages against her swimming cap, thickening layer upon layer. They cover her chin, her lips, stopping just short of her nostrils. The world grows mute, indistinct. She can't gesture or speak. The giantesses retreat to the back of the room, and she can't even call for them. How long has it been? Don't panic, she tells herself, don't panic. With her head jacked up high, she can't see if the rest of her exists. She is disembodied.

IN THE dressing room, she weeps under the hot shower. Anechka soaps her back, scrubs the white residue between her shoulder blades. "Was it bad?"

Kat doesn't answer, because isn't it obvious? Anechka should've been there. Maybe it wasn't the gypsum smell that made her mother queasy. Maybe it was Kat herself, the image of her naked on the scaffolding, her crooked body swathed in bandages.

"No throwing up tonight," Anechka says. Kat nods in a dumb, noncommittal way.

Anechka says, "It's a deal. If you don't anymore, I won't either."

The very next instant, she has to clamp her hand over her mouth and dart into the smelly toilet cubicle next door.

It occurs to Kat that something's wrong with Anechka. Horribly wrong. She might even have cancer, like Vika Litvinova's mother. Mothers get sick all the time, Kat knows that now. They languish in hospitals, perish during messed-up surgeries, come back to haunt their daughters, like in the scary bedtime stories Nina Petrenko tells the girls. And some, like Igor Zotov's real mother, leave and never return.

"Stop whimpering," says Anechka. She is back, wiping her mouth and looking rather peeved. "So you had your molding done. It's hardly the end of the world."

She doesn't understand that Kat's now sobbing for her.

Mothers get sick. Mothers die. Mothers abandon you.

5

WEEKS GO BY, AND KAT CAN'T TELL IF ANECHKA is getting better. Since the molding appointment, she hasn't seen her throw up again. But that in itself doesn't prove anything. There could be other symptoms. Anechka takes long naps on Sundays, and when she isn't napping, she seems sad. She and Misha have tense conversations behind the closed kitchen door, and Kat feels excluded from their secrets. And it's not just the secrets. She's unsure of their schedules, can't place some of the names they mention, those of their new students and colleagues that Kat isn't likely to meet. She's a transient presence at home: a visitor, a stranger.

It is now the end of October. "A somber time, the eyes' enchantment," wrote the poet A. S. Pushkin, but what did he really know of autumn? He never had to live in a school-sanatorium, get up at the crack of dawn, do calisthenics in the school's frosted courtyard. The light in the morning is meager, and in the afternoon it rains. When it rains in the evening, their walk gets canceled.

"It's just as well," says Rosa, hearding 1A into the classroom. They have a lot of work to do. They are preparing to become Octobrists. Once received into the Octobrist organization, they'll wear red-star pins. They won't be mere children anymore, but vital participants in their country's great ventures. It is an honor, Rosa tells them. It comes with duties, tasks. The first of which is to prepare for the initiation ceremony, with a montage of patriotic poems, songs, and chants.

Rosa has already selected the poems, written them out on long paper strips:

> *A star burns on a soldier's hat.*
> *A star speaks of our work and sweat.*
> *And on the flags of our land*
> *Our Soviet stars shine lights ahead.*

It is a poor, incompetent poem: A star, a star, a star.

"Is there a problem, Knopman?"

Kat says no. "It's just . . . It's so short." She's only got one poem, while some kids got two or three each.

"You can have one of mine," says Igor Zotov.

Rosa bristles. "What do you think you're doing? Swapping gum wrappers? Is that how you're going to act when your country entrusts you with a special task? Are you going to haggle with your country?"

The class says no—empathically, in unison. No, no, no! A fiery assurance from every one of them.

"Russian people don't haggle," says Rosa.

Kat isn't so sure. She's gone to the market in Kratovo, she's seen Valentina haggle, and her mother, and the old women with callused, dirt-encrusted fingers who plunk radishes on duck-shaped metal scales. The only one who never haggles is Misha. He has a delicate constitution, an overdeveloped sense of fairness. Faced with inflated prices, he simply walks away.

After the poems and songs come elections. Soon they'll be more than just a class. They'll be an Octobrist detachment. Rosa explains how each detachment needs its leaders, those the class respects the most. A detachment commander and a class elder.

"What's the difference?" asks Sonya Bronfman, and Kat tenses instinctively. She hates being Bronfman's cot partner. She has nothing in common with this dormouse Sonya, but their proximity makes Kat complicit in every stupid thing her partner says.

"It shouldn't concern you, Bronfman," says Inna Smirnova, a spindly, mean-spirited girl. "You're not eligible."

The elder, Rosa says, is responsible for practical matters. Cleanliness, attendance, the schedule of housekeeping tasks. The commander's job is more ideological in nature.

They select Tanya Kushina to be their elder. The vote is unanimous, except for Bronfman who abstains. Tanya Kushina is neat and even-tempered, with short, curly hair tucked behind her ears and small, clean hands. She has the best handwriting: substantial, blocky, each letter at a perfect slant. You don't expect such a diminutive person to have such forceful handwriting.

Next comes commander. Alina Nesterenko nominates
Kira Mikadze, and Kira nominates Alina, which is a cour-
tesy and a big mistake. The majority votes for Alina. It's not
that surprising. Alina is prettier than Kira—prettier, in fact,
than all of them. She is like a princess, with her long, wil-
lowy body and hair.

"It's unfair," says Vika Litvinova, when they retreat into
their dorms. She's sitting cross-legged on Kat's bed, chomp-
ing on an apple, the last of Kat's treats for the week. "Kat's
the sweetest, the kindest, the fairest person in our class. She
should be our class commander."

"You didn't nominate me," Kat reminds her, and Nina
adds maliciously, "That's right." Vika's flattery is trans-
parent, and lately even Nina has been refusing to share her
snacks with Vika.

Kat says she doesn't care; she didn't want to be elected.
Power, her father says, corrupts. She wouldn't want to be
corrupted. Her parents disdain fervent activists, those poor
unprincipled sods who'll throttle themselves for a sought-
after Party post or chance of career advancement.

Though now that she thinks about it, Galochka P. is a
class elder and neither of Kat's parents seems to mind. They
both adore Galochka, who's beautiful and smart and comes
from a troubled family. So maybe the rule isn't absolute, or
at least doesn't apply to everyone. And maybe Kat's parents would have liked her to be a commander or an elder—
someone special, valued, respected—and since she wasn't
even nominated, she's failed them once more. She resolves
not to mention the election, not unless one of them asks her.

―――――

EVERY SATURDAY, Misha comes to collect Kat. If the weather is good, they might walk part of the way: visit the store that sells electrical goods to look at fancy lamps; stop by the Culinariya to pick up éclairs; check up on Anechka, who's teaching auxiliary classes at her and Misha's school.

Kat's classes end early on Saturdays. By noon the vestibule is packed: parents and grandparents idling on foot, the lucky ones reclining in armchairs. You can't miss Misha, though. He is taller than everyone else. It usually takes Kat a second to scan the crowd for his curly head. Except today he isn't there.

Kat wills him to hurry. Though he's famously distracted, he hasn't been late in the past. She watches her classmates depart. "See you later," she tells Igor Zotov. "See you later," she tells Alina Nesterenko, who is leaving with her father. A plump, blue-eyed woman comes out of the coatroom, pushing Vika Litvinova and giving her a hearty smack. She looks remarkably like Vika.

By the time Misha arrives, there's no one left in the vestibule. Kat's waiting by the bust of Lenin. She and her good pal Lenin and no one else. Misha halts when he sees her standing there, but he doesn't say he's sorry and doesn't explain why he's an hour and forty minutes late.

"Are you ready?"

"My suitcase," she says.

He goes to fetch her suitcase from the coatroom. There is something odd in the way he behaves. He doesn't hug Kat or

rumple her hair like always; doesn't gasp, "Eh, my dear slab
of oak," while lifting her suitcase. When they come outside,
he doesn't sing to her "Madame, the leaves already fallen,
the autumn's in its mortal rage." Which is also strange—he
loves to sing Vertinsky.

"You know," she says, "I was worried."

He looks like he's thinking about something else.

"Yes," he says. "Yes. Be gentle with your mother, Button.
She had a little surgery this morning."

Cancer is the first thing Kat thinks of, the worst sickness
on earth. Masha Sivova says young people die from it. Her
mother is a nurse; she sees it constantly. Young women come
in and you just look at them and know it's too late. "Doctor," they say, "please, I have children at home." The doctors
cut them open, glance inside, then quickly stitch them up
again. They send them off to die at home.

Kat bursts into tears.

"Oh, Button. I didn't mean to scare you. It's just a teeny-
tiny operation. A little stomach thing. She's home already."

"Not cancer?"

"Not even near," Misha swears.

They take the bus home, which also reassures Kat. If
Anechka's life were in danger, they would have flagged
down a cab.

"It's best if you stay in your room today," says Misha.

ANECHKA LOOKS LIFELESS. She is resting face down
on the sofa, covered in blankets and several shawls. After

a while she shifts, and then an odd choked-up sound comes from under the mound of fabric.

"Is she crying?"

Misha shakes his head. He pushes Kat gently in the direction of her room. "Remember what we talked about?"

Kat waits until he leaves to buy some bread, then tiptoes out to check on Anechka. She stops by the living-room door; she doesn't intend to go any farther than that. Except that from where she stands, she can't tell if Anechka is breathing. She steps forward a little and listens again. Then moves ahead some more. Soon she is kneeling beside her. She places her hand on what she figures is Anechka's back.

The heap of blankets shivers.

"Who is it?" says her mother. Her mussed-up head pokes out from under the coverings.

"Does it hurt?" Kat says.

"What?"

"You. Your operation."

Anechka's gaze wanders, confused, uncomprehending. She grabs Kat's hand, holds it against her breast. "This," she says. "This is where it hurts. You understand?"

She lets go of her roughly. "Just leave me be," she says, burrowing again under the blankets. And now it's unmistakable—she's crying. These hard, strangled sounds forced into the pillow can't be anything else.

IN HER room Kat sits amidst her books. She has them organized by title, catalogued as in a real library, with a shoebox full of index cards. The ones in front of her are tattered picture books. Anechka's been itching to recycle them. In return for twenty kilos of recycled paper one can get a brand new volume of Dumas or Conan Doyle.

Misha says, "Looking for something?" He's brought her supper, noodles in milk, which she usually likes.

She tells him she's not hungry.

He sits next to her on the carpet, leafs through the books fanned out in front of her. "Want me to read to you?" he says.

On any other night, she would have found the offer insulting. She does her own reading now, real books, not these childish scraps. But tonight she allows it. They huddle together on the carpet and he reads to her, one by one, *The Tale of the Golden Cockerel* and *The Little Black Hen*, *The Steadfast Tin Soldier* and *The Scarlet Flower*. It's past Kat's bedtime, but Misha is unmindful of the hour. He seems to love these silly illustrated tales, where every dilemma is solvable and every choice is clear-cut.

6

A NECHKA NEEDS A NEW DRESS, NO QUESTION
about it. Not for a special occasion, an anniversary or
New Year's Eve, but simply because she deserves one, damn
it. Especially after everything she's been through in the last
few weeks.

"You mean the operation?" says Kat.

"I mean a baby. A child. A little sister or brother for you.
But since that wasn't permitted, I'm getting a dress."

"And the baby?" says Kat.

"No baby."

"Ever?" Come to think of it, Kat wouldn't mind a little brother or sister. Or a puppy. A puppy would be great.
Could they possibly get themselves a puppy?

"Shut up, Kat. Don't be daft."

Most of Anechka's dresses are from before she was married, dating back to her institute days. Faded knits, stretched-
out synthetics, plus one crisp black number with red stripes
along the hem and a row of white plastic buttons. What

she needs is something warm and durable, good for the approaching winter months. Raised shoulders, a simple cut.

It's a Saturday evening. They are walking along deserted, frosty streets, the streetlights casting thin pools of electricity. Each apartment block they pass is lit up by hundreds of windows. Behind each window, life sizzles—warm, intimate, impossibly mysterious—while out in the streets there's only the chill and stillness and occasional crunch of footsteps.

They are going to meet Anechka's dressmaker, and the word itself, somehow antiquated, makes Kat feel grim. She wanted to stay in, to have a cup of egg-flip, to watch *The World of Animals* with Misha. She's been away at school all week. But Anechka said, "Come with me, baby," and Misha gave Kat one of those looks that seem to say they have an understanding.

Ever since her operation, Anechka's been in a state. Misha keeps saying "fragile," but Kat, if asked, would call it "all-out mad," except that no one is asking. The week after the operation, Kat came home with two "satisfactory" grades; when Anechka saw them she slapped her with the back of the school diary. Later she cried and said sorry and told Kat about the "murdered" baby, hacked out of her belly with knives and garden shears and God knows what else. It took Misha days to convince Kat there had been no garden shears, and the baby itself hadn't become a real baby yet. They just couldn't risk it, he said. Not with Kat's scoliosis in the picture.

The dressmaker's apartment is in a fancy complex of tower-style blocks. She's been endorsed by a colleague of

Anechka's, a young, silly woman nicknamed Moth. She's a lousy teacher, this Moth, but she does know fashion. When she's not at work, she stands outside the Shoes & Furs store, waiting for some once-in-a-lifetime delivery, boots from Yugoslavia, men's leather gloves.

The dressmaker greets them in the hallway. She's wearing what looks like silk pajamas, though since she's friends with Moth, it could be the latest squeak of fashion. Her name, she says, is Nelya.

"We're doing something for the girl?"

"The girl is just along," says Anechka.

"Charming," Nelya mutters. "Simply charming."

Kat sees nothing charming at all.

Nelya leads them into the kitchen, where, amidst tea and clutter, Kat sees no sewing implements. A phone rings, a slick red contraption with buttons, and Nelya motions for them to sit down and wait. She is speaking to someone called Bunny. "Yes, tomorrow. Let me write it down." She scribbles a reminder directly on the wall.

"Now, where were we?"

The dress, says Anechka. She starts describing what it is she wants, but Nelya interrupts her. "Let's see the fabric first." She rubs the edge of the blue nubbly fabric they brought, and even Kat can see it's better suited for upholstering couches. "Domestic production?"

Anechka says, "It's all I've got."

"Well then," says Nelya. She gets a tape measure from a cupboard and tells Kat she can look at catalogues. There are several thick catalogues on the counter, pages full of lovely blond people in bright coats. Women, men, children. German or Swedish. The colors in the *Working Woman* magazines are dismal in comparison, and the women, the mannequin girls, how strained they seem in retrospect, how mannered and uncomfortable.

In some parallel universe, Nelya takes Anechka's measurements, and later the two of them discuss payment, make the next appointment. Anechka dictates their phone number, which Nelya commits to the wall. "Roshdal," she says, jotting down Anechka's last name. "I knew some Roshdals once. They went to Palestine. You're not related, are you? Probably not. Her husband, I think, was an accountant."

"WHAT'S A JEW?" Kat asks Anechka on the way to school next Monday. It's not as if she's never heard the word; in the kitchen discussions it popped up quite a lot. She just never figured out what it meant, or what the discussions were about.

"Jew is a nationality," says Anechka. "Our nationality, to be precise."

"Aren't we Russian?"

"We're Soviet citizens, if that's what you're asking. That's not the same as nationality. You know there are many nationalities, Ukrainian, Moldavian, and so on."

"The fifteen republics?"

"That's right," says Anechka. "Except there's more than fifteen nationalities."

"We don't have a republic then?"

Anechka sighs. "We don't have squat."

"It's not a bad thing, though, is it? To be a Jew?"

"Why should it be a bad thing?"

Kat drops the subject. Some girls at school don't make it sound like a good thing. Lida Kravchenko whispers "Yid" when she walks by, and Misha later tells Kat it is an ugly word. And also, why do they have such odd last names?

Ahead of the Octobrist ceremony, Rosa divides their detachment into groups. The groups, called little stars, are supposed to compete with one another in grades, deportment, adherence to medical procedures, and daily chores. The first little star is the best: it's got, among others, Alina, Igor, and Kira Mikadze. The second one is also good. The third has the weepers and is clearly inferior. But Kat's little star is by far the worst.

"Tell your father about your little star," says Anechka.

"What should I tell him?" Kat stalls. They're having their normal weekend supper—cubed potatoes, small bits of "Doktorskaya" sausage fried in sunflower oil—and she'd rather not discuss the latest of her failures.

"Just tell him who's in it."

"Vera Dinnershtein," Kat starts slowly. "Sonya Bronfman—"

"Oh, for God's sake!" says Anechka. "Dinnershtein, Bronfman, Knopman, Falikman."

"Also, Seryozha Mironov."

Mironov was added at the last minute. "Why me?" he tried to argue. "Why put me with those freaks?" Some girls in the front row started giggling. Didn't he know what he looked like, the poor freaky thing?

"Could Rosa be any more blatant?" asks Anechka.

"You're jumping to conclusions," Misha says.

"Knopman, Falikman, Dinnershtein, Bronfman?"

"And don't forget Mironov. A simple Russian name."

"An outlier," insists Anechka. "An exception that only proves the rule."

"Could be a coincidence. We don't know about the other groups."

"Sure!" Anechka sneers. "A whole class full of little Jewish girls. Next you'll tell me we'll have communism by the year 2000."

"Won't we?" Kat asks them, and her parents both say no, at once, in unison.

"Communism is a utopia," says Anechka. "A fairy tale, that's all."

"She really needs to know this now? You want her to repeat that at school?"

"She knows better," says Anechka, and Kat assures them she won't repeat it.

"She's a child," says Misha.

"She's an individual," says Anechka.

"Okay, Button, be an individual now and go to your room. You must have some homework to do."

"I've done it," Kat says, but she goes. She's disappointed them again, this time by not rising above her weird surname, the way Misha and Anechka rose above theirs. This wouldn't

have happened if she had managed to excel in something—
math, reading, nature studies, art, or gym. Instead, she is
just average.

ANECHKA SAYS she dislikes the dressmaker. She'd rather
not go back to her. "That woman," she says. "That woman
with her innuendos." But the appointments have been made,
the dress is partly paid for, so it appears she doesn't have a
choice. She makes Kat come along with her—the fittings are
always on Saturdays—and Misha also pushes Kat to go; her
mother, he says, needs her moral support. Kat sits at Nelya's
kitchen counter, looks at the catalogues, imagines what it
must be like to live in such opulence, with such a wealth of
colors around you.

She has her own fittings now. Once a week she returns to
the brace shop, where her technician tries on her the newly
made brace parts. She likes her technician. She's glad he's
not the one with missing fingers, nor the clean-shaven buf-
foon who flirts with the older girls. Hers is a serious, taci-
turn type, and she mostly doesn't mind when he touches her
bare arms and shoulders, or when he jostles her hips into the
pelvic enclosure. She never says a word. Even when he pulls
the belt too tightly and the uneven edges pinch her skin, a
small grunt is all she'll allow herself.

Pain is becoming her companion. She goes in for vitamin
injections every day; the school dentist fixes her two cavi-
ties; and then, despite Anechka's conjectures, she is given a

plaster-cast bed. It's molded to her body, and after it dries for a couple of weeks, it's fitted with hard wedges that bite into her back when she lies down. It hurts so much, she can't sleep. Other girls in her dorm ditch their plaster-cast beds once Rosa goes out for the night. They stash them underneath their normal beds. They can't understand why Kat prefers to suffer. Is she showing off? Is she afraid?

But Kat is testing her resolve, her character. "Live up to the heroes' example!" It is imperative to prove that she's a hero, that she is stalwart, brave, impervious to pain. She must be diligent in class and generally well-behaved, and she must always volunteer to sweep the floors or air the classroom. "Only those who toil and sweat get to join the Octobrist set."

They are swimming in slogans these days. The one they hear the most is, "The school is your new family." Thumbelina says it when they quarrel. The school principal says it when she inspects their class. And Rosa? Rosa says it at every opportunity.

"Why do I need a new family?" Igor Zotov asks her.

Rosa considers that a show of impudence and sends him to stand in the corner for an hour. Then she tells them the story of Pavlik Morozov, the pioneer hero who exposed his kulak father. "Loyalty to one's collective is more important than familial love."

"What if my mama dies," starts Vika.

"Your mother's fine," says Rosa. "I spoke to her last Friday."

"That was my aunt."

"You don't have an aunt, Litvinova. And your mother, incidentally, doesn't have cancer."

So now they have to decide what to do with Vika, whether she can be forgiven for deceiving the class, whether she deserves to join the great Octobrist organization. This isn't a minor infraction, Rosa tells them. Because Octobrists don't lie.

The night of the Octobrist ceremony, neither Misha nor Anechka comes. There's no one to marvel at Kat's prettiness as she stands outside the classroom in her new blue skirt and white silk blouse. Her hair has grown out a little. Thumbelina brushes it and ties up one section with a borrowed rose-bow. "Such lovely soft ringlets," she murmurs. The weepers ask if they can touch Kat's hair, and then Igor Zotov comes closer too.

Inside the classroom, someone's father is blowing up balloons, someone's mother is arranging flowers.

"Your parents are here?"

Kat shakes her head, Nope.

"Mine neither," says Igor.

When it's time, they line up in the hallway, and the Junior Pioneer Counselor leads forward her troops. The banner is carried in, to the roar of drums, the squeal of bugles. "Octobrists are diligent children—they love the school, respect their elders." Songs are followed by poems, poems by short songs. "Octobrists—honest and deft, brave and adept." Even Vika is permitted to participate, and she is not exactly honest. "Octobrists—a friendly gang—read and draw, play and sing, have much fun with everything." And finally, the private moment comes, quivering with meaning, when each of them faces a Young Pioneer, a girl or a boy from the fourth grade, and the needle of the pin is threaded through the fabric on their chests. Something is altered in every one of them, something important is bestowed.

In the canteen, they celebrate with tea and cake. Kira Mikadze's mother brought the cake; she is the head of the parents' committee. She sits sprawled on a chair, and other parents keep asking her what they can do to help. Nothing, she says. It's all taken care of. Don't fuss so much, for God's sake. Sit down, have a piece of cake.

Then Rosa taps her watch and says, "All good things in good measure," which means that it's time for the parents to depart. Rules are rules and schedule is schedule, and homework isn't going to wait. Though in recognition of this outstanding day, the children may stay in their party clothes for the rest of the evening.

And this is the best part: the blouse, the bow, the skirt, the devastating lightness as Kat pirouettes rather than walks through the remaining evening hours. She turns out her shoulders and keeps her back straight so that everyone can see how perfect she is, how slim is her mannequin-girl body.

After supper the girls beg Rosa to allow them to dance. They put on a record and for the next twenty minutes they become one and the same—sweaty, happy, flailing—singing along with the stereo. "Summer, oh Summer!" And Kat is among them, perfect and weightless, dancing as if in her sleep, as if this joy would never cease, as if this moment could be endless.

THE BRACE she's given is unwieldy. It smells of leather, metal, glue. It seems to be intended for a much larger person. Kat puts it on in Dr. Bobrova's office, and once she's all trussed up, Dr. Bobrova tightens the bolts at her sides. She has a wrench in her desk for just this purpose. She tells Kat the rules: always put it on while lying down, never while standing up; never walk with the head collar unlocked.

Kat stands frozen by the doctor's desk—because this can't be it, this heaviness, this ugliness, this roughness.

"What are you waiting for?" Dr. Bobrova asks.

It is a long, slow walk back to the classroom. To be sure, she's not the first to be lumbered with a brace. Nina Petrenko has hers, and so does Seryozha Mironov. It's been months since school started, and now the braces on others don't seem all that ghastly and strange. Yet how different it is to be inside one. With every step, the bolts squeak at Kat's waist. The metal slats support her head, so she can only move it up or down. How massive it feels, how rigid, despite the strips of leather that cover the slats and the rosy fabric of the corset part.

By nap time the brace has rubbed her body into a red, blistery mess. Even her chin is red and scraped. "You've got to break it in," says Nina, while Kat sits on the bed examining her sore spots. Nina gives her a spare handkerchief to line the inside of the head collar.

After nap, Kat has to put the brace on by herself. It takes her half an hour. The lacing gets tangled, and the clamps on the shaft-bows get stuck. She misses evening snack and has to go hungry until suppertime.

In the morning, the process is just as long and intricate. She has to skip morning calisthenics, which doesn't bode well for her disciplinary mark. The only good news is, it's Saturday. "Try practicing," says Thumbelina. "You'll get the hang of it." A kind-hearted creature, she makes an exception and doesn't mark Kat down for tardiness.

"Oh, Button," Misha says, when he sees her downstairs in the vestibule; then just as quickly he backpedals: "You can barely see it. It's really not that bad. I bet you'll forget it's even there."

But how can she forget when every squeak, every pinch, every step keeps reminding her? People stare at her—on the bus, at the Culinariya, where Misha buys éclairs and almond cakes. Quick, sneaky looks or prying, lengthy ones. At a crosswalk, a small boy gapes at Kat. "What's wrong with her?" he asks, and his mother explains in the same loud whisper: "She's probably broken her neck. I bet she didn't listen to her parents."

This weekend Kat is grateful not to go anywhere. She picks one of Misha's thick scarves to disguise her head collar. She plans to wear it forever—let people think she has mumps. She once heard her parents talk about a book they read in college in which a man gets turned into a bug. At the time it seemed silly, improbable, but now, studying herself in the mirror, Kat is struck by how insectlike, how unnatural she looks.

She knows she must practice and she does. By the end of Sunday, she's mostly mastered it, easing herself onto the carpet, pulling down her panties, stretching out the edge of her camisole, lacing up the corset, fastening the stubborn locks and clamps.

"I think I'm pretty fast," she says, when Anechka comes home from her final appointment with Nelya.

The new dress is ready, and Anechka hovers before the wardrobe mirror. "It's not too boring, is it?"

The dress came out well, neither too staid nor too frivolous. It has some solidity to it, which makes it appropriate for work, but also some girlish grace—raised shoulders, pleats, an elegant blue bow at the neck. Nelya has done her best.

Kat tries to count how many fittings they have been to, how many brace fittings *she* had. Her mother got a dress, and Kat got a brace, and no matter how you look at this situation, it's unfair.

Anechka turns this way and that, frowns a bit at her reflection, though anyone can see she's pleased. "You think it's attractive? Not too frumpy or matronly?"

And seriously, what does she expect? Here's Kat in her brace, all sore and shivery, a monstrous, miserable thing. The dress, Kat says, looks like a sack. A boring, shapeless sack, something Rosa might wear. In fact, Rosa dresses like that every day.

"You don't mean it," Anechka says, stunned, and Kat, also stunned, stricken by her own meanness, runs off to the bathroom and slides the latch closed.

How quickly a person can change. A bright and sparkly girl, perhaps a budding genius, becomes a sickly, mediocre slug. A girl who was formerly kind becomes a dark, vindictive creature. She is a bug, inside and out, a gruesome, despicable bug. Is it any surprise that her parents have grown ashamed of her?

KIRA MIKADZE SAYS, "You've really done it, Knopman."

It's Monday afternoon, classes have just ended, and Kat is not aware that she's done anything deplorable. In fact, she feels she's held up rather well. But Kira's looking furious, sticking her finger in Kat's face, and beside her, the others appear just as mad. Alina Nesterenko. Lida Kravchenko. The viperish Inna Smirnova.

"You've disgraced all of us," Kira says.

Kat asks what she is being blamed for.

"You're such a retard, Knopman."

"Can't you see she's pretending?" Lida Kravchenko says.

"At physical therapy," says Kira. "You pulled down your panties, and all the boys saw it."

"I didn't . . ." Kat starts. But of course! She was putting her brace on. With all that practicing at home, she'd forgotten about the boys.

"She's smiling," says Inna. "She's enjoying it."

It's true, she can't control it. Her lips are creasing into

the semblance of a smirk, which happens sometimes out of
nervousness.

"They *totally* saw it," says Lida Kravchenko.

"The way they were whispering and pointing." Inna covers her face. "That horrible Mironov—"

"Zotov, at least, wasn't pointing."

Kira says, "She's either a retard, or she did it on purpose.
Either way, I'm calling for a boycott. No one talks to Knopman from now on."

"I didn't," says Kat, and what she means is, How could
it have been on purpose? But the girls spin away from her
in a motion so smooth you'd think they'd choreographed it.
A splash of arms, twitching shoulders, a turn. Through the
doorway and into the classroom, where they will speak to
every girl in confidence.

All conversations hush when she enters, and the girls
make a show of scattering away. Even the weepers won't talk
to her. And Igor Zotov . . . How studiously he avoids her,
how promptly he averts his eyes. When Kat asks to borrow
his eraser, he acts as if he hasn't heard her.

She tries to be stoic about the boycott, too proud to let on
how much the silence hurts her, too mortified to dare complain. It can't get worse, she tells herself. It simply can't. But
it is getting worse, each day a little more so. Spitballs land
in her hair, doors are slammed as she approaches them. Her
towel gets dropped into the toilet. Someone puts salt in her
tea. And everywhere she goes, there's the cursed Mironov,
circling around her, monkey-like. "Take off your panties,
Knopman. Show it to us." He is loving this boycott. He

steals her notebook, draws naked pictures on the cover, and later the notebook makes rounds through the class. They know it's his work, but they all pretend it's Kat who did the drawings.

A week goes by, another one starts. Mironov won't let anyone forget about the boycott. If it weren't for him, they would have grown bored with it by now; but no, he won't let them move on. He shadows her everywhere and even waits for her outside the girls' room. The moment she comes out, he resumes his hollering. "Show it, show it, show it to us."

She dreams of hurting Mironov. Hurting him physically, drawing blood. Never before has she had such primal urges. She'd like to push him down a staircase, or punch him really hard, so hard that he'll fall over and lose consciousness.

It happens at the end of medical gymnastics, just a few days before the autumn break. She's putting on her brace, flat on her back, at her most vulnerable. But because it's almost break and the day's been relatively quiet, she doesn't expect an attack. Even when the boys start gathering around her, she thinks they're mostly playing and that their game, whatever it might be, won't go too far.

She is the mammoth and they are the hunters. They brandish their exercise sticks, do their stupid indigenous dance. There are only two of them this time, Mironov and his sidekick Eremeev.

The boys are trying to provoke Kat. They prod and strike her feet and shoulders with their sticks. They've done it before, so she knows it's best to ignore them. But the blows of the sticks are persistent and not so light anymore. When one catches her knee, she can't keep from crying out: "Stop it!" It's more of a squeak than a scream, and anyway, their therapist, the young and bored-looking Evelyna Borisovna, left the gymnastics room a while ago.

They draw back briefly, but soon return. And now the game is different. The blunt tip of a stick touches her thigh and inches upward. It is her panties they're after; they want to hook them and drag them off. "Show us, show us, show us." You can tell it's Mironov who's thought it up. The whole class is watching: Will it work? In the back, someone whispers, "Disgusting," and Igor Zotov leaves without a glance.

Disgusting. The word seems to echo. What would her parents think of her? It's two o'clock on Wednesday, which means they have . . . what? A pedagogic council? Their once-a-month union meeting? She doesn't know, can't remember anymore. How did she end up here—on her back, in a brace, on this floor, abandoned among these wicked creatures? Is it because she is also wicked? Or maybe simply weak? "Disgusting," Anechka would say. She can't abide weak people.

Her brace undone and clunking, Kat gets up on her knees. "You freak," she shrieks at Mironov. "You worthless freak of nature, you ugly dwarf, you miserable crippled hunchback!"

She sees her words connect with him; he shrinks from the impact, recoils. They're better than a punch, these words. So powerful and solid. They are bubbling inside her, she can't contain them anymore. "You're a hunchback, hunchback, hunchback."

~

SHE DOESN'T REMEMBER IF IT HURT. There's the glimpse of him swinging the stick and the quick burst of panic. Some time after: the shine of a pen-light in her eyes. The stick hit her just above the temple; an inch lower and she'd be gone. Years later she can still recall his face, pasty and hideous, twisted with hatred. How odd, she remembers thinking, to be hated like this, so completely. But not the pain, never the pain. Just the swift, blissful darkness that comes a second later.

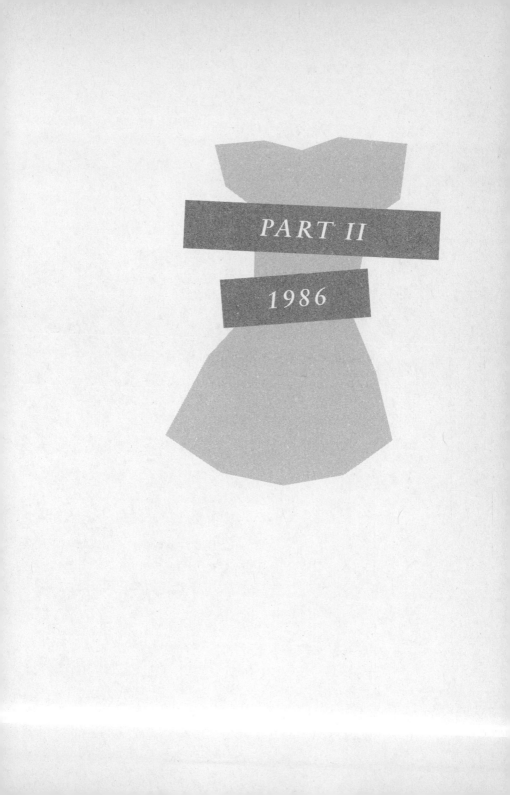

PART II

1986

7

NO NEW STUDENTS TURN UP AT ASSEMBLY. KAT is certain of that. She and Jules scrutinize the whole of 7A and find not a single new face. "Figures," says Jules, and Kat says, "What did you expect?" But she is also disappointed. Their class is rotten, everyone hates them, they haven't had a new non-loser person since Jules joined the class in fifth grade. They are bad, truly bad. There have been rumors of splitting them up, redistributing them amongst the other classes, and Kat wouldn't mind that—as long as she and Jules can stay together.

It's the first day of the new school year, and like every year the courtyard is awash in bouquets. The school population, lined up in rows for assembly, braces for forty minutes of tedium. A big-time baritone climbs onto the wooden podium. His daughter is starting first grade at their fine institution, so hurray, they've got themselves a celebrity. The baritone is portly, with a sweaty and bloated face. For decades now he's been singing of plentiful Russian fields and unrestrained steppes, and no one has any respect for him anymore, save maybe for some patriotically minded pensioners.

"Sing for us, birdie!" a boy calls from the back.

The assembly breaks into titters, and it's fun to watch the teachers as they try to maintain their composure. Everyone's turning to look at whoever's been so brave.

Kat doesn't need to turn. She knows. How stupid do you have to be to pull a prank like that? At assembly, no less. "Imbecile," she mutters.

"What do you care?" Jules says.

Kat tells her she doesn't care, she just hopes he finally gets expelled.

Jules, a first-rate skeptic, jacks up one eyebrow. Kat has never told her what happened between her and Mironov, and Jules, bless her careless heart, has never asked. All she knows is, they hate each other.

Jules is runty and skinny and looks harmless enough. That was the first thing Kat noticed when she spotted her at assembly two years ago: a sunny disposition, a warm and mirthful smile. But Jules has a hard center too. You might miss it at first; it takes a day or two to realize. But it's there in her sure bearing, the way she throws back her shoulders, her flippant opinions, her sharp, unsentimental eyes.

The moment of hilarity is stifled, and the rest of assembly plays out according to plan, with neither a knot nor a hitch. The speeches carry on, the pupils languish. At last the baritone's small daughter is released into the wild: she runs through the courtyard shaking a tinny cowbell, signaling the end of assembly.

No matter what's listed on the schedule downstairs, the first class of the year is always the Peace Lesson. This year 7A gets Kapitolina P. (code name: Creampuff). She's nearing retirement, which Kat feels can't come soon enough. She looks like a giant flaky pastry, with her pompadour hair and bulging eyes. Her subject is biology. She's been at the school since forever; she's one of the old guard.

The old guard toes the Party line. They are loyal to the legacy of Lenin/Stalin, enthralled with the heroic past. The old guard is leery of the liberal press, of ballyhoo artists, of anyone who doesn't appear sufficiently Russian. You can be sure their Peace Lessons are carefully planned: unmask American imperialism, denounce the arms race, expose the capitalist system, then spend the rest of the period singing praise to the virtues of their Socialist society. Freedom to all people! Workers of the world, unite!

Lately, though, the requisite points must also include perestroika and acceleration—which isn't something the old guard particularly likes.

Acceleration's a new factor
But it failed our old reactor.
Now our fine atomic wreck
Has all of Europe caked in dreck.

Kat herself doesn't mind perestroika or acceleration. It's just that you can't turn on the nine o'clock news anymore without getting an earful of it. Talk, talk, talk. She is applying to Komsomol this year, so she tries to keep abreast of current events. But the news is often taken up with Gorbachev's speeches, and he's so long-winded she gives up and goes to sleep. It's too confusing, really. Is acceleration a good thing? There is Chernobyl, and there is a girl in 9B—not from Chernobyl, but near—and now her parents won't let her go home to Ukraine. There you have it, some people might say. There's your acceleration.

In the back of the classroom Lena Romanova (code name: Bones) begins to sing: "Felicità." As if to say, We don't care about acceleration, we don't care about American imperialism. We prefer Italians! Which in itself is ridiculous—Italian pop is by now obsolete. But Bones has such a lovely silvery voice, who can resist?

Creampuff applauds in a mocking way. "May I now get on with my lesson?"

"You may," Bones allows, inclining her head like a queen.

She has this ethereal face, a voice that turns you inside out, and a horrible wreck of a body. A shortened torso and grotesque long limbs. How do you reason with a girl like this? How do you reason with any of them?

ALL OTHER classes are like families: solicitous, sisterly, a little bland. 7A alone is an aberration. They are the most-despised class in the whole school. There's meanness in them that is almost pathological. Deep-seated, private meanness.

They arrive in the canteen jiggling with agitation, and soon there are insults and bits of food flying across the table, and whoever's supposed to be in charge is asking them to for God's sake behave, while the headmistress up front looks displeased and impatient. Can't anyone control these deviants?

Not Anechka Roshdal, that's for sure. No one at school loathes 7A more than Anechka Roshdal. They are vulgar and soulless. Language and literature enrage them; they see no value in art. A mob, she says, is what they are. Your basic mob, with its small sordid needs and just a few stunted emotions.

They cram into her classroom at the end of the day, like some bored, maladroit cows, and she stands there, arms folded, eyeing them with contempt.

Anechka and Misha joined the faculty two years ago, when the school was expanding. For Kat's sake, they said. To be with her, to monitor her treatments. They promised they would never teach her class. That would be awkward and unethical. But there are some things a new faculty member doesn't get to decide, and Anechka has been Kat's teacher since last year.

"Well then," Anechka says, "if it's not the infamous 7A. I'm sure you've wasted no time this summer. I'm sure you've all worked relentlessly on bettering yourselves."

The girls look at her, bull-like. They don't appreciate her irony.

"That summer reading list I gave you? I bet you've covered everything on it."

7A stays silent, and Anechka stays silent, and the pause—

excruciating in its futility—lasts several minutes until Nina
Petrenko breaks wind and several girls begin to giggle.

"Oh, right," says Anechka. "I have forgotten who I'm
dealing with. 7A—the model of refinement."

There is that humming sound now, the humming that
fills every classroom 7A is in—pervasive, unnerving, insipid
like static on the radio. The sound of a dozen small animals
attending to their small animal needs: Carry on, Anechka.
See if we care.

Anechka has no choice but to get on with her teaching.
It's Pushkin again. Every year starts with Pushkin, and this
year they are reading *Eugene Onegin*. They've finally graduated to the lovely turmoil of *Eugene Onegin*, and it pains
Kat that her classmates will foul her favorite book.

Anechka walks back and forth at the front of the classroom in her oversized sweater and striped, bell-shaped
skirt. These floppy wools and tweeds are like her uniform.
She is cold all the time; everything, she says, is cold—her
classroom, their apartment; even in summer she was cold.
It seems like a sign of her recent health problems, or maybe
she's always had poor circulation.

The floorboards creak softly as she walks, a song to go
with her story, and it's this story, this creaking, the tim-
bre of Anechka's voice that make her teaching so magical.
Here's young Pushkin in St. Petersburg, Pushkin the fop, in
his modish black tails *à l'américaine*. Pushkin the carouser,
the lover of champagne and women. Beloved Pushkin, really
just a boy, speaking at the meeting of a secret society. And

here he is, exiled and slandered, poverty-stricken and alone. "I saw my life ennobled," he writes to a friend, "my future meaningful."

Teaching has always come easily to Anechka. She has a huge following—back at her old school, and here as well. Her popularity is unrivaled even by Misha. Misha has his own following, though it is smaller, more intellectual in nature. With Misha you can discuss politics, a *Literaturka* article, an obscure book, Sakharov's return to Moscow, *Doctor Zhivago* in samizdat editions. It takes some courage to approach him, though. He has this pensive, nearsighted look—you sense he can't quite place you; you sense you might be keeping him from something more important.

There are no such barriers with Anechka. Her girls adore her, and it's easy to see why she's loved. She is like a sister to them, or a girlfriend. They kvetch to her about other teachers, entrust her with the secrets of their hearts, share their problems at home (accidents, sickness, divorce). And she encourages these confidences, remembers every story, and even intervenes on her girls' behalf. A few of them have spent weekends at the Knopman–Roshdal home, the orphans, the unfortunate ones with violent stepfathers and no place to go.

After class, Kat stops beside Anechka's desk. She doesn't know what to say to her, unsure whether to apologize for the atrocious behavior of her classmates.

When Anechka and Misha joined the school, Kat thought it was a dream come true: the three of them together at last. And at the beginning, at least, it was good. They were new, they had a lot of questions. Kat showed them around the school, explained how the daily schedule worked, warned them about the canteen food. For a week or so, she was important, indispensable. But it wasn't the way she'd imagined it. No one fussed around her here the way people had at her parents' old school when she, not yet seven, recited scenes from *The Inspector General*. She wasn't a kid anymore. She was an adolescent now, and it didn't suit her. She wasn't attractive or particularly gifted, only well-read and moderately smart.

As for her parents, they still had their magical spark. Within a week the school was buzzing—they were young, married, and dazzling. They wrote plays. They used to be on stage themselves. Rumors abounded. Was it true, a girl asked Kat in the canteen one day, that Anechka was once a famous actress? "She did some theater in college," Kat explained.

Anechka herself was always glad to share her tales of student acting. She'd tell her girls anything, really: how her mother passed away, how she and Misha met, how they saw each other from a distance in the lobby of their institute and instantly knew it was fate.

It's only with Kat that she holds back these days. Like now, for example: Kat asks her if she's upset about her class, and Anechka just looks at her as if to say, Why even ask? Then she checks whether Kat's got her textbooks from the library and whether she's put away her snacks. "You don't want the apples to go moldy like last time." Never mind that last time was almost a year ago.

Then, before they can attempt a normal conversation,

Sveta Vlasenko from 10B arrives. She is Anechka's best pal, the prettiest girl in the school, the perpetual princess of every drama club production. She often stays at their apartment on weekends, though not because she is an orphan. Her parents are abroad, and when they're not away, she doesn't get along with them.

"You're looking tired," she tells Anechka. "7A again?"

"The bane of my existence."

Sveta sits next to Kat on the nearest cot. They have things to discuss, she and Anechka. They always have things to discuss. Sveta flicks something off Kat's shoulder—a speck of dust, or dandruff. She herself is perfect, with her long and symmetrical body, good clothes, heart-shaped face. Her tangle of long corkscrew hair is held back with velvety headbands. She is soft in all the places where Kat is rough and awkward. She doesn't move but flows, forming soothing and brilliant shapes, and her voice purls like silver, a splash of small fish in clear water.

"Some aspirin?" she offers.

Anechka says yes, and downs two dry pills without water. She does look exhausted. Her complexion is sallow, her lips are chalky. Her hair, short, boyish, sticks out awkwardly, like she didn't have a chance to brush it properly this morning. Maybe she shouldn't be so careless with aspirin. Maybe she ought to see a doctor instead. Kat wants to say something, but before she can muster the courage, Anechka packs her bag, puts on her coat, and Sveta says she'll walk her to the bus.

"Wait," Anechka says, and looks at Kat. "What about

your birthday?" They were going to buy éclairs for Kat's class, but as often happens, they've forgotten.

Kat says it doesn't matter. Her classmates don't deserve éclairs. She'd rather celebrate at home anyway. They don't do much for birthdays, but maybe they could get a cake. Maybe her mother could arrange to take Kat home? She's waiting, but Anechka doesn't suggest it, and it's clear she has other plans.

"All alone on your birthday," Sveta Vlasenko says sadly.

Kat shrugs. It's not that bad, she's got her Jules.

"Jules who?" Sveta says.

"Oh, you know her." Anechka gestures dismissively. "The diplomat's girl, the skinny one."

JULES AND KAT. Kat and Jules. With names like these, they were destined for each other. Jules's real name is Yulya Smolkina, but she insists on Jules. She lived in England with her parents for a while, and she claims to love everything English: English names, horseback riding, English cottages, *Ivanhoe* and *Jane Eyre*. Her father is a diplomat, her mother an ex-opera singer, and Jules herself is a budding polyglot. She knows some Italian, a little French, but English is what she's really good at. Her English is better than Kat's. They like to speak it between classes, swapping quips to the great irritation of their linguistically challenged classmates. They've nicknamed their classmates "the gaggle," a moniker that conveys exactly their dumb, gabbling nature.

Kat's parents don't think much of Jules and her family, though they've met them only briefly. Too successful, they say. Misha says you don't become successful in this country without sacrificing something of your decency. You have to be ruthless, you have to step on bodies in order to move up the Party ranks. You adapt by betraying your principles. The country is full of these adapting people—spineless, materialistic. "Look around," says Anechka. "Look around your own class." Kat does, and it's true, the gaggle is a miserable group. But Jules, she feels, is different.

She finds Jules waiting out in the hallway, her elbows propped on a windowsill. "I have to go see my dad," Kat says.

"Don't be an idiot," Jules warns her. Classes ended twenty minutes ago; they are already late. Margo, their evening matron, gets suspicious when they dawdle. She likes them to return to their homeroom right away. They are in seventh grade, and still she insists they tromp to the canteen together.

"She'll kill you, just so you know," Jules says, but Kat tells her, screw it. "Tell her I went to the infirmary. Tell her I'm already dead."

She sprints across the hallway to Misha's classroom. He is there, in the back, rummaging in the shelves and drawers of the wall unit. His glasses, as usual, are pushed above his forehead. It's the first day of classes, and already he has misplaced something.

"Button!" he says. "Do you have any idea how many copies of *Woe from Wit* I own?"

"Three," Kat says.

"That's what I thought. Turns out I have five of them. Do I donate them to the library?"

"Maybe you can sell them or something."

"Five bedraggled copies of *Woe from Wit*? Unlikely. Have you seen your mother?"

"Of course," Kat says. "She and the gaggle got reacquainted."

"Was it bad?"

"Same as always."

"Poor Button," he says. "Do you think your mom could use a copy of *Woe from Wit*?"

"I don't know," Kat says. "She just left."

"Already? Ah, yes."

She thinks he looks crestfallen for a moment, or maybe she's simply imagining it. Anechka is always in the spotlight, and Misha, so unobtrusive, is easy to forget. Talking to Misha is easy. There's a softness to him, and a haplessness. He's a genius, and like all geniuses he needs to be looked after.

"Do you want me to help you?" she offers.

"Nah," Misha says. "It's just a book I used to have. It might be good for our new play." He's been writing a new play all summer, and he's agreed that this year Kat is old enough to have a real part.

"What do you think of me?" she asks.

"Meaning?" he says.

"Do you think I have a strong personality?"

"Is this because of your birthday? Or did your mom say something?"

"Just a general question," she says.

Misha mulls it over. He's careful with his pronouncements. "I think so," he says, eventually. "You stand up to your class. That takes courage, if you ask me."

Actually, she doesn't. She bears the gaggle's anger, absorbs their insults. She's learned not to react, not to complain, to dress up her hurt in opaqueness. They don't like her. They've never liked her. They've nicknamed her Kysya: a searing, dismissive hiss. "Kysya, drop! In your box, Kysya!" Meaningless doggie commands. She puts on the stolid, faraway expression of a Lermontov hero—exiled, misunderstood, estranged, gazing up at the peaks of the Caucasus mountains. She hopes it looks courageous.

"Seriously, Button, how did your mother do today?"

Kat says, "She took two aspirins."

They look at each other and feel a hazy sort of dread. They've long ago learned to recognize the signs of Anechka's malaise: the sleeplessness, the moodiness, the headaches. The irrational upswings of happiness. And then, of course, the blood. It always ends in blood, even in the months when it doesn't arrive as expected. They look at each other and know that Anechka isn't all right.

THE FIRST loss happened when Kat was in fourth grade. There had been much excitement right at the beginning, a lot of talk of the new baby and how it was growing, and then one day the talk just stopped and the pregnancy books disappeared. For two or three days, Anechka stayed in bed. Once she got up, it was as though there had never been a baby.

The next time, it took longer. Something must have jammed inside Anechka, and months after her last appointment she kept circling back to the fresh devastation of the loss. She and Kat would be leaving school on a Saturday, crossing over the curved bridge in the park, and Anechka would begin to weep. You couldn't talk to her when she got like this, unstoppable, almost hysterical. She'd say, "Shut up, Kat. Just shut up." That bridge in the park behind the school—they both knew it wasn't safe. Icy in winter, pointlessly steep. There was always an unfrozen patch of water underneath, and there were rumors of women—always women—who had slipped.

Why is it so important? Kat tried to ask Misha. Why is Anechka so hell-bent on having another baby? But it was always too untimely or indelicate, and surely Misha had no answer; surely it was something he would have liked to understand himself. Unless—and it's too difficult to even contemplate—he also wants to have another child.

He and Anechka have dropped their dissident activities. Misha says that the movement has ceased to exist—the journals are shut down, the dissidents imprisoned or exiled. At last year's Human Rights Day demonstration, twelve people were detained, right at the center of Pushkin Square. Anechka stayed home that year, and though Misha was there, he didn't get close; he watched the demonstration from across the street. Without the movement, the two of them have grown aimless, their ambitions truncated, their concerns too domestic, mundane. Misha works on drama club plays, while Anechka longs for a baby.

Stuck at school, Kat spends countless evenings worrying about Anechka, about the park and the bridge, about the likelihood of yet another pregnancy (so far there have been six), and what it will be like if one turns out to be viable. No one has asked her if she'd like a sibling (the honest answer would be no) or shown concern for her feelings. With each loss, her mother has gotten more brittle, their relationship more faltering and tense, and at times Kat can't escape the sense that Anechka is somehow blaming her. If only Kat hadn't fallen sick. If only she were more exceptional. More like Sveta Vlasenko, less like herself. And maybe if Kat can astonish her mother and prove that she's unique, she won't pine for this other child, this second chance, this saving grace.

"You REALIZE what time it is?" Margo says, when Kat sneaks into the canteen.

"Sorry," Kat says, in a tone that makes it clear she's not particularly sorry. "I had to see my father."

"You *had* to?" Margo mocks her. "You mean to tell me he, poor thing, can't function without your help?"

Everyone knows she despises Kat's parents, their dissident leanings and liberal tastes, the fact that they read Solzhenitsyn and Orwell in class instead of the district-approved authors. Their grooming is questionable, their manners too informal and generally lax. They are not even properly Russian. No wonder their daughter manifests all sorts of strange affinities and can't keep to a common schedule.

Margo is a machine, an automaton; her carriage is impeccable, her every gesture is exact. She looks pretty good for her age, which Jules says must be in the area of fifty-seven. She dresses the same every day: flat shoes, white turtlenecks, dark skirts (all cut the same), tan stockings that never get stained, even in autumn when it rains constantly. She's never sick, she's never late.

Kat, on the other hand, is often late. You can say it's a bad habit, an affliction. She's late for dinner and she's late for nap, and when she gets to the dorm, she's greeted by the gaggle's mayhem.

But how on earth did they become this gaggle? They were diligent girls all through the early grades. Their marks were above average. They got pennants and honorary notes each May, naming them the detachment of the year.

In fourth grade they left their old classroom. They now had to shuttle from lesson to lesson—alone, uncared for, adrift. No longer contained by Rosa, or loved by Thumbelina. They had too many teachers. Their evening matron was a flake. There was a series of substitutes, which didn't help with the already unraveling discipline.

It is uncanny how they've all ended up in one class, a gang of wretched girls who have embraced their deformities, grown to crave everything angry. Anechka says it is because they are unwanted. They stay at school for five days, and on the sixth day they return to their imperfect families. Mothers, divorced or abandoned. Mothers, remarried or otherwise engaged. Mothers who drink. Mothers who can't stand the sight of their daughters' bodies.

In fifth grade they got a new matron, Margo. She'd worked with juvenile delinquents in the past, and she treated the gaggle with the same steely distrust. Some said it was exactly what they needed—a firm, unyielding hand. But Margo with her militant ways has only made them more embittered.

Here's Inna Smirnova (code name: Snake)—a psychopath. Here's Vika Litvinova (Cherub), one of the former weepers, famous for her compulsive lies and thieving, including that time in first grade when she convinced the whole class that her mother was dying of cancer. Lida Kravchenko (Shrew)— given to furious outbursts. And not to be forgotten: Kira Mikadze (Little Hog), their fat, despotic, self-appointed leader. Nina Petrenko, the second of the weepers, is doing a vile imitation of Anechka, jerking her shoulders, shaking her nonexistent hips. "Look! Kysya's mother!" It looks nothing like Anechka, and Nina Petrenko *is* vile. Slippery, freckled, she's learned to make her smallness obscene. She sucks in her cheeks, streaks naked through the dorms. She peels herself open for everyone to see.

"Ignore it," Jules mutters.

"That's what I get for my birthday?"

"Just wait," Jules says. "Maybe Mironov will get expelled."

Mironov has been gone most of the day, ever since his stupid escapade at assembly. "Wouldn't *that* be a great birthday present?" Kat says.

Regrettably, he reappears in time for evening snack. In the canteen he bumps Kat with his shoulder. On purpose, she is sure. "Pig," she mutters, though quietly and mostly to herself.

She tries not to see him, pretends he is not even there. But he exists nonetheless, perpetually mediocre, flickering in and out on the periphery of her vision. His cot is in the back of the classroom. On evening walks, he joins the boys from other classes. Climbing trees, running with sticks, whatever inane activity they seem to be fond of that week.

"Slim pickings," Jules sighs, as they spy the boys escaping through the broken fence into the park. There are movies at the House of Culture, at the opposite end of the park, and other classes go all the time. But 7A isn't allowed to go. Margo is like a bloodhound, scouring the campus every night, waiting for them to get in trouble.

"Let's try it," Jules says. "In honor of your birthday."

Kat says, "Don't even start." It's not worth the risk. Besides, there are movies at school every other Friday.

"*Amphibian Man?*" says Jules. "The bloody *Elusive Avengers* they show every quarter? Honestly, Kat, you're such a mug sometimes."

But she is not. She's simply being cautious. The old guard is watching them all. Any stumble on her part will get her parents in hot water. It's hard to be a rebel when you have others to protect. So she tries to be perfect. She never wears makeup, breaks curfew, or busts her brace on purpose. She's the one person in the school who's always got her brace on, even when she's in a play, even when there's a disco, when other girls put on miniskirts and stow their braces in closets.

She's gotten used to the discomfort of the brace: the blisters, the bruises, the withered spots of skin on her hip bones. She's used to nonplussed glances, pity from the neighbors, the local boys with their catcalls. No boy will ever find her pretty.

"All in its time," Misha usually tells her. "Someone will love you for who you are inside." As if Kat's outward beauty were now out of the question.

Those careful, tenuous promises: someday, sometime. What she wants isn't abstract or tenuous. The boy she likes is real, and he is three grades older.

Kat has a foolish heart. In first grade she loved Igor Zotov, and the next year, after Igor Zotov was discharged, she loved her second cousin from Leningrad. That's how it went, a new infatuation every year, until last year, in sixth grade, she met Nikita. Her love had been always unrequited, but until now it wasn't real love. Now it hurts, and that's how she knows it is real.

The first time she saw him was at last year's play rehearsal; it was the second rehearsal of the season. Kat had missed the first rehearsal—she had been home with chicken pox—and she was slightly late for this one. She entered the assembly hall and stopped. There was this person on the stage, this boy she'd never seen before, standing atop a shaky coffee table. He was playing a villain, apparently. Misha had told him to do this, to leap up on the table, to use the coffee table as a prop, and who could have predicted the effect would be so dramatic? He smiled, breaking out of character, and his face, somewhat crude, a little sheepish, came inexplicably alive. Imperfect it was—imperfect and strikingly familiar.

To him, she must be nearly invisible. He hardly knows she exists, and if he thinks of her at all, it's simply as Misha and Anechka's daughter. Sometimes she imagines writing him a letter, a confession, *Eugene Onegin* style: "I write to you, what more is there to offer . . ."

Jules says, "How about we call him over? Tell him it's your birthday. I could go fetch him if you want. We can play spin the bottle."

Kat tells her to stop it. "Don't be so—"

"Yes, dear?"

"Trivial."

"Ah," says Jules. "Trivial. All right."

Jules is hopelessly unsentimental, unlikely to swoon over a person, verse, or movie star. "You know me, darling," she likes to repeat. "I'm an inveterate cynic." But Kat knows that Jules cares. She got her a chocolate bar called Inspiration for her birthday, a tube of pink lipstick, and a card. She helps her to apply the lipstick, even though she knows Kat's going to wipe it off before they go inside.

"Child," Jules says, "you've got to loosen up. They're your parents, I get it. But sooner or later you'll have to dis-appoint them."

"I disappoint them all the time."

"So what's the problem?" Jules asks, and Kat can't

explain it, or maybe doesn't want to. Jules is nothing like the kids Kat's parents tend to like—not romantic in spirit, not upfront with her emotions. She mostly reads what gets assigned in class, and even her cherished *Jane Eyre* she prefers in its televised version.

"Tell you what," Jules says. "Let's go to the oxygen café." It's a new type of therapy they have, a small basement place by the library that serves frothy drinks made of air.

Kat nods. It's not much, but it's safe.

SVETA VLASENKO finds Kat in the canteen at suppertime. "We have a surprise for you, Kitten. Come to the drama room, okay?"

"You can't go," Jules whispers, and points with her eyes to Margo. It's the first day of school, which means that tonight Margo is primed to deliver her start-of-the-year harangue: where not to be, what not to do. "She'll never let you go, even if you beg her."

"Who's going to beg?" Kat says.

Jules stares at her, flabbergasted. "You won't come with me to the movies, but this Vlasenko character crooks her little finger and suddenly you're not afraid?"

"It's not the same," Kat says, because the truth is a lot more complicated. She belongs with the drama kids, with Anechka and Misha's favorites. They speak the same language; they share passions and ideals—all of which have to do with being noble and a little hapless, and somehow helping humankind. None of them is rich like Jules or has careerist parents.

After supper, Kat runs off to the drama room. It's far enough away, behind the boys' dorms, that no one will stumble across them by accident. Inside, there's an old piano in need of tuning, a scattering of mismatched chairs, old props and set decorations stacked randomly against the walls. In the center, a pair of plain canteen tables.

"The birthday girl," says Sveta, when Kat enters. On one of the tables there's tea and a cake. Bought with Anechka's money, Sveta whispers in Kat's ear. Anechka has arranged it all. A small group of drama club regulars has gathered: Sveta's best friend, Ritka Mavrina. Sveta's boyfriend, Vlad. And here is Nikita, too, with his broad, freckled face (some might say pitted), his slouched shoulders and coppery hair that always falls into his eyes. He nods at Kat shyly, then moves to the side, sits with his back against a wall while strumming his guitar.

Sveta, the graceful hostess, passes around napkins, cuts the cake into thin slivers so everybody gets a taste. They talk of doing a new play, which hasn't been announced yet, and ask Kat if she knows what it's going to be this year. She says Misha has sworn her to secrecy, and they tease her and then attempt to guess.

After a while, though, their attention drifts. They talk of other things, to which Kat was never invited: a trip to Peredelkino, where famous writers live; the party Ritka had that summer. No one thought to include her, because she is three years younger and not their equal yet. But all of this is

going to change. She is about to surprise them. In the meantime, it's her birthday. She is happy. She is fourteen but wise
beyond her age, and Nikita is playing the happy birthday
tune for her: "How sad that a birthday comes only once
a year."

8

WHEN ANECHKA AND MISHA WERE HIRED TWO years ago (a full-time load each, plus half-time extra for the drama club), no one at the school expected real theater. Their duties weren't that extensive: to arrange pageants for all the major holidays, to prep the gym for the quarterly discos, to act as DJs, and to make the discos more educational in nature.

They started modestly. For Teachers' Day, they did a potpourri of short poems and comedy sketches, and most of the teachers were pleased. They said it was refreshing, and the kids got to do something creative, which in the past hadn't always been the case.

For Revolution Day, Anechka and Misha staged a few scenes from *Ten Days That Shook the World*, and though the younger faculty members enjoyed it, the old guard expressed concern. "This ain't the Taganka Theater," Creampuff announced, and the others from her group concurred. They hadn't asked for this buffoonery. They wanted what they'd always had: the carrying of the banner, declamation of poetry, heartfelt singing of patriotic songs to the sound of an accordion. They wanted their boys and girls dressed up as proper Pioneers.

Kat's parents dialed down their efforts. For March 8, they went back to pop song parodies: a humorous ode to the school nurses, a moving tribute to the canteen's female personnel. And for the Victory Day pageant, they even dug up an accordion. Still there were rumblings among the old guard: it was the fortieth anniversary of the victory over Germany, they had expected something grander.

The week after, a playbill went up by the canteen entrance. The play would be a modern fairy tale. Anechka and Misha had been planning it in secret for most of the year. There were stage sets and costumes on loan from an actual theater. There was real theater makeup. On opening night, girls appeared on stage with rouged cheeks and upswept hair, touchingly delicate with their exposed, skinny elbows and long lace gloves. Sveta Vlasenko played a princess, Vlad Borisov a swineherd. With not enough boys to go around, some girls had to take male parts. They wore frock coats and pantaloons, and some sported penciled-in mustaches.

Kat didn't get a part that year, not even as an extra; her parents said she was too young. She'd sat through every minute of every rehearsal and knew each scene by heart. On opening night, she watched from the front row as Professor Fabri came up to embrace Sveta Vlasenko. He held a large bouquet of flowers, and there were tears in his eyes. "Our beautiful mannequin girl," he called her, and Kat knew he meant it, because even then Sveta Vlasenko was beautiful and had only a nominal degree of scoliosis.

Later, the old guard questioned whether the play had been necessary and whether such spectacle promoted unhealthy competition and early fondness for makeup, though what they really objected to were the not-so-subtle messages: the villain dressed to look like Stalin, the masses marching with red flags. But the school administration liked the play, and Professor Fabri commented on the positive effects of the dramatic arts on the students' attitude to treatments.

Next year, everyone wanted to be in a play. The girls from the top grades swarmed over Anechka and Misha, but they remained selective. Sveta Vlasenko played a princess again; Vlad Borisov, an absentminded scientist. They had a thing between them now, a real-life romance. Nikita, new to school that year, was in the play as well. Kat played a villager, a wordless part. Her costume was a poncho and a wide-brimmed hat, and she wasn't allowed to take off her brace, because Anechka said the brace wasn't affecting her performance. Even without the brace she wasn't much to look at, clumsy and awkward, her hair sticking out of her ponytail in short, unruly tufts.

Still, it was the best spring of her life. They rehearsed every Wednesday at night and on Saturdays in the afternoon, and once again she memorized each part, on the off chance that an actor might fall ill and she'd be asked to step in as an alternate. When they weren't rehearsing, she watched Nikita strum his guitar or play cards with Sveta Vlasenko and Vlad.

She spoke to him twice: once to ask whether learning guitar had been hard, and another time to tell him Misha needed his help in the drama room. He and Misha bonded instantly, Nikita often staying to talk to Misha after class, so after a while Kat knew just when to visit Misha's classroom.

It wasn't just Nikita. She felt close to everyone. They would huddle together at the end of each performance, giddy from applause, a little stunned. It seemed unthinkable for them to ever be apart. They'd stay for hours in the assembly hall and sing their favorite guitar songs, about the rose blooming in a brown beer bottle, about the last midnight trolley, about the beloved courtyards of old Arbat, despite the fact that none of them had ever lived near Arbat. They'd all grown up in the unsightly new developments in remote corners of Moscow.

Before the school year ended, they'd given three performances. Afterward, some of the students got discharged. Sveta Vlasenko went to a tourist resort. Kat got dispatched to Kratovo, as always. To sleep and to laze in the sun, to swim in the nearby lake whenever the weather allowed, to wait for her burr of a body to soften and blossom so that she also one day might be worthy of love.

Summer that year was overcast and lonesome. She paced in the woodsy back of the property, reciting the play to herself. She knew it was pointless—the year was over, the play was over, she'd never be asked to step in as an alternate—but the play was a part of her now, vital like an internal organ.

It was then, while reciting the play, that she decided acting was her calling. She had a lot of time to ponder it, and she figured it had to be true. She'd once asked Misha how he knew that teaching was what he had to do, and he said that time disappeared whenever you were doing what you were meant to. Time certainly disappeared for Kat that summer as she gulped down Chekhov, Ibsen, and Shakespeare, memorizing pages' worth of monologues. She was Nora, or Nina, or Cordelia. She could probably be Hamlet. She'd found a paper-wrapped book in Misha's classroom, the fictional diary of a young man enrolled in acting school, and after she read it three times in a row, she started practicing its theories and exercises.

Looking back at the drama club contingent, she could easily see who her parents took under their wing. It was either great talent or great need. There were the girls who'd lost their families to accidents and who sometimes had no place to live. There was the girl from 9B who couldn't go home to Ukraine. There were others shipped in from far-flung towns—because schools like this didn't exist anywhere else—who knew not a soul in the capital and spent their weekends in strangers' apartments.

Mostly, though, it was talent: a professional dancer who used to perform all over the country, a trained ballerina or violin player, even a twelve-year-old prodigy who could compose her own songs. Ritka Mavrina was an artist. Sveta Vlasenko looked good on stage, though in Kat's opinion she wasn't a great actress. She always played the same old character and seemed to have no range. Kat could imagine outshining her, leaving the audience shaken, her parents proud and impressed. Proving once and for all that she was one of them.

ONE WEDNESDAY after nap time, three weeks into the autumn term, Jules helps Kat get ready for the first rehearsal. She lends her a pink sweater and puts her hair in a tight French braid—so tight that Kat's scalp itches and she's feeling the beginning of a tension headache. Some blush? Some lipstick? Some eye shadow? Kat says, "No, thanks." Makeup looks tacky on young girls, in Anechka's opinion—that is, unless they are on stage.

Kat doesn't bother asking Jules to come with her to rehearsal. She's tried in the past and she knows the answer. "Don't like amateur dramatics," Jules usually says. No one from 7A is in the drama club, apart from Kat. In theory, one doesn't need an invitation; it's a school institution, open to every student. In practice, though, the workings of the drama club are secretive. You must be in the loop to know about their upcoming auditions and new plays, and you are only in the loop if Anechka and Misha want you there. Jules must know she isn't wanted, not for her talents anyway. As Kat's best friend, sure. But anyone can tell it's not the same.

Kat goes to the bathroom to check her reflection. The brace is like a military jacket; it makes her look square and squat. Her face, pinched by the brace, looms large and unattractive, and her pulled-back hair only accentuates her ugliness.

"Nonsense," says Jules. Kat looks exotic, Georgian

maybe? There must be someone Georgian in the play. Didn't Pushkin write about some such lady? "A jug held high, the Georgian lass her way was slowly making . . ."

"That's Lermontov," Kat says. She's strangely irked by this mistake, and even more so by the suggestion that she looks Georgian. She knows she is darker than most other girls, dark in a Jewish way, and whenever they celebrate Friendship of the People Day, she always has to dress up like someone from the Caucasus.

Kira Mikadze (Little Hog) overhears "Georgian" and thinks they're making fun of her. She claims her father was from Cyprus (God rest his soul), not that they understand the difference, the ignorant cows. The gaggle pretends to believe her, because no one's willing to provoke her. She's thick-set, muscular; she can easily squeeze you into a corner. There are bruises on her legs, her sides, her arms. The gaggle never asks about those. There is no need; they've seen Little Hog's mom.

Inevitably Little Hog will run to complain to Margo. Knopman, she'll say, was making fun of Georgian people. Not that Little Hog herself has anything to do with Georgians, but for her it's a matter of principle, you understand? She is hurt on behalf of the homeland.

Margo, in turn, will say she's not surprised, *some* people don't appreciate their country's spirit of inclusiveness. *Some* people (namely Jews) make a lot of fuss about being perse- cuted, whereas in reality it's simply not the case. And maybe if they contributed more to society, instead of trying to slan-

der it every step of the way, others would have more respect
for them.

Margo is unhappy because the drama club is back in session. A waste of resources, she calls it. She says it has gotten too easy to criticize the past, and it's people like Kat's
parents, the ungrateful, unpatriotic kind, who've been too
eager to exploit the fad for glasnost. Why must they focus on
controversies? Why not celebrate successes instead? Whenever the drama club meets, Margo tries to come up with
competing activities, or else she tells the gaggle the drama
club thinks them unworthy.

She needn't bother: the gaggle has no desire to join the
drama club, and as for Kat, she's been a lost cause from the
start. Tonight, Margo reminds her, they have a class hour
scheduled. They'll be discussing how to apply to Komsomol.
Kat tells her she can't stay, she's got a previous engagement.
Margo squints at her as if to warn her, as if to say, "You'll
only have yourself to blame." She doesn't actually say it,
though—just folds her arms and walks away.

Kat leaves ahead of supper and asks Jules to save her some
food: a slice of cheese with bread, a pastry wrapped in napkins. She's excited, impatient, but also sheepish about leaving Jules, who'll have to endure the class hour on her own.
"You're sure you don't want to join me?"

"And miss Margosha's pearls of wisdom?" Jules snickers
and pats Kat on the back. She seems unconcerned, but Kat
still feels like she's betraying her.

Jules settles on her cot, cross-legged, and opens a packet

of potato chips. "Don't worry, thespian," she says. "Go and be daring."

THE DRAMA ROOM is small. They really could use a bigger room, something more centrally located; but given how the old guard feels about Anechka and Misha's undertakings, they are lucky to have a room at all. The two canteen tables are pushed together in the center. Those who got to rehearsal early are huddled close to the tables, close to Misha, who's shuffling through the mess of his typewritten pages, and Anechka, who's knitting, a little distanced but engaged.

The new play is about Pushkin, and Misha has written it himself. There is no Pushkin in the play—which is a shame, Anechka says, because Misha would make a perfect Pushkin. Instead there are Pushkin's contemporaries: his enemies, his loves, his friends. Sveta Vlasenko is playing Pushkin's wife. Asya Matusova from 10A, nicknamed Medusa, is cast to play her sister. Vlad Borisov is Baron d'Anthès, who is destined to end Pushkin's life. Nikita is a secret police spy. Alex Goldin, who finished school last year, will play the tsar. Even Ritka Mavrina, who always insists she's not an actress, has scored the small part of the postmaster's wife.

Kat's character is nameless, identified only as Society Lady #2. In her first scene she comes to Pushkin's house for a visit. She is greeted by Medusa, Pushkin's sister-in-law. In the back, by the mantelpiece clock, posing as a servant, stands Nikita. The two ladies share a few lines of gossip; then, using a tome of Pushkin's verses, they play a fortune-telling game. Kat names the page and line, and Medusa divines Pushkin's future:

I've learned the voice of other longings
And sorrow I've relearned anew.
The former brings me no atonement.

Nikita completes the quatrain from the back of the stage:

Old sorrow, I am mourning you.

For now, there's no mantelpiece or stage; they are clustered around these old canteen tables, under a single bare light, Kat and Medusa next to each other, Nikita across from them. They haven't memorized their parts yet, so their eyes are mostly on the pages. They look up only occasionally, and sometimes both Kat and Nikita look up at the same time. He smiles. She flushes, painfully.

Some girls, she knows, find Nikita too rough-hewn and menacing. His shoulders roll forward; his hair falls over his brow—he jerks his head backward to throw it out of his eyes. He looks mature, manly, and also his voice is kind of gruff. You get all sorts of wrong ideas when you meet him, but if you wait, the outer shell will crack and you'll see the real Nikita—a little shy, obliging, tender.

If only this brief hour could last forever and they could stay like this, in the small, square room with its poor, hard chairs, all fifteen or twenty of them. The drama kids. They live for the sound of prose, verse, and music, for the beauty that can turn your soul upside down. Catharsis, Misha calls it, that moment when art brings you to tears. They live for the theater also, though few of them think of it as something they'll do in the future. It's more of a place, an escape. They can enter the drama room, or the assembly hall when they rehearse in earnest, and discover a world that is perfect and glorious, where there are no nagging matrons or grouchy night nurses or mandatory evening walks, a world where none of them is sick, where Ritka's hips are not askew and Nikita's back isn't bowed because of his kyphosis. In this world they are counts and princesses; they converse in a language that is respectful and old-fashioned, share books, exchange clever remarks. Here they can be themselves, they can be individuals and intellectuals.

No one else at the school is like them. The rest of the students are land-bound, practical, more than content to act en masse. They worship cheap pop music, yearn for trendy clothes, keep photos of their hackneyed idols, long-haired heartthrobs with guitars or the most recent crop of doe-eyed foreign actors. That doesn't mean they are wrong or immoral, Anechka always clarifies. In fact, it's an easy existence for them. You'll find that they're mostly happy and more than pleased with their uncomplicated lives, their souls impoverished, their hearts perfectly empty.

Right now, Anechka says nothing, even though Kat's scene has just finished and she thinks she's delivered her lines rather well. But no, not a word from Anechka. She's just knitting, knitting endlessly, and it's as though the pink ball of yarn in her lap is the only thing worthy of her attention. She started knitting back in May, and since then she's turned out three baby caps and two pairs of booties. She knits everywhere and openly, in classes, at meetings, and doesn't bother with excuses that she's doing it for a relative or friend. It's easy to see what she's making, and it gives people ideas. "Is your mother expecting?" some teachers have asked Kat. They look at Kat with pity, even those who don't know of Anechka's miscarriages.

"Good work tonight," says Misha. "Good work, ladies and gentlemen." Rehearsal has ended; it's now ten past nine. The usual gang congregates around Anechka and Misha: Vlad and Nikita, Sveta and Ritka. Alex Goldin and some other kids who have graduated. Medusa, whom no one actually likes. Sveta leans over and whispers something in Anechka's ear, something that makes Anechka smile. Ritka Mavrina whines, "Darlings, I'm dying for a cigarette." In a moment the whole gang will go outside. They'll stand behind the big canteen, where no one can see them from the windows, laughing and smoking in a knowing, world-weary way, the girls complaining of the autumn cold, the boys being gallant and giving up their jackets. Anechka and Misha will linger among them, acting cool and informal, impressively young. They won't be like teachers, won't even mind the smoking. The gang will walk them to the edge of the campus. Those who have already graduated will say goodbye as well. The rest will slink back into the dorms. None of them ever gets caught. Maybe they're lucky, or maybe it's because they're older. Whereas Kat is probably in trouble already, late for dorm check-in and all.

Anechka says, "Are you still here? I don't need another earful from Margo."

"Chin up," Sveta Vlasenko says, in her heartfelt and trilling manner, which Kat has never learned to trust. "You'll be a hit this season, Kitten. I can feel it."

BUT IT'S not so easy to be a star, a hit, to outdo someone like Sveta—Sveta who is beautiful and perfect and never had to wear a brace at all. There are others at the school like her, and you take one look at them and wonder whether they even have scoliosis. What they have, you realize, is parents with connections and resources, who have managed to propel their progeny beyond every medical council and lengthy waiting list. Where else can you find a boarding school like this, with a rigorous curriculum and swimming lessons three times a week? There are no boarding schools for healthy kids, not anywhere in Moscow.

Kat tries not to be envious of Sveta. At least *she's* at the school due to her illness and not because her parents just wanted to get rid of her. But it's tough to keep things in perspective, especially on weekends, when she leaves the protective school gates and every gawking passerby reminds her she's defective.

For exactly this reason, Jules refuses to wear her brace on weekends. Kat, though, thinks that's unwise. It's the pivotal year for most of them in seventh grade. They are going through puberty, the peak of their development, their bodies shooting upward like stray grass. The problem is, it puts too much strain on their musculoskeletal system, which is already compromised. Their curvatures might worsen overnight, by as much as twenty degrees on the Cobb scale. Once puberty is over, the bones ossify, and then there's nothing to do but to accept whatever you've been left with.

Every Sunday, Kat stands naked before her wardrobe mirror. The slope of her left hip is slighter than the right one, as if cast by a negligent sculptor, and when she turns sideways she can see a protrusion around her right shoulder blade. It gets a little worse each year—she knows this because of her X-rays—despite the almost maniacal discipline with which she follows her regimen. "Your back!" Anechka snaps whenever Kat forgets to pay attention, when she's doing homework on Sunday at the kitchen table or slumps on the sofa while watching TV. "Your back!" Anechka's voice rings with frustration. "For God's sake, mind your back." She turns away as if it pains her.

"Are you ready?" Misha calls from the kitchen, and Kat pulls on her brace and her clothes, hiding the head-holder with a scarf. Every Sunday they go to visit Zoya Moiseevna. Every week they do this, like clockwork, while Anechka stays at home, sometimes cooking, but lately mostly resting on the sofa, working or reading or taking long naps.

Kat's often tempted to stay with her, but deep down she knows it's useless. She has tried to relate to her like Sveta and the others do. She told her what Shrew said about Kat being a Jew and what Margo said about the drama club being decadent, and when that didn't work she tried to talk about books.

Anechka said there wasn't anything to be done about Shrew and Margo. A stronger person might be able to stand up to them, but Kat wasn't strong, she was soft, and it was better if she just kept quiet, better for everyone involved. And as for the books, was it not enough that Anechka talked books all day at school? She had a headache now. She was tired. Or else she resorted to nagging, and when that happened anything would do: a mistake Kat made in last week's dictation, a poor mark in algebra, a missing button or a new tear from her brace. "I'm just a chore to you," Kat said to her.

"Cut your mother some slack," Misha asked her. "She's struggling. She's not herself."

"Is she pregnant again?"

"I don't know," he said. "She's unhappy and searching for something. The doctors say it's her thyroid or hormones, but I think it's deeper than that."

Kat saw he was upset and dropped the subject. Illness scared him. It had taken his father away back when he was a boy, and now it was everywhere around him.

AT FIRST they thought nothing of it when, three years ago, Zoya Moiseevna started to get forgetful. It was normal, they figured, a natural sign of her age. She was, after all, nearing seventy. But her confusion grew and they became alarmed at the worsening state of her health, especially after she fell in the stairwell. Misha would go over to her apartment and there would be something rotting on the kitchen counter, maybe a plate of chicken bones left sitting for a few days; or he would find a kettle on the stove with all the water boiled away. Some days she might forget to flush the toilet, and other times she'd simply stay in bed.

Misha goes to check on her every few days, and he pays a neighbor to look in on her between visits. What they really ought to do is swap their two apartments for a bigger one, but no one's got the time to organize the swap. It can take years, anyway, years of going across town to the housing bureau, years of making phone calls, collecting documents, stringing together a long chain of interested parties, and even then the swap might fall through in the end.

Kat tries to help whenever she can, during school breaks and every Sunday, though not because she's fond of her grandmother. She's grown to crave these afternoons with Misha, the hours spent on the train, their heart-to-heart talks, and most of all his gratitude. "Where would I be without you?" he says, and she knows he means it. He relies on her, leaving the nastiest tasks till the end of the week.

As they ride on the train, they talk about theater and acting: affective memory and Stanislavsky, how one can perfect one's technique, and whether Misha ever wished to be an actor. He says no, not really (he's always been more drawn to writing), though Anechka once did. She almost quit their teaching institute.

"Why didn't she?" Kat says.

"It's not that simple, Button. For a Jewish person in this country to make it as an actress, you have to be obscenely talented, not moderately gifted or well trained."

"Like who, for example? You think we have someone at school who's that talented?"

"It's too soon to tell," Misha says, and Kat doesn't press him, though she hoped for a different answer.

For the rest of the trip they talk about Zoya Moiseevna, and how she's deteriorating and can't continue to live by herself.

"I bet it's not so bad," Kat says.

But you know it's bad the instant you step inside Zoya Moiseevna's apartment. There's the smell, for one thing. The sweet, dirty, rotten-fruit smell.

"When did you wash last?" Misha asks.

"Yesterday," says Zoya Moiseevna. She has a dumb smirk on her face, and it's impossible to tell whether she actually believes it or if she's just pulling his leg. She sticks out her tongue at them.

There's a racket out on the landing, the clank of a lock and chain. Of course, Kat thinks, the neighbor. She's calling out for them: "Yoo-hoo? Anyone there? I saw the door ajar, so I thought I better check." At least she's paying attention.

The neighbor's pretty old herself; they can't expect much from her, apart from looking in on Zoya Moiseevna and making sure she is safe. If only she could help her bathe once in a while. But Misha, ill at ease around the domestic stuff, has never specified his demands, and now it's too late. The neighbor is angling for more money. She's saying how hard it is these days to survive on one pension, how things aren't as they used to be, how in the past the country cared for its elderly but now no one gives a damn. "I switch on the news at nine o'clock, and it might as well be in Chinese for all I get from it."

Misha hands her a ten-ruble note and she goes away.

Once she is gone, they start setting the place in order. It's unbelievable how much dirt one person can accumulate. There's dust on top of everything, dust underneath the furniture, and behind Zoya Moiseevna's sofa they find some slices of stale bread. They take out the garbage, collect up her soiled clothes. "You think we maybe ought to wash the windows?" says Misha.

Kat tells him, "It's three o'clock, Dad."

They know exactly what's left to do.

"Oh hell," Misha says, and goes off to run a bath. "Sometimes I wish I had a sister."

"Or maybe Mom could help?"

"Very funny," he calls through the noise of running water.

It takes Kat much cajoling to get Zoya Moiseevna out of her housecoat. "What are you doing with my clothes?" her grandmother demands.

"I'm stealing them," Kat says. "I'm going to sell them."

Her grandmother grabs for her rags, and her long, hardened nails dig into Kat's forearm.

"Let go," Kat yells. "I'm going to wash them, you moron."

She lets her keep her slip and underpants.

"I've only just washed," Zoya Moiseevna protests, as Kat guides her toward the bathroom.

They get her in the tub and Misha lathers up her hair; she coughs dramatically as he sluices the soap off her head. She's acting like a frantic cat, thrashing all over the place, scratching, and splashing water. She tries to take the loofah away from Kat. Her slip comes off, and then her panties, and Misha steps away, leaving Kat to take care of the delicate bits.

The key is not to think about it. Kat finds she mostly doesn't mind giving her grandmother a bath, except for the scratches that cover her forearms and wrists. They take a while to heal, these scratches. On the way home, she'll show them to Misha and watch his eyes turn watery and sad. "I'm sorry," he'll tell her. "You're shouldering more than your share. It must be terribly upsetting to see your grandmother like this. But you, you're so kind and patient and never seem to get upset."

"I'm just a good actress," she'll tell him.

9

"THERE ARE NO SMALL PARTS, ONLY SMALL ACTORS." This becomes Kat's mantra for the next several weeks. At home on weekends, she locks herself in the bathroom and tries to convey complex feelings while remaining entirely still. Because, even motionless, the actor must be able to captivate the audience. Hers is a small, composite character, and she goes to a great deal of trouble to invent her backstory. What is actually known about Society Lady #2? Is she young, is she rich, for example? Does she live with an elderly aunt?

In her most significant scene, Kat dances at a ball, and later she pleads with the tsar to pardon Pushkin: "Don't punish him, Your Royal Highness, and spare him your wrath." She tries to put all of her ardor into her words and even wrings her hands to telegraph her desperation. Though sometimes, to her dismay, her awareness lapses and suddenly she can't remember what she's begging for. Has anyone noticed? She checks Misha's and Anechka's reaction. Anechka is knitting and Misha's making notes. They neither commend nor correct her performance—probably because her part is so small.

Sveta, of course, gets a lot of attention, though this time she, too, struggles with her role. Pushkin's wife is a complicated character, unfaithful, willful, splendid. Here she is, entering briskly and squinting in the limpid candlelight. "Less charm," Anechka says. "And a bit more impatience."

In this way they get through the end of the first quarter and reach the autumn break. The week before the break, rehearsals are canceled. Instead, the drama club must organize a disco—there's one at the end of evey quarter—the one event the whole school always eagerly awaits.

ANECHKA AND MISHA used to take the discos seriously. They came up with contests and special themes, and in general they seemed to believe they could elevate the discos, make them into something artistic and meaningful. Kat remembers one time in particular when they did a whole sequence on the history of dance: minuet, waltz, foxtrot, tango. It took a lot of effort to train the students to perform all these routines.

Since then they've lost interest, or maybe they finally figured out it wasn't worth their energy. The students don't like the disruptions, don't need prizes and quizzes. They only want to dance, though really it's more like bobbing in the dark, to the unrelenting tunes of Modern Talking. "You're my heart, you're my soul," or as the students prefer to translate it phonetically: "You're my bread, you're my salt."

These days it's the gym teacher who installs the lights and mounts the spinning mirror ball. Vlad Borisov supplies the tapes, since neither Anechka nor Misha can tell C. C. Catch from Sandra. After that, all they have to do is sit at the front of the gym, feed the tapes into the outdated sound system, say a few things into the microphone.

For the students, though, the discos have always been important. The girls come in on Monday with dresses and blouses propped daintily on hangers, with small arrays of lipsticks and extra knapsacks. They usually have until Friday to fiddle with their outfits and hair, to go through their baggies of cosmetics, to fret over scuffed pairs of heels they've swiped from their mothers' closets. Do they clash? Do they fit? Will the music be good? Will there be slow dances? And if so, will anyone ask them this time?

The odds are never in their favor. In the whole school there are maybe half a dozen boys that look halfway decent—the son of the head of orthopedics, the nephew of the music teacher. These are the best prospects, the healthy boys. They are here because of the swimming, and also because the school has the best ranking in the district.

And if these boys are not to your liking, there are always the local boys. They lurk in the park outside the school bounds, and only the most abject, wildest girls dare to join them in the overgrown shrubbery or out on the deserted playground.

The local boys are curious about the crippled girls. The discos allow them to sneak inside, briefly dissolving in the gym's pulsating darkness. But they are easy to spot on the dance floor. Everything gives them away: their street clothes, their smell, their strong, stocky bodies. Still, for a song or two, a girl might find herself pressed to a stranger's sturdy form, her cheek crushed against the metal-studded denim, his breath on her neck thick with cigarettes and booze. And for weeks afterward, she'll dream he might return for her.

ON THE day of the disco, Anechka doesn't come to school. "Feeling out of sorts" is how Misha puts it. It happens. It's happened before. A few days at home feeling ill, or feeling blue, and later a note from a cousin who works across town at a district policlinic.

"Is she okay?" Kat whispers, and Misha shrugs as if to say, who knows!

The day has gone haywire anyway. The schedule's been thrown out of the window, and no one pays attention in class. The girls pass notes and even practice their dance moves. Mironov rips one of his notebooks and sends out a score of paper planes. The teachers let out empty threats, but even they don't care. The quarter is practically finished.

After nap, Margo relents and lets the girls stay in the dorm and primp before the disco. The girls lounge in their pajamas or get their outfits prepped, darting to the room down the hall to borrow the iron. In the hallway, Jules has set up her makeshift beauty parlor. She is a pro with makeup brushes and hair implements, wielding them with ease, stepping around lightly. She seems strangely fragile in her flowery pajama pants, but also somehow indestructible, like a chess piece en route to a checkmate.

Kat perches on the couch nearby to keep her company.

"What are you wearing?" Jules asks.

Leaving for school that Monday, Kat plucked a blue skirt and white blouse out of her closet. Now, upon closer inspection, the skirt appears rather shrunken (she's had it since before fourth grade), and the blouse isn't any better—tight under the arms and with a small darn on one side that she hadn't noticed. But in the dark, she reasons, it won't matter. What matters is the overall impression, the full effect, which, she believes, is light and airy.

"What are you," says Jules, "a snowflake? Honestly, child, it's like I've taught you nothing."

Kat's never been too good about clothes. The stuff she wears is usually hideous, ill-fitting, badly made. Patched-up button-down shirts, corduroy pants, a few stretched-out sweaters that used to be Anechka's, and a particularly ugly brown jacket. She knows her wardrobe is atrocious. In part it's because of the brace, which turns everything into rags with its bolts, joints, and planks, so there's never any sense in buying her good clothes. Besides, month after month her parents say they're short on cash.

"We've got to find you something else," Jules says. "And absolutely no brace."

"You're dreaming," Kat answers, but then she thinks, Maybe? If Anechka were here, she would notice, but Misha's not the most observant person, so it actually might work. Week after week Kat's been rehearsing in her brace, aware of how much it dwarfs and limits her. Without it, she could soar.

Jules, in the meantime, is working on Vika Litvinova's hair. Vika Litvinova—a pest, a parasite. You'd think after the whole thieving business, after all the times she's been caught in extravagant lies, she'd be the leper, the black sheep of the class. Instead, she is more of a white sheep. Sweet-faced, soft-spoken, docile, she plays up her angelic attributes, poses as someone helpless, childlike. It's no accident that her nickname is Cherub.

Kat thinks it's repulsive the way she lisps on purpose, curls up in the fetal position, and even sucks her thumb at times. There's a slickness to her, a silky sheen, that makes her appear trustworthy, especially to those who haven't known her for long. She sidles up to Jules, and Jules, who's lived through only *some* of Cherub's debacles, considers her amusing.

Right now, Cherub's blubbering some nonsense: how everyone despises her, how she feels misunderstood and sad, how when everyone leaves for the disco she'll stay behind and hang herself with the belt of her bathrobe.

"Is it sturdy?" Kat checks.

Jules says, "Don't encourage her."

"It's the same song and dance every year. One day it's razors, the next it's the gas." Kat straightens up.

Jules says, "You're going?"

"I'll be inside," Kat says. "Just let me know when the melo-drama's over." She doesn't know why she's letting Cherub get to her. Maybe because she once believed her. Or maybe

it's the fact that Cherub has broken every rule without incur-
ring any real penalties. Her brace is perpetually busted or
hidden; she routinely skips swimming and other kinds of
therapy, but you'd never know it from looking at her back. A
normal, slightly chubby back, maybe a little uneven. In the
six years they've been here, Cherub has barely changed.

Kat doesn't mean to fall asleep. She isn't sure how it's even
possible, given her irritation and the gaggle's noise. She is
reading in bed, and the next thing she knows it's an hour
later and someone's thrown a hairbrush at her. "Rise and
shine, Kysya. It's party time."

The gaggle is rigged out and ready: Shrew's dressed in
jeans and a red leather vest, Snake in a miniskirt and fish-
nets. Cherub, it seems, has scrapped her suicide plans for
the time being. Her hair is crimped into tight little ringlets
and she's sporting pink banana pants. Even Bones—poor
skeletal Bones—has spruced herself up, donned a billow-
ing, big-shouldered jacket and put a small ribbon in her
hair. The rest of the girls are in dowdy skirts or cotton summer dresses, in high-necked blouses their grandmas wore
when they were young themselves. Kira Mikadze, her bangs
pinned back above her protruding forehead, swaddles herself in a big wooly cardigan.

Out in the hallway, Jules is still in her pajama pants,
doing some witchery over Nina Petrenko's stringy orange
hair. "You're next," she says to Kat.

There is no time to hesitate. Kat leaves the brace off and
pulls on her snowflake costume: the shirt that gapes between
the buttons, the skirt that puckers at the waist. The sleeves

are too short. Her tights are white and unattractive. One of her shoes has come unglued.

But Jules is undeterred. She rolls up Kat's sleeves, untucks her shirt ("It's not a parade, it's a disco!"); from somewhere deep inside the wardrobe she produces a pair of black nylons. She paints Kat's face, back-combs her hair and pins it on both sides with red barrettes.

"Observe!" she says, posing Kat in front of the big mirror in the bathroom.

Kat slowly takes in her transformation: bright lips, skinny arms, eyes big with mascara and kohl. There is something woeful about her, as if she's a young urchin, a tragic, large-eyed creature from Hugo's *Les Misérables*.

AT THE DISCO, the gaggle occupies its own corner. They always dance together, in a large and disorderly swarm. It's the way Margo wants it. She stands not at a distance with the other matrons but directly across from the gaggle, her gaze unwavering, her back straight as a board. Margo the prison guard. You know it's driving them bonkers. You see it in the way they dance, huddling together, squaring their bodies, pushing against other clusters of girls, hoping to provoke somebody.

Kat walks aimlessly around the gym. She locked up her brace in Anechka's wall unit, for which she has a spare key, then waited until the last possible minute, until the lights were dimmed, hoping Misha wouldn't notice her. It seems to have worked, though she must avoid the pair of hulking speakers behind which Misha has marooned himself. He's there with Vlad and Nikita.

It annoys Kat sometimes that Nikita is so devoted to Misha, so awed by his ideas, so keen to embrace his every plan. Of course, it makes sense; Misha is brilliant. But some afternoons when she comes into Misha's classroom and finds the two of them discussing something abstract, she feels superfluous, beside the point. Jules always tells her to speak to Nikita, but what, apart from Misha, would they speak about?

Kat and Jules always split up at the start of the disco. Jules goes to the gaggle's corner, while Kat, they both know, will latch onto the group of drama club girls. It feels wrong every time, but Kat can't possibly include Jules. It's just not her scene. She might feel awkward or unwelcome among the older girls.

The older girls are loose-limbed, self-possessed, insouciant. They accept Kat's presence like it's natural. A couple of them wave or wink. They're doing some synchronized sequence of steps, which Kat can't hope to copy. At first, she just shifts her feet—utterly lost, trying to find her rhythm—and smiles like a moron. But then the music loosens her and she begins to feel the beat. Her steps become easy. The song pulses through her. She is nimble, she is weightless and lithe, a ball hitting the pavement. A bounce for every note, for every name. "I know five names." She is normal again. She is in sync with the other girls.

KAT FINDS Jules resting outside the gaggle's circle, fanning herself with a small handkerchief. "Too little oxygen," Jules says, "too much exertion." Kat is sorry for having abandoned her, but Jules is not resentful or even remotely upset. She is her usual unruffled self, and not even slightly spectacular in a simple white shirt and stylish tapered pants. Despite her magic touch she has done nothing to augment her own body, staying sticklike, athletic, razor-straight. Not a curve on her, not a hint of soft womanly plumpness.

They go outside to get some air. On the way to the second-floor bathroom, Jules complains that the music is lame. "Have a word with your dad, or your boyfriend." "He's not my boyfriend," Kat retorts, though she'd like nothing more than to be Nikita's girl. Whenever there is a slow song, which isn't often, she gets this shaky, hopeful feeling. But it's stupid, she knows, because Nikita doesn't dance at all. Whenever he emerges from behind the speakers, it's only for a cigarette or a sip of water. She might catch a glimpse of him returning, pausing briefly at the edges of the gym, so big, so out of place, a bulwark of a person, looking forlorn amidst the dancing throng. She'd like to go to him, to throw her arms around his sloping shoulders—but that's such a romantic, improbable notion. Because who is she, really? She is no one to him. She watches him retreat behind the speakers and later curses her pathetic lack of courage.

She and Jules enter the bathroom. A group of girls Kat doesn't recognize have crammed themselves into the anteroom, their hairspray canisters crowding the sink. They give her and Jules dirty looks, as though they own the bathroom.

The anteroom is empty when Kat comes out of her stall. Alone, she studies her reflection. Maybe it is the semi-darkness, or Jules's handiwork, but despite Kat's strange urchin-girl getup, her image in the mirror suddenly seems attractive. There's a certain sharpness to her features, a certain deep and brooding look. Here in the drafty public bathroom reeking of pee and hairspray, she discerns in her face the traces of Anechka's angular beauty, the softness she inherited from Misha.

She gazes at her face, her body, and murmurs the lines from the play: "My sadness is interminable. There's so much baseness in the world." Looking like this, she could be more than a bit player or a soubrette. She could be unforgettable. Entrancing.

She shivers for no reason. How long has it been? The bathroom is perfectly still. She calls out Jules's name, quietly. All of a sudden she's convinced that Jules has left.

Outside, the long corridor stretches in front of her: murky, unbearably vacant. She runs alongside closed classroom doors, her heart beating fast, her steps echoing in the emptiness. A door opens abruptly and, startled, she nearly trips.

She doesn't recall whose classroom this is. What she knows is: a) it's not theirs and b) Mironov, who is standing at the threshold, has no business being there. He and his ilk lurk outside the gym, ogling the dancing girls inside, smirking when one of them comes out for some air.

He is not smirking now. It's hard to make out his expression in the dimness of the corridor; suffice it to say it isn't anything Kat's seen before. Perhaps it's just a trick, a play of shadows, but she can swear his face looks almost handsome. And he is *not* a handsome boy. He'll never be one—not with his hideous body or the ugly grimaces he seems to favor. But tonight there are no grimaces. Tonight his expression is solemn and stark. He's just looking at her, as though he's never seen her in his life.

Something or someone shifts inside the classroom, and then it is like ripples over a pond and his face once again clouds with malice. "What are you gaping at?" he says, his voice sour, raspy. Before she can begin to answer, he steps inside and shuts the door.

She stands there for a few seconds. She has an eerie feeling that if she were to glimpse inside, she'd find no one in the classroom. Werewolves, she mutters, thinking of Nina Petrenko's ghost stories at bedtime. She doesn't normally believe in werewolves or ghosts; nevertheless, she gets chills and a frantic desire to bolt. This time she doesn't run; she walks fast to the end of the hall, and when at last she's at the stairwell she dashes downstairs, where the music is thumping relentlessly and everyone's bopping and sweating in the pools of blue and orange light, and where later, under the slowly rotating disco ball, Vlad Borisov will slow-dance with Sveta.

THE DORM is subdued tonight. No one's throwing fits or tossing pillows. The gaggle have changed into pajamas and nightgowns, and now they seem emptied out and pleasantly sedate, as if they've stomped off all their rage and left it on the dance floor.

Nina Petrenko is telling a story, something she's seen in a video—a pornographic video, most likely, full of the smutty scenarios she likes to describe. She gets to see a lot of videos. Her mother is too busy for Nina. The mother has boyfriends (a new one every quarter), her own private life. When weekends come, she sends her daughter off to stay with distant relatives. They seem to have a lot of boys, these relatives. Teenage boys (or older), and always a video player. The boys show Nina the videos and later get into her bed, though she swears she never lets them do anything nasty.

"You're fibbing," says Kira Mikadze.

Nina, predictably, gets mad. She says she never lies, she's not like Cherub. And if they don't believe her, it's their problem—'cause now she won't tell them how the movie ends.

The girls yell at her to keep going; Shrew says she'll smack her face; and when the threats don't appear to be working, Jules throws Nina a decent chunk of chocolate.

Jules isn't picky when it comes to entertainment, a fact Kat has learned to accept. She's one of the land-bound ones, as likely to enjoy Vivaldi as the pop music TV program *Morning Mail*. And yet from the start, she and Kat have been inseparable—getting up in the morning together, sitting at meals together, shouldering each day together like a tight little crew. Every evening they walk, from four thirty to six, traversing every path within the campus. The bleak autumn light thickens slowly toward nightfall. One by one the streetlights come on, early and not yet strictly necessary. They start along the central alley, but soon escape into one of their favorite nooks, the space behind the swimming pool, with a swing and a view of the park, or the secluded corner outside the dorms that has the giant oak tree.

In the dorm, they routinely stay up well past midnight, snacking on Jules's chocolates, slathering their faces with cucumber astringent that is supposed to cure spotty skin. If asked, Kat would be unable to explain what keeps the two of them together.

It's strange how time moves at night. An hour can last forever. Kat drifts off, only to awaken to the sound of high, nervous voices and frantic footsteps outside. When, despite the late hour, the matrons and night nurses don't bother to walk on tiptoe or lower their voices, you know it must be an emergency.

The lights come on abruptly. The door, flung open, hits the corner of the wardrobe. Margo walks in, followed by two night nurses. "Where's Litvinova?" she asks.

Cherub's bed is unmade, which is probably why no one noticed that she's missing. They must have glanced in passing at her bed, noted the crumpled blanket, and deduced from it that she was in the toilet or brushing her teeth.

"Cherub?" the gaggle clamors. "Where's Cherub?"

There's a brief, rather pointless discussion of who saw Cherub last. Jules says she did her hair. Cherub stuck around for a while, watching Jules do Shrew's makeup.

"May I ask what she's done?" Little Hog inquires. "As the chairperson of our detachment council, I feel it's my responsibility—"

"You *may* shut your mouth," says Margo. It's clear to her that no one here knows Cherub's whereabouts.

She and the nurses leave shortly thereafter. But the girls, agitated, can't rest. Was Cherub at the disco? Some say she was, at least in the beginning. And later? No one can say. Perhaps she did go back to the dorms. "Girls, check your belongings," says Snake.

They go through their assorted canvas sacks, the wardrobe shelves stacked with soap dishes and toothpaste. They don't have much, but most keep at least a few rubles stashed here or there, enough for a movie ticket or a packet of potato chips.

In the past Cherub stole earrings, hairclips, a watch, twenty rubles in cash, innumerable snacks, a pair of jeans. And that's just what they'd managed to recover. Countless other treasures have never been found, their disappearance never officially pinned on Cherub—though the suspicion remains.

"What if she did it?" Kat whispers to Jules.

"What? Kill herself? Don't be stupid."

Just as they start winding down, someone quietly raps on the door. This time it is two girls from 7B. "Can we come in?" they say. "We have the info!"

And the story unfolds: Sometime after the disco, the gym teacher locks up the gym. Then he stumbles up into the attic, because that's where he keeps his liquor. Right now he really needs it—although he's had some already, a big swig in the afternoon. So anyway, up to the attic he trundles, and at first it's too dark to make out any shapes, except he's pretty sure someone's there. And when his eyes adjust, he sees them, the pair for all time: Mironov and Litvinova. Stark naked and drunk out of their minds. Doing you-know-what.

Really doing it?

Don't interrupt. They're so drunk, they don't hear him at first. He has to cough or something to alert them. Next thing you know, Cherub flees.

And Mironov?

Too sloshed to move, apparently. Got taken to the infirmary.

Or else the sobering-up station. I heard his mother is a total lush. An apple doesn't fall far from, you know, the cherry tree.

I'm sorry, but these two are finished. Expelled in the morning. *Finito!*

Gross! Mironov and Litvinova.

You think they actually did it? All the way?

Girls, can you picture Mironov undressed?

Sick!

No really, do you think he's . . . what do you call it . . . well-endowed?

Sick, sick!

And Cherub, damn! She looks like such a demure little thing.

Devils live in still waters.

On and on it goes, this senseless conversation, long after the girls from 7B depart. Jules falls asleep. Kat gets up twice to use the bathroom. She keeps thinking about Mironov, about that classroom on the second floor. Was Vika Litvinova with him? Was she the shadowy presence that broke the odd moment between them? And the attic. The cold, dingy attic, the cold cement floor—she can only imagine, she's never actually been there. The groping in the dark and drunken giggling. What did it feel like: the rub of the fabric, the touch of a probing index finger, the warmth of the skin underneath. It should feel disgusting, but it can't be. It isn't.

THE FOLLOWING DAY, no one openly mentions the incident. You catch a group of students snickering and you figure it's probably about *that*. The teachers act as though nothing happened. Not one of them asks about Cherub or Mironov. It's the last day of the quarter, so why dwell on such shameful things?

Cherub was found shortly after midnight. Earlier this morning she was seen exiting the premises, her face swollen with tears, her suitcase in tow. As for Mironov, no one has seen him yet.

Anechka makes it to work, despite her illness. Both she and Misha seem a little tense. It's not their job to monitor the students at the discos. That's what the matrons are for. Still, the discos are their responsibility.

"Have you heard?" Kat asks, which is a silly question.

"I wish they'd expelled the whole class." Anechka scowls. "That girl's just revolting, and the boy—"

"Yes," Misha interrupts, "the boy. You've seen his back, Anya? Where's he going to go with that back? A local school? Some no-name sanatorium for invalids? There's no father in the picture, and the mother's the sort you wouldn't wish on a kid."

"I see you're well informed about him."

"Yes," Misha says. "I checked. He won't last outside. He needs his treatments. Most likely surgery as well. And at the very least, he needs a decent education."

"You suggest we cram it down his throat?"

"I suggest we give the boy a chance. Do you realize, Anya, he's been Kat's classmate since first grade, and we barely know him. We barely know his name."

Kat interjects, "Mironov."

"*Seryozha*," her father corrects. "Sergey Mironov."

"I still don't understand what you're advocating. You've seen his grades?"

"You're missing my point, Anya. *We've* failed him. The *system's* failed him. It's what we used to talk about, you and I, how our system doesn't work for everyone, how we don't do enough to reach these broken boys and girls. And honestly, I don't know anyone as broken as this one."

And that's when Kat speaks, to everyone's surprise. She's been standing there quietly, listening to Misha, to his talk of justice and compassion and Mironov's sad fate, and suddenly she's had an inspiration. Here is her chance to distinguish herself, to prove that she shares her parents' ideals and that, like them, she can be selfless, brave.

"What if I tutor him?" she says, and for a moment no one speaks.

Anechka touches Kat's forehead. "Have you lost your mind, baby?"

Then Misha says, "No, she hasn't." He's nodding slowly, as if he's probing Kat's idea. "It's not a bad strategy. What if we talk to the principal? He's a reasonable person, our principal, as long as we can make a solid case. A trial period, perhaps? Some way to measure his accomplishments? Anya, don't you think it makes sense?"

But Anechka has turned her back to them. She's looking out the window, her fingertips flat on the cold pane of glass. What can possibly be so interesting there? The edge of a glassed-in walkway, the well-trodden path? The same unchanging scenery. She wipes her eyes.

"Anya?" Misha says.

She swivels on her heels, unsteadily, and now Kat can see that she's really sick. "You're a good person, baby." She leans in and kisses Kat, a clumsy, sloppy kiss. Rising, she staggers a little, and Misha has to catch her by the elbow.

"I'm losing it, aren't I? I didn't use to be like this. You know me, I used to care."

Misha says, "You still do. You've just been feeling ill."

"I've become this Fury, this Megaera."

He smiles. "You have not." And then he holds her for a long, long time, until she gets her bearings.

And that's the most amazing part—these strange and

errant moments when, despite everything, Kat's parents come together and you can see how, amidst domestic drudgery and gripes, they're still these beautiful young rebels, still true to their dreams and their principles, and still tremendously in love. Together they leave the classroom. Together they walk downstairs, where no door or sallow-faced secretary can keep them away from their goal. They are invincible—as long as they remain together.

10

ON THE DAY KAT RETURNS AFTER THE BREAK, the mood at school is hushed and cautious. Cherub is no longer there. In the past, back when she was a nuisance, her absence would have barely registered. Now it seems momentous, and Kat feels as though everyone is giving her dark looks.

"It's like they're blaming me," she says to Jules.

Jules says, "Don't be insane. No one knows you've sold your soul to the devil. Where is he, by the way?"

"Who, Mironov?"

"No, Grandpa Mazai and his rabbits."

Oh yes, it appears that Mironov is missing as well. At the start of the break, Kat still felt great about her decision. She'd be a hero, a celebrity. The teachers would admire her pluck. She'd do such a bang-up job with Mironov that they'd ask her to help with their other challenging pupils. By Wednesday, though, she began to lose her nerve. Some of it had to do with Anechka, who all week was skeptical and irritable. She'd be doing the ironing, for instance, and without much preamble she'd start in on Kat again. "I just don't know what you were thinking," she'd say. "It's a noble idea in principle, but someone else should do it. Your own grades are not that great, and I'd rather you focused on yourself." On another occasion they were returning from the local grocery and Anechka said, "Don't you have enough conflicts at school?"

By the end of the week, Kat was in agony. She didn't know a thing about tutoring, and yet she was stuck with Mironov now, responsible for his atrocious grades. She'd have to approach him, she'd have to *interact* with him.

"Maybe the deal fell through?" Jules speculates.

"Blessed is he who keeps the faith," Kat quotes from *Woe from Wit*. And she is right: Mironov turns up before second period, in a new zip-up cardigan and his usual ratty sweatpants.

"I think we'd better start tomorrow?"

Jules pats her on the shoulder. "You're on your own, pal."

Second period is geometry. At the end, just before letting them go, their math teacher, Beatrisa P., calls Kat and her nemesis over. Calls openly, in front of the rest of the class: "Knopman! Mironov!" She is a bitter little person, Beatrisa, thin-voiced, imperious, merciless in her remarks. She had a stroke three years ago, and the left side of her face twitches whenever she's displeased.

"Knopman," she says once Kat and Mironov approach

her, "are you aware that your friend here failed last quarter?" She speaks as if Mironov has always been Kat's burden. "The next exam is in two weeks. If he flunks, you're
getting a fail also."

"But—" Kat begins.

"It's non-negotiable."

This *wasn't* the deal, Kat wants to scream. But you don't
scream at a teacher, and furthermore, you never scream at
a disabled person. Beatrisa will grimace as if Kat were a
disgusting small thing and say it's not her job to deal with
Kat's emotions. "You want to shriek, shriek at your parents;
but spare me your hysterics," she will say.

She is not part of the old guard, not one of Kat's parents'
sworn enemies, though neither is she their supporter or personal friend. She is simply one of those who wanted Mironov
expelled, and now that Kat's parents have prevailed, she's
seething with frustration.

"Go study," she tells them.

"Where?" Mironov says. His voice snaps from nervousness, and Kat sees how desperate he is. "Where do we go?"

"Doesn't matter to me," says Beatrisa. "Not my problem."

The scene repeats itself in other classes. No one's as
openly malevolent as Beatrisa, no one else threatens to
fail Kat. Still, the teachers make it clear: they want rapid
improvement, they don't intend to mollycoddle them.

By the end of the day, Kat is falling apart. What Mironov
needs is an army of tutors. Misha has gone home early, and
since she doesn't have a choice, she stumbles, near tears, into

Anechka's classroom. "Why do they hate me?" she demands. "There's no way to do this tutoring. No time, no place."

Anechka watches her coldly. "You can always back out," she says. "I told your father this was more than you could handle—"

"I'm handling it," Kat says. "I'd just like a little bit of help."

"Help," Anechka scoffs. "You should have thought of that before." Then she sighs and tells Kat not to go anywhere. She is gone for at least twenty minutes, but when she returns she's in a better mood, like maybe she's now amused by Kat's predicament. She dangles the drama room key before her nose. "There," she says. "One of your problems solved. The rest, of course, is up to you."

MANY YEARS AGO, when Kat was little, she used to love cloaking herself in Anechka's old shawls. But it is one thing to play school, to make up fake class registers and lecture rows of invisible students, and it's another thing entirely to tutor an actual boy. Minutes into her first session with Mironov, it's obvious to Kat that she is no good at teaching. She's got neither passion nor patience. She lacks grace in the face of his obstinacy; she expects gratitude.

When she told him, discreetly, to meet her outside the drama room, he just shrugged and grunted something unintelligible. Because they were in public, she was inclined to excuse his response. But now, in the drama room, it's not that different. He doesn't acknowledge her instructions, doesn't say thank you. He doesn't even look at her.

They are doing geometry drills from the hand-bound book of supplemental problems. Kat shows him how to do it, then lets him try one by himself. He scribbles something. She paces. The drama room is cozy: there's a small electric kettle, and Kat finds a half-empty packet of cookies left from before the break.

She can feel herself flushing. It's disturbing to be in his presence, to feel the familiar mix of old guilt and disgust whenever she thinks of their feud, the first-grade incident that led to her concussion.

"Are you done?" she says, when she sees that Mironov has put down his pencil. But when she checks the page, there's nothing there, nothing but a picture of a smirking cat with a cigar. It's outrageous: he is mocking her, while *she* is doing *him* a favor.

"What's this?" she says, in the tone Anechka reserves for the most worthless of her students, usually the ones from 7A.

"Don't know," he says, and she can tell from his voice that, like her, he doesn't find this ordeal amusing. "I fucking hate these stupid riddles."

"Watch your language," she says. "They're *problems*."

She sits down next to him—even though he's smelly and unpleasant—and they begin again. Soon she discovers that it's true what Misha said about the system having failed Mironov. There are awful gaps in his schooling. He's got no grasp of geometry. Plus, for whatever reason, he still won't really talk to her. She asks him a question, and he answers with something like a groan. Would it kill him to speak like a regular person? Or show some respect for her?

The system has failed him, so now it's her job to suck it up and help him. She gets out her calico notebook, the one she's been keeping in preparation for next year's exams, each question numbered, each page cut with scissors to form a side tab. It's actually better than their textbook.

They start with the axioms, the parallel postulate. By six o'clock they have reviewed ten pages and done a handful of corresponding problems from the book. Kat says they're getting somewhere.

"Right," says Mironov. "I'm practically an academic. Why bother if they're gonna boot me out anyway?"

It's the most he's said to her all day, which Kat thinks must be a good sign.

AND THIS is what her life has become: at four fifteen she sneaks into the drama room for tutoring; afterward it's homework (always done in a hurry), supper, the tedious class hour, the survey of the news. She spends hours designing the tutoring sessions, laying out detailed lesson plans, thinking of theorems and proofs. Even at play rehearsals, she catches herself puzzling over obtuse and acute angles.

She's not suited for this. Anechka was right about that. There are others at school for whom learning comes easier. They gulp down new knowledge instantly, commit it all to memory, wrap up their work in half the allotted time, and their grades, as if shaped by a lathe, are identical, effortless fives.

Gone are the days when anyone thought Kat a wunderkind. She's become plodding: for hours she pores over her textbooks, and always runs out of time. On tests she makes careless mistakes, because she's so often anxious. She has the diligence, but diligence alone isn't enough. The last thing she needed was a pupil of her own.

And not just someone, but Mironov—Mironov, who has always despised her, who grunts and scoffs at her instructions and offers no response. Their situation is unworkable. Their only joint concern is to keep him from flunking. They study in secret, during the evening walks, because it's too embarrassing for both of them.

How secret these sessions are, to start with, is up for debate. One day Sveta Vlasenko and Ritka Mavrina drop by the drama room and don't seem too surprised to find them. Sveta drifts over to the piano, while Ritka unrolls a sheet of Watman paper and sets about sketching the poster for their play.

Ritka is an artist, a real honest-to-God artist. Teachers always ask her to do posters or decorate their wall displays. Why pay a professional when a student can do it for free? Ritka says it helps her practice. She's got her eye on the Stroganoff Art Institute, and she's constantly practicing. Everyone says she's destined to get in.

It seems they're all destined for something: Vlad for medical school, Nikita for the Institute of History and Archives. Sveta Vlasenko, who is a middling student, is mulling over a degree in education, and when the time comes, Jules, with her linguistic prowess, will join the Maurice Thorez Language Institute.

As for Kat, she continues to refine her acting. She has been working on imagination exercises, picturing a tree in Kratovo (a rowan tree or possibly a birch), the park behind the school, a fence with an intricate pattern. She has begun a notebook of observations—because an actor must notice the smallest details, the wing of a butterfly or a spiderweb or the little rolls of fat on the tops of Creampuff's feet. She tries to keep the notebook private, which means that by the time she gets around to it, her memories have often grown stale. Sometimes she's so tired that a whole day goes by and she forgets to "notice" anything, and then she worries whether she's cut out to be an actress.

She pictures herself at eighteen, already a sensation, a star of the Sovremennik Theater or possibly the Lenkom, putting on makeup in her dressing room before a rosewood vanity, having a late supper with a lover at a small bistro down the street. She draws her fantasies from something she's seen on TV, a film based on a book by Maugham. The truth is, she's never met a single actress. She doesn't know how they get discovered, what they do, where they live—or even what a bistro really is. But she's sure their lives are dramatic and glamorous, and it's sweet to imagine the satisfaction of fame: the admiring whisper of Sveta and Ritka; the gaggle, starstruck and full of hard regret. The poor, miserable gaggle, condemned to dumb menial labor, a life of drunkenness and ugly spats. No one will ever mistake Kat for one of them. As for Mironov, he'll take to drink and go to seed by then. She'll never have to chance upon the likes of him.

"WHY DO they call you Kat?" Mironov asks on Saturday.

They have gone through two weeks of clandestine study dates, devoting them mostly to geometry and algebra. The geometry test is on Monday, and while Mironov is still iffy on congruent triangles, Kat thinks he will probably pass.

Today they're starting to tackle Russian grammar. Since everyone's gone for the weekend anyway, they decide to use Anechka's classroom. Kat goes up to the blackboard and copies sentences for them to diagram. "Not far from us, in a coastal ravine, a shallow river skittered rapidly over the rocky bed."

It is the first time he has asked her anything, and she is feeling a tiny bit distrustful. "It's just a name," she says, "a name like any other." "Apart from rivers, Meschersky region is rich in canals."

"No, really," he insists. She checks his face, but can't spot any signs of ridicule or malice. They have worked hard these past two weeks. She gets why he used to hate her. It's been seven years since she was forced to wear a brace and she is now used to being stared at. She's learned how to repel frank, prying glances, how to answer with her own hateful look, how to set her jaw when faced with insults. Still, it took her years, while he, in first grade, was already a pro, his whole short life spent as a circus freak. And she—she called him a hunchback. She hopes he has forgiven her, or possibly forgotten the details. "Friendship is not a favor, it doesn't require gratitude."

So she tells him. She tells him about the old house in Kratovo, about her grandfather with his translations and his cane; his declining health; his desk set up on the veranda, where they have English lessons all summer; the trays of tea and bread and cherry jam.

"Fancy," he says. "See, here I thought you and Jules were just stuck up or something. Making up screwy names."

Screwy? she thinks. She's an idiot for opening her mouth.

"So what's my name? In English?"

"There isn't one," she says.

He seems disappointed, but then he tells her it's okay. "I guess I'm not cut out to be, you know, English. Like Sherlock Holmes and Doctor Watson in *The Hound of the Baskervilles*. You seen it on TV?"

"I've seen it," she says, unsure what to do with his sudden effusiveness. Is she now supposed to be his friend? Is she supposed to forget how vile he's been to her? His clothes smell rank, and his face is still the same—bleached out, insolent, with freckles and thin scabby lips. She wishes she hadn't told him anything. She wishes he'd go back to his bottled-up, barely mumbling self. That, at least, she knows how to deal with.

He is still talking about the movie: the moors, the butterflies, the hound with its phosphorus mark.

"Make it brief, Sklifosovsky," she tells him. "I'd like to get home eventually. You see those sentences up on the blackboard? Go underline the subject and the predicate."

It comes out harsher than she meant it, and he's looking at her as if stung. After that, he shuts up. He diagrams each sentence, he watches her correct his errors—all of it in total silence, not a sigh from him, not a grunt. He won't speak to her even when she asks him to explain a particular grammar rule, and for a long time after that it continues to ring in her ears, his silence.

THIS WEEKEND, Kat is struggling. She feels rotten about the Mironov fiasco and tells Misha they're not getting along. He says, "Teaching is tough. I'm proud of you, Button." But he doesn't seem proud, just distracted, absorbed in the production of the play. He's thinking of entering it in a regional contest. Anechka's no help either. She still doesn't believe Kat's efforts are worthwhile or that she has it in her to succeed. "Make sure your own grades don't slip," she warns her.

Kat's been thinking about a name for Mironov all Sunday, trying to find him an equivalent in English. Seryozha. Sergey. She's even checked the dictionary. It seems imperative that she locate it, as if it's a question that's certain to come up on an exam.

It comes to her later that evening as she is flipping through their play. *Mon Dieu. Au revoir. Ma chère.* Their characters often speak French. Of course, she thinks, why should it be in English?

"Serge," she says, when she and Mironov meet again. She's genuinely happy about this name. It's got a good and noble ring to it. "Give the boy a chance," said Misha, and that's what she is doing. She's giving him a chance, and a new name.

"What's that?" he says, suspiciously.

"You asked for it, your name. Except it's French instead of English—"

He spits right there on the floor and cusses at her.

It's been an agonizing day for both of them. They had their geometry test in the morning (more difficult than Kat expected), and after lunch he got called out in biology and failed. All day they haven't spoken—they never speak in public anyway—and Kat can only hope that he's managed the geometry test.

But maybe he hasn't? He's looking pissed, his lower lip is busted, and now, up close, she sees a cut below his left eye.

He calls her a psycho and tells her he's done with her.

"You asked for it," she says again, meaning not just the name but the cut and the bruises, the busted lip, the poor grades. He was supposed to study this weekend, not get in a brawl with some street rabble. "You're totally worthless," she says.

He's looking at her the way he did before he hit her on the head, his hatred vast and irrepressible. Without thinking, she steps back.

"Scared?" he says. "You're scared of the hunchback?" And now she knows he's not forgotten anything.

He grabs for his bag and she flinches, because in that second she really believes he might hit her again.

Of course, it's a mistake.

"You know," he says, "I could kill you."

"I know," she says.

He slams the door so hard that a piece of stage set collapses in the corner of the drama room.

11

THE PLAY IS SLATED TO OPEN BEFORE THE WINTER holidays, and once December comes everything quickens. At first they rehearse twice a week, on Wednesdays after supper and Saturday afternoons, but after Misha enters them in the district contest, they add Tuesday and Thursday nights as well. The most surprising thing is Anechka. After months of gloom and moodiness, so bad that her students were starting to take note, she is suddenly crackling with energy. She's become indispensable at rehearsals, choosing the music, choreographing the waltz, tirelessly coaching Sveta, who's still having trouble with her part. Even Kat gets a tip or two about her performance: "Avoid unnecessary gestures, and stop wringing your hands. It makes you look like an amateur."

Kat has no more time to do her acting exercises, what with the rehearsals and the tutoring, which on Saturdays has to be pushed back. It took some work to reinstate the tutoring. Misha spoke to Mironov in his office, a sensible man-to-man talk, about the realities of life and the value of good schooling. At least that's how Kat imagines it. For all she knows, they might have talked about dialectics and the mystery of being. Their first conversation was fruitless. A day or so later they spoke again. By Saturday that week, they'd come to an agreement: Mironov would resume his tutoring, and as for literature and grammar, Misha would tutor him himself.

Mironov returned to the drama room. He and Kat exchanged no apologies. They simply set to work, immersing themselves in the subject at hand and steering clear of any superfluous discussion.

By now everyone knows about the tutoring, so they don't need to hide it anymore. Margo, who had to know from the start, said nothing on the subject. The gaggle, as could be expected, embraced the news with zeal and great excitement, spinning atrocious tales about Kysya and Mironov and what they must be doing in the drama room, behind the closed door. "Kysya the slut," they say whenever she enters the dorm, and Nina Petrenko pantomimes something ugly and lewd. Often they do these things in public, in the canteen or in the hallway at recess, and Kat finds that hardest to endure—anyone could happen by and get the wrong idea about her.

Lately, with Misha's encouragement, Mironov has started sneaking into the assembly hall. Holed up in the back and nearly invisible, he watches rehearsals and then delivers his reports. He's developed opinions, mostly shortsighted, and he's especially invested in the character of Pushkin's wife.

"Why is everyone so up in arms about her?" he asks, as if he's somehow missed the part where Natalie caused Pushkin's duel.

"She was selfish," says Kat. "It's obvious she never loved him. She married him because she had no dowry. Then she went around with d'Anthès, even though everyone warned her about him. She even flirted with the tsar himself."

"So you're saying she's a whore?"

Kat wrinkles her nose at the jarring word. "It wasn't really about her. She was convenient, you understand? The tsar, society, they went after Pushkin, and she . . . she kind of played into their hands."

"It wasn't her fault then!" Mironov says, triumphant.

It's because of Sveta Vlasenko, Kat thinks, because she's the one playing Natalie. At the mere sight of Sveta, all boys immediately lose their brains.

"You're being willfully obtuse," she says.

"And you're full of shit," Mironov counters.

She backs away from this sensitive subject, before the thin ice of their mutual politeness springs new, dangerous cracks.

But a week later, he returns to it again. He says he's visited the library. "There are letters," he says. "A whole book of them. Thick like three encyclopedias stacked up. There's this letter in there that says that d'Anthès sort of trapped her. And the tsar—I checked about that. It says the whole story is a lie because she never went to no balls that year. She was, you know, big with child."

"Pregnant?" Kat says. "You've told my dad about this discovery?"

"You tell him," he says.

"Why should I? I don't even think it's correct."

"It is." Mironov sighs. "I checked. I don't want to upset him, though, like his whole play is now wrong or something."

They talk for a while about the play: how it's basically a good play, even if it's not completely accurate; how the final scenes are poignant, and even Natalie is kind of sympathetic at the end.

Mironov laments that they have no Pushkin. "You think I could play him?"

Kat bursts out laughing. She simply can't contain herself. "No, no, wait," she says, seeing his lips pale and tighten. "Don't make a beastly face. I don't mean you'd be bad. It's just that you don't *look* like him. You know what he was like, dark-eyed and swarthy."

"Who do I look like then?" Mironov says.

She thinks for a moment. "Yesenin!" Another poet, from this century. Blue-eyed, light-haired, troubled. " 'I'm a rakish Moscow idler.' Remember?"

He doesn't.

She recites some other lines from memory. "You even have his first name," she points out. "Scrgey."

"How did *he* die?" Mironov asks.

She tells him about Yesenin's tumultuous life: his early successes and setbacks, several marriages (including one to Isadora Duncan, who also died in a horrible way), his drinking, and finally his suicide in 1925. He hung himself. In his room at the Angleterre Hotel—so stupidly, so hopelessly young.

"How young?"

"Barely thirty."

Mironov nods. "Fits like a glove. I'll be kicking the bucket round that time. A gypsy told me at Kazansky terminal last summer. They know their business, the gypsies. Said I'll die from drink in a back alley. Or else get stabbed. Which do you think is a better way to go, Knopman?"

"Don't be morbid," she scolds him.

He chuckles. "Yeah, I know. It's not as classy as the Angleterre Hotel."

They go their separate ways, but Kat keeps wondering about what he said, about death and chance and how in their play the character of Natalie has just that sort of moment of foreboding. Except when it comes, it's too late and the machinery of fate cannot be stopped, and all you can do afterward is question what set it in motion, which one of your past errors or bad choices is to blame.

"Do you believe in fate?" Kat asks.

She and Anechka are making waffles, using a clunky contraption to bake thin, round cakes which they roll with a fork into tube-shaped crispy structures. It doesn't happen very often that Anechka elects to do this. There must be something in the air: the first nips of true wintry weather, the crunch of well-packed snow underfoot, the smell of pine needles and tangerine peel, the crinkling of chocolate wrappers. Soon it will be the holidays.

Anechka seems milder, gentler. They talk about fatalism

and fortune-telling, which she admits might be a sham—
even if it does feature in so much Russian literature. But
Kat, she says, Kat has nothing to worry about. She's a mirror image of Misha, and it's common wisdom that girls who
resemble their fathers turn out to be the happiest of all.

Anechka's eyes are burning. This weekend she is churning with excitement, the sort of excitement that a short trip
to the local haberdashery just isn't enough to assuage. "Let's
go to Arbat," she keeps saying. Arbat is a pedestrian street,
strewn with buskers, break dancers, and artists. Peddlers
sell amber necklaces and nesting dolls set up on trays. But
it's the artists Anechka is after. They sit on folding chairs,
making cheap soft-pastel portraits for tourists. Fluid, fantas-
tical pictures of starry-eyed women and men. Anechka's got
it in her head that she needs a portrait.

In December, though? Will the artists be there in the cold?

A movie then, Anechka says. Something lively and foreign, a musical comedy, an Indian love story. No, wait! Let's
go to that new cosmetics store and buy some cherry lip gloss
from Poland.

In the end they stay home, eat their waffles and two cups
of egg-flip, curl up together on the green living room sofa.
There's a game show on TV, a bunch of city girls trying to
milk a cow.

"I have a secret," Anechka whispers. "Shall I tell you? Or
can you work it out yourself?" She counts the months on her
fingers: January, February, March . . .

Kat's heart flips unpleasantly and her skin under the brace
begins to itch.

". . . July, August, September. A little present for your birthday, Kat."

"You're kidding," she says.

"What would you like, a little brother or a little sister?"

"As long as it's healthy," Kat says—the only acceptable answer.

Anechka presses her lips together as if trying to keep back a smile. She hasn't had the test yet, but she is sure of its outcome.

"You were sure before."

"This time it's different, baby." Her body's given her all sorts of signals, and she's already thrown up a bunch of times. "Trust me," she says. "I know what it feels like."

"All right," Kat says. "But why not see a doctor? Just to be certain it's developing correctly."

"And jinx it? No thanks!"

Their talk leaves a bad taste in Kat's mouth, as if she has somehow been duped. She dropped her guard, allowed Anechka to lull her with her playfulness. She thought things were finally changing between them, that they were becoming equals, close pals, and Anechka was seeing in her something, maturity perhaps, as opposed to the usual source of aggravation. But she was mistaken once again. There's only one reason for Anechka's excitement and only upshot of her news: Kat is being replaced. Replaced for good.

For the next few days, she watches Anechka and Misha. They are caught in a constant leapfrog of activity: classes, rehearsals, assignments to grade. The day of the play is approaching. The playbill has already been posted by the

canteen entrance—a beautiful playbill, done in a florid, old-
time scrawl—and later Anechka and Misha go off to fetch
costumes from a theater studio in the southwest corner of
Moscow. Kat offers to come with them, but they go alone.
The snow thawed a bit the other day, but then it got colder
again, and now Kat watches as they both slip on icy patches.
They're laughing and Misha is especially protective, his arm
wrapped tight around her mother's waist. He knows, Kat
thinks. He knows and he's happy.

THE WEEK of the opening, Sveta Vlasenko comes down
with pneumonia. On Sunday night she calls Misha and
Anechka at home and pleads with them to wait for her, vows
she'll be at the opening anyway, despite her raging fever and
the risk of complications. Kat's parents put a quick stop to
this foolishness. There can't be any talk of that, they say.
Sveta must remain in bed; pneumonia is not a thing to toy
with. They sound decisive and confident, but afterward
they're at a loss.

"What do we do?" says Misha when Anechka gets off
the phone.

The situation leaves them with few choices. They can wait
until after the holidays and miss the district contest, or they
can try to replace Sveta. But how do you replace your leading
actress with only a week of rehearsal left? Never mind that
she wasn't the right actress and that most of her scenes rang
hopelessly false. In the past, she was good at playing princesses. She could do goodness, wide-eyed innocence, even

a bit of comedy sometimes. But the part of Pushkin's wife has been eluding her. First she played it too sweetly, then too peevishly, making Natalie into a shrew. She couldn't seem to capture her complexity, couldn't grasp that she was bad *and* good, that a person could be like that, at once big-hearted and self-centered.

Kat always knew *she* could be Natalie. For weeks now she's had the whole play memorized. Not on purpose, but unconsciously, just as in previous years. It happened seamlessly, without her really noticing. She can play any part, stand in for anyone. She'd play Natalie right, the way she and Mironov discussed it, not as flighty and selfish but misunderstood, trapped. She'd turn the whole play upside down, if only Misha would allow it.

She corners him that Sunday night, once Anechka has gone to bed, and, as might be expected, he's startled.

"It's a big part," he says. "The biggest one. Without it, there is no play."

"Test me," she says, and right there on the spot she recites for him a monologue that has always confounded Sveta.

"I don't doubt your memory, Button. But darling, you're only fourteen. This role requires life experience."

"Does one have to be a murderer to play Lady Macbeth?"

"We can't be rash, Button. Most likely we'll have to reschedule for after the holidays. It's not fair to Sveta to go on without her. She's put a lot of work into this play. We have a rehearsal tomorrow, so why don't we shelve it until then?"

"Should I practice some scenes?" Kat asks, and Misha tells her, "Might as well."

The next evening, Kat does what she never thought she would. After nap, she takes her brace into a bathroom stall and loosens two screws at the side. It's the most common break and also the easiest to fake, and it will only take a minute to fix when she goes to the repair shop next morning. For now, though, the brace is broken, and a break is a break.

At rehearsal, she sits in the back and hopes no one will notice her, not until she is on stage performing, her voice, unhindered now, resounding through the assembly hall. She is nervous. In her head she's going through Sveta's lines. Not that anyone's paying attention to her. You can tell that the drama kids have heard of Sveta's illness, and, judging by their funereal expressions, they don't think their play has a chance. Little do they know that Kat's about to astound them. Once she's given the spotlight, they'll never look at her the same again. She'll be something miraculous. They'll all want to speak to her, to have her as their confidante and friend, and she, in turn, will be straightforward, unafraid. She won't hesitate to get close to Nikita. He's sitting at the end of the first row now, in a thick knitted sweater that adds to his bearish bulk. She could sneak up behind him, put her hands over his eyes—Guess who?—and he would know; he'd be in love with her.

Then Misha and Anechka enter—enter briskly, energetically, as if nothing is amiss. It makes no sense, but they appear almost happy. They sit side by side on the edge of the stage, their feet dangling. "Why the long faces?" Misha says. "Cheer up, ladies and gentlemen." Yes, he admits, it's sad that Sveta's fallen ill, but in their line of work it happens.

And then he reveals the new plan: one show at school, one at the district contest, and then two more, with Sveta, when they come back after the break.

This means, Kat thinks, he must have listened; he's actually giving her a chance. She must have impressed him with her recitation last evening.

"But who will play Natalie?" asks Ritka.

"Ah," Misha says, "that's our big surprise," and now he is positively beaming. He bumps Anechka's shoulder with his shoulder, and she smiles a bit shyly and waves to the group. Misha fakes a small, officious cough. "Ladies and gentlemen, please welcome our veteran actress, our incomparable Anna Alexandrovna."

IT'S STILL a shock, not just to Kat, but to everyone there. There have been stories, of course, stories of Anechka's acting and her talent, but no one has seen her perform. So now they watch her with some hesitation. Will she stumble, or take a wrong turn? And how will the rest of them hide their embarrassment?

Kat in particular feels that this casting choice is wrong. Not because she herself has been ignored, but because Anechka is pregnant. She should be sitting quietly and resting, nurturing the creature inside. But perhaps she's been chosen precisely *because* she is pregnant, because she and Misha both know that it will work this time, and the play is their way of celebrating. They are starting over together. They're passionate, hopeful, young.

Then Anechka begins a scene, and it turns out that she's good, really excellent. Her mastery on stage is unmistakable. There are no extraneous gestures, none of the simpering or artificiality that Misha often cautions them against. She is confident, natural. Within minutes of watching her you forget she's your mother or your teacher, you stop noticing her age.

She is tender on stage, stirring in her fury and her helplessness, and that makes you root for her—root for Natalie—even though she's not as virtuous as other characters. You see how she's tied down by her marriage, how she grasps for something greater and casts about for somebody to trust. You can understand, finally, why Pushkin was so obsessed with her.

ON THE day of the dress rehearsal, the borrowed theater costumes are carried from the drama room to the assembly hall. The boys are ordered to get out; the doors at both ends are barred with brooms. The long drapes make perfect changing rooms. Behind the drapes, the girls transform themselves—shed their braces, don their nineteenth-century finery. They emerge looking hesitant. There are no mirrors in the assembly hall, so they have to rely on one another. "Does it fit in the shoulders? Does it show too much of my back?" Ritka Mavrina pins their hems, takes care of their makeup.

Kat leaves her brace behind the drape as well. Her dress is white with silvery embroidery. There are rows of small metal hooks on the sides and in the back, and these take a long time to fasten.

The boys come in, their costumes simple in comparison: frock coats, tailcoats, overcoats. Under their eyes, the girls become a tender, chirping flock. They twirl, or spin each other in a waltz, or simply walk without purpose to and fro, as if attempting to relearn their bodies. They love these beautiful new bodies, encased in bombazine and marquisette. They relish the sway of their skirts and the percussion of their shoes on the assembly hall parquet.

The set is arranged on the stage: a papier mâché pillar, a fainting couch, and in the background a cutout silhouette of St. Petersburg, steeped in violet twilight. Everything is in place. Everyone's gathered. Only Misha and Anechka have yet to arrive.

Kat catches sight of Nikita, who's looking especially anxious and scanning the assembly hall—not for Kat in her beautiful gown, but for the comforting figure of Misha. No wonder, she thinks. Even in this dress she's still herself, a minor character.

"I'm sorry it didn't work out," Misha had said to Kat on Monday, after rehearsal ended and Anechka left the stage.

Kat had wanted to tell him that he could have at least let her try, but, after seeing Anechka, she knew that she could never be as great.

"I spoke to your mother and we both think you're fabulous, but, Button, you wouldn't be right for this part. There will be other parts, of course. You're so young. And besides, we're all counting on you to be our Society Lady. I mean, someone would have to replace you if you took Sveta's part, and frankly, no one but you could do it right."

Kat nodded to show that she got it, and she really did, though not in the way he would have liked. She saw through his flattery, saw it as kindness, saw also what Misha left unsaid. She was not like her mother. She could play pleasant, episodic characters: modest maidens, obedient daughters, simple but loyal servant girls. But she would never be the magical, erratic star who has the power to mesmerize an audience.

Thinking of it now, Kat slips into the stairwell. Outside sits Mironov, a dismal figure on the stone steps. At first she assumes he's come to pester her about math, about the wretched polynomials. Doesn't he know it's dress rehearsal? Can't he for once give her a break?

"I just wanted to see it," he says, rising.

It looks like he didn't expect her to come out, at least not in a lavish dress like that.

"Why are you sitting here?" she asks him. "Why don't you go inside?"

"I didn't think I was supposed to. You know, your mother—"

"She'll be on stage. She probably won't see you."

He is still hesitating, so she gives him a push.

"Go sit with my father and keep an eye on how he reacts."

"You want me to *spy* on him?"

"Not spy. Just pay attention."

"You're worried he won't like your acting?"

"I'm not worried," she snaps. "I don't care. You can go

inside or you can stay here and freeze. It doesn't matter to me either way."

She turns and walks away from him abruptly, but she can hear him scrambling after her. "Don't get all psycho on me. Jeez! You goddamn crazy actors."

Except she's not. She'll never be an actress, no matter what Misha or anyone else says. If she can't be the best, she'd rather not be anything. She won't toil in obscurity as a noble but bleak understudy, an overgrown Snow Maiden performing at children's matinees. How foolish she was to believe she could assume the role of Natalie. She actually thought her whole life was about to change. Now the mere idea of it makes her cringe. Misha was wise not to give her this chance; he knew she'd never crack it, never come close to Anechka's perfection, never match her talent or her grace.

She enters the assembly hall and stops. Anechka is standing in the middle of the stage, in waves of white organza. Her hair is done up in a fancy chignon and she's wearing a circlet around her forehead, just as Natalie did in all her best-known portraits. The stage lights are on, and she's up there all alone. Even now Kat knows that this is how she will remember her, unbearably beautiful, shielding her eyes against the sudden brightness. She doesn't really belong in this assembly hall, on these crude wooden boards, in this play that suddenly seems trite and unimportant. She is a muse, she is the Madonna with child, beyond reproach, above them all.

THE LIGHTS in the assembly hall come on, and after what seems an infinite pause but must be only a few seconds, Misha gets up and applauds. "Bravo! Bravissimo!" He punches himself in the chest. "You really got me, you devils!"

When he gets up on stage, there's another upswing of excitement, a whirl of embraces and pats. "Good job. Well done. Decidedly not bad."

The actors close in around Misha and, like a good director, he doles out criticism and praise. There were only a few mistakes: Medusa missed her cue, Nikita skipped a line. But mostly they rose to the challenge, and even improvised a bit at times. They're pleased, extremely pleased, but also full of questions: Were they loud enough? Were their soliloquies distinct? Did Misha like that little moment at the end of the second act? Did he catch that one particular inflection?

It's good that Misha is, for once, the center of attention. He's so often overshadowed by Anechka. At least now he's getting his due. But it's unlike Anechka to shy away from the revelry. It takes Kat a few moments to locate her. She is still elegant and swanlike in her ethereal costume, poised by the St. Petersburg cutout and gripping its wrought-iron frame. She seems disoriented, though, oblivious to the celebration.

Kat calls to her, but she's too far away. There are dozens of people between them. She jostles her way to the back of the stage. "Mom?" she says, though at school she's not supposed to call her that, not even when they are alone together.

Anechka tries to straighten up. Her fingers grapple

with the frame, and in the light of the overhead lamps her eyes appear large and vacant. Then she is falling, falling, falling—pulling the set along with her, her head thudding horribly against the wooden floor, the set breaking in half over her body.

12

THEY LIVE AT THE HOSPITAL, SLEEP ON THE COT in the orderly's room or sit in the hallway. They eat whatever they can find. There's a grocery across the street; they buy bread, kefir, rolls of bologna, farmer's cheese in small packets. They eat with their hands, drink from the bottle—there are no utensils or cups. The nurses are merciful; they don't make a fuss. When there are rounds, they hide Kat and Misha in the linen closet.

Here's what the nurses told them when Anechka came out of surgery: she had been pregnant, but it hadn't been right. The pregnancy—atypical, they say, ectopic—was never meant to thrive. It ruptured, and now, post-surgery, there are complications. It's unlikely she'll have another child. Maybe a one percent chance.

"As long as she's alive," says Misha. Anechka has mostly been unconscious, and he's worried. Worried about septicemia, pneumonia, high blood pressure, clots. He tells Kat he doesn't trust hospitals.

Kat herself tries not to think about the pregnancy, or whether she's somehow willed this loss. Nor can she think of Anechka not making it. It's better not to think at all, just go from one task to the next: sit on a banquette, stand, check Anechka's temperature, ask Misha if he's hungry, walk up and down the hallway, sit again.

It takes them two days to track down the Roshdals. There's a pay phone in the downstairs lobby, next to the coatroom. It is usually busy or out of order. The phone line in Kratovo is new. Listening to the long infrequent beeps, Kat tries to guess whether the line is down again or some-one's turned down the ringer.

The Roshdals arrive on the third day. Valentina takes Kat in her arms and calls her and Misha "poor children."

"You couldn't send a telegram?" says Alexander Roshdal. Not waiting for their lousy excuses, he walks away. Some-how, without asking, he knows exactly which room is his daughter's.

He comes out looking even grimmer. "We're taking Kat home. A child has no business at a hospital."

"I'm not going," Kat says. "We've *agreed* not to leave her."

"Don't fight it, Button," Misha whispers, even though they did agree. "Go home for a bit, and then I'll come and get you."

KAT ALMOST falls asleep in the bathtub. She's tired and she stinks of sweat and hospital. She feels as though she hasn't been home in months. It's a relief to take the brace off, to scratch at the chafed bits of skin. "I can help wash your hair," Valentina offers, but Kat says she can manage. Afterward, in her slippers and bathrobe, she shambles to her room. She just needs to lie down for a moment.

She wakes up by suppertime and at first she can't tell whether it's night or morning. Valentina has cleaned the whole apartment, changed the sheets and towels, made a supper of sausage and mashed potatoes. "Feeling better?" she asks.

Kat jerks her head impatiently. "Why did no one wake me?"

It turns out she slept through Misha's phone call; he was the one who told them not to wake her. There's no reason to worry; there has been no change.

Alexander Roshdal, in the meantime, has made his own phone calls. The son of an old army friend is a surgeon at the Institute of Obstetrics and Gynecology. If Anechka doesn't get better by morning, they will arrange a transfer.

"If only you'd reached us sooner," says Roshdal. "Oh, Misha—you foolish, foolish boy."

They sit in the kitchen and pick, without appetite, at the fatty chunks of sausage. "It's all I could find," says Valentina. "There were cutlets in the fridge, but really I wouldn't dare. They didn't look too fresh."

"My mom's in the hospital!" Kat says. "So maybe, you know, you shouldn't complain." She's never been so short with Valentina, but something in her voice, a note of insincere plaintiveness, has felt to Kat like an attack.

"You're being disrespectful," her grandfather warns.

"Taking a leaf out of your mother's book? Showing your loyalty? I thought I knew you better."

Kat produces a muffled apology and Valentina says she understands. To think what Kat's been through! she says. A grown person would have gone to pieces from so much stress. But our girl is a real stalwart; she's been such a help to her dad.

Kat cringes at the praise. She doesn't understand her own feelings. There's never been bad blood between her and Valentina. They've always gotten along just fine, though perhaps in recent years they have drifted apart. It's natural, Kat thinks. She's growing up. She finds herself restless in Kratovo, bored with the card games, not really amused by Valentina's jokes. She's a simple person, Valentina, without much in the way of education, and now that Kat thinks of it, she's never seen her read a book. How hard it must have been for Anechka when Roshdal brought her home, this perfectly average woman, meant to replace Anechka's mother.

They watch the news after supper, and the TV is playing "Manchester et Liverpool," the melancholy, heartrending tune that serves as a background for the nightly weather forecast. There's always mild frost in Belarus. Sixteen to twenty-one degrees in Georgia. Slight rain in Leningrad. Westerly winds in Moscow. So familiar. So imprecise.

She must have been no older than five. They were coming home from a store, she and Anechka, both dressed in summer clothes. No rain had been mentioned in the forecast the previous night. It started fast. They ducked into the nearest doorway, a normal doorway smelling of urine. They tried to wait it out, at least the worst part, watched hard bubbles pop over the sidewalk. But the downpour wouldn't let up and the smell in the doorway was horrible. "What are we waiting for?" said Anechka, and then she said, "Let's run."

Oh, how they ran! Squealing at the rivulets of water that trickled down their bare backs and arms. Afterward, drenched to the very last thread, they laughed and laughed and no one could stop them. "Just look at us," said Anechka. "Like two wet chickens." She kissed Kat on the nose.

"Like wet puppies," Kat added. "Like wet mice."

"Like two silly girls."

IN THE MORNING, Kat discovers that first of all it's Monday, and that secondly, the quarter has ended without her being involved. She calls Jules after breakfast, and Jules says, "Thank God! I kept calling and calling your apartment. We've been worried sick here, you know."

Kat gives her the morning's update: Anechka's better, but only a little. Today she's being transferred. The new hospital is militant about visiting hours. No sneaking around in there; even Misha can't stay. She doesn't name the hospital, doesn't reveal what's really wrong with Anechka. "A burst appendix," she says. She and Misha have agreed that's what they'll say when people ask them.

Jules fills her in on what she's missed the last few days: the chaos surrounding Anechka's accident, the speculations and concerns. The play's been postponed, the disco canceled.

"Do you want to come and stay with us?" Jules offers,

but Kat, though tempted, says she can't. She's needed here. Misha needs her. She tells Jules she must go. Jules says to keep them *au courant*.

Waiting for news at home isn't easy. At the hospital, Kat had a sense of purpose—talking to the nurses, waiting for the doctor, darting to the store and back. Even sitting in the hallway seemed important. At home, though, she is useless. In the kitchen Valentina is cooking up a storm: soaking bread, cutting onions, putting meat through the grinder for new cutlets. Kat should probably help, but the smells are revolting and the onions make her eyes water and sting. And why is Valentina cooking so much? It's not as if they starved without her.

Misha comes home in the evening, looking exhausted, grimy, gaunt. He tells them Anechka is stable. There's something wrong with her blood count, though—red cells or white cells, he can't quite recall. Some supper? No thanks, he isn't hungry. He does need a shower though.

Ten minutes later, Kat finds him asleep face down on her bed, a stack of fresh clothes next to him, a towel clutched in his hand. He never made it to the shower.

That evening in the living room, Kat watches TV until late. The Roshdals make their bed on the green living room sofa. For Kat they set up a folding bed. It must have been like this in the old days, back when they all lived in a single room, though now, instead of Anechka, it's Kat who's feeling displaced. Stifled by Valentina's kindness.

———

THEY VISIT Anechka on Wednesday, two days after her transfer. She is better, the danger is over, and she is now conscious and awake. Misha is the first to go in, followed by Alexander Roshdal. Kat stands against the door and listens.

"You can't give up, Anya. You have your family, your daughter."

"Yes, family, daughter, whatever that means." Anechka's voice, still frail, goes up a notch. "I'm done, don't you see? I've got nothing."

Kat isn't allowed to see her. "Maybe next time," says Alexander Roshdal. "Today she is still very weak." Before they leave, he goes to speak to the head doctor, and Kat spots a plain white envelope peeking out of his coat pocket, presumably filled with cash.

Kat's father says, "I'll pay you back."

But Roshdal just brushes him off. "For God's sake, Misha, stop your nonsense."

On the way back, they talk of the doctor's prognosis, how if everything continues according to plan, by New Year's Eve Anechka should be able to come home.

Roshdal says he doesn't trust doctors. "That's what they said about Anya's mother, before she got pneumonia and passed away."

"Same thing with my dad," Misha says.

"They stop paying attention, get over-confident."

"Or it's just basic neglect."

"That's why we give them a little something in an envelope. A bit for the doctor, a bit for the nurse. A modest present for the janitor so she won't leave the window open by accident. I understand your scruples, Misha. But trust me, it's how things work. You can't at your age view the world through those rose-tinted spectacles."

"But that's the problem, don't you see? We're so deeply steeped in bribery, we've come to see it as par for the course. I mean, if it weren't for Anechka's current condition—"

"Yes, her condition. Let's stay focused on that."

After a while they calm down. It seems as though now, with the contents of the white envelope circulating among the hospital personnel, Anechka's recovery is all but guaranteed. To Kat, this is a dangerous error. Bad things happen when you stop watching your back. That's when the phone call comes—when you're least prepared.

When the phone rings later that evening, Kat is convinced: This is it.

"Kat, it's for you!" Valentina hollers. She stands outside the kitchen door and winks. "A gentleman caller."

Kat's hands shake as she takes the receiver.

"Hello?" she says, but there's silence on the other end. "Hello? Who is it?"

"Me," says the voice, too faint to be Nikita's.

"Speak up, please. Who is it?"

"Serge," says the voice, and it takes her a moment to put it all together. Mironov? What has possessed him?

"How's your mom?" he asks.

She tells him, in brief, about the burst appendix, the positive prognosis, the improvements in Anechka's health. Where did he get her number to begin with? And why all of a sudden is he calling himself Serge?

"Guess what? I passed algebra." He reads her his grades, mostly "satisfactory," with a couple of "good"s thrown in. "I looked up that book, by the way. The one by that fellow, Yesenin."

She doesn't know what to say to him. It all seems so far away, the tutoring, the play, the name.

"I liked it a lot, especially the one about the maple. 'Oh my dear maple, frozen stiff and bare.' " He reads to her some of his other favorites: "Not regretting, not calling, not crying," "Here it is, silly happiness," "Are you still alive, my old girl?"

"He wrote it for his mom," he says about the last one.

"I know," she says automatically.

She stalls and he stalls and the whole conversation feels suddenly nonsensical.

"I probably should go. We're waiting for a call."

"Oh," he says, "I didn't know. Sorry."

"Don't be," she says. "It's not your fault." She wants to tell him that she's glad he called, glad about his grades, glad that he is reading poetry. That she is grateful for his care, his concern. Of all the people in the world, he is the one who thought to call her.

But before she can wring from herself a single kindly word, the line clicks off, and all that is left in her ear is a string of short beeps.

ANECHKA CONTINUES to get better. On Monday she is coming home. Sveta Vlasenko calls to find out the hospital's address, but Misha tells her not to bother. She can visit once Anechka returns. Kat hears them discuss the "burst appendix" and she is pleased that Misha's sticking with their story, pleased that even Sveta won't know the truth.

After one night on the folding bed, Kat is back in her room, with its firm, almost mattress-less bunk, extensive desk, her notebooks and textbooks. But the apartment feels congested. She used to love it when the Roshdals stayed with them and the apartment took on their distinct noises and smells, the soft fragrant leather of their suitcases, the scent of Valentina's creams, the rhythmic creaking of Alexander Roshdal's cane.

But now she finds everything they do disturbing. She listens to Valentina's footsteps. She eats her food. She notes the various improvements that she's made: the stacks of clean bedding, the dusted bookshelves, the patched elbow on Kat's favorite sweater. Valentina does it all unasked, as always. To Kat it seems as if she's forcing her good deeds on them, each task calculated to garner their praise, to show up Anechka's defects, to prove that she, Valentina, is more competent.

Kat knows it's stupid, the way she's winding herself up, but by Saturday morning she is shaky with resentment. She dials Jules's number. "Get me out of here," she says.

Jules says, "No problem. Eleven thirty, at the Avenue of Peace. Meet you across from the subway."

An hour later, Kat is picked up by Jules's parents in their spanking new Moskvich. Jules is in the back seat, sporting a blue Adidas tracksuit ("You wear Adidas today. Next day your country you'll betray!"), a tape player perched on her lap. Kat climbs inside and also settles in the back. She tends to get sheepish around Jules's parents. They are so imposing and big, which is strange considering that Jules herself is so scrawny. Jules's mother is particularly regal in her black patent-leather coat.

She asks after Anechka's health. "Appendix at this age! It must be horrible. I had mine taken out back in high school. Ate too much candy. Or was it sunflower seeds?"

"Candy, I think," says Jules's dad. The two of them met while in high school. "Could have been anything, though. Everyone knows, Murzik, that you can eat."

"That's true," says Jules's mother, whose actual name is Marusya.

It's pleasant to be driven in this voluptuous automobile, to lounge on the padded seats and listen to bouncy music. They seem to have no destination, nothing to buy or see. They're just cruising—stopping at random places for chocolates or *chebureks* or *ponchik* donuts or, at one point, a bottle of perfume for Murzik. Such a kittenish name for such a solid person, though it does match her apparent joie de vivre. Jules plays pop tunes on her tape player and Murzik sings along, not a bit embarrassed to squander her great operatic voice.

Is it wrong to enjoy this and even like these people, who, according to Anechka and Misha, have long ago sold their souls, who are money-obsessed and too successful, and who probably detest Gorbachev's reforms because the old system worked so well for them? But if you put that aside, they're just normal, pleasant folk. They like music, cars, good food;

they seem to like each other; and it's clear that they also like Jules. Nothing overt ties the three of them together, not even physical resemblance, and yet you can't miss that they are family and Jules belongs with them.

Jules herself seems different, not the way she is at school: sticklike, almost plain, in her uniform pants and light blue jersey, and the brace, which she wears with the head-holder mostly open even though it's against the rules. There is no brace today. Jules has put on violet lipstick and eye shadow, tucked her hair under a jaunty beret, and suddenly she's enigmatic, even beautiful. Mostly, though, it's her confidence, that invisible pivot that holds her up, makes her impervious to setbacks, immune to insecurity. Maybe she learned it from her parents, or maybe it's something innate. Whatever the case may be, Kat has been relying on her self-assurance. Being with Jules calms her down, sets her chaotic mind at ease—though not until now has she known how vital it is, how much it helps her sanity.

Around four o'clock, they end up at the Exhibit of People's Accomplishments. In summer it's one of Kat's favorite places, a vast and stunning park with wide paved alleys and palace-like pavilions. In winter, though, it looks neglected. The stone fountains are silent, and there are no Pepsi stands or pony rides. They find a show of folk art, and afterward they shop for souvenirs. Kat buys a florid shawl for Anechka. For Valentina she selects an apron, pale yellow with a bright rooster appliqué, and when she comes up short Jules's mom spots her some money.

Back at the subway station, they part ways. Murzik makes sure that Kat has the subway fare, checks whether someone will be there to meet her at the other end. Her father? Her grandfather maybe? Kat's already starting for the station when Murzik rolls down the window and calls out her name. "Here," she says and presses the bottle of perfume into her hands. "Give this to your mom. It will make her happy."

THE SUBWAY ride is long and the bus doesn't come for a while, so when Kat returns home it's almost eight o'clock. Valentina is nearly hysterical. "You know what time it is?" she asks her.

Kat shrugs. "It's not that late." What's the big deal any-way? She was just out with the Smolkins.

"I don't know any Smolkins."

"So? That's your problem," Kat says.

"Don't lie to me. You went to see that boy. I know it!"

"What boy?" Kat says, incredulous.

"The one that called the other day. No 'please,' 'no how do you do,' not even a basic 'hello.'"

"Mironov?" Kat starts laughing. "He's, you know . . . he's nobody."

Valentina calms down a little and changes her tack. "No need to be ashamed, my dear girl. It's perfectly normal at your age to have a certain curiosity, or feelings."

"Feelings?" Kat says. "You must be out of your mind."

"Kat dear, don't be rude. Your grandfather and I, we're

your family. We have a right to be concerned. You're
going through puberty. You need someone to guide you
toward the proper path, and your mother, in her current
circumstances—"

"Leave my mother out of it! She's fine!"

"Of course she is. I didn't mean to—"

But the more Valentina stumbles, the angrier Kat gets.
"It's not your place to interfere."

"Now, darling, I think I've been patient enough. But
really, you're pushing all the limits."

What limits are there? There aren't any limits. Just the
growing fury that sweeps Kat along.

"You're not one of us. You've simply glommed on to our
family!"

Valentina shuts down. She touches her face and says,
"Oh dear." And then she simply stands there and seems not
to know what to do. Kat briefly feels sorry for her, she's so
pitiful. Then she panics, like a kid who's mouthed off to
grownups. But on the heels of the panic comes more anger.
Valentina *is* devious, Anechka has been saying so for years.
She has been undermining Anechka, slowly ruining her life.
Why couldn't Kat see it?

Cloistered in her room, Kat waits for the sounds of pack-
ing, the tears in the bathroom, the sharp rap of her grandfather's cane. What she hears instead are voices in the
hallway. Roshdal returns from the hospital, Misha from
Zoya Moiseevna's. There's the noise of running water, the
clattering of plates. "Get in here, Kat! It's suppertime."

For supper they're having stuffed eggplant. Valentina herself doesn't join them, but busies herself at the stove. "Come eat with us, Valya," Roshdal calls.

She says, "I have no appetite."

Tomorrow Anechka is coming home. The doctor says she needs a sense of normality, and what can be more normal than a plastic New Year's tree tied to a kitchen stool with laundry ropes? They dress it up with an assortment of glass ornaments, and at the base they place clumps of cotton wool.

"How about some tinsel?" suggests Valentina.

Kat turns away and gets a broom. Misha starts picking up empty wrappers.

"Tinsel! To make things more festive?"

They're trying not to look at her. Because it is embarrassing. How can she not know after all these years? How can she be so blundering, so uninformed? She's been with them on every holiday.

"Anya hates tinsel," Roshdal tells her.

BACK FROM the hospital, Anechka's installed on the living room sofa, propped up on pillows, swaddled in blankets and shawls. There are books all around her, cups of tea on the floor. She's looking peaked and hardly speaks at all—asks for another cup of tea, but then forgets to drink it; complains the room is stuffy, so they crack the ventilation window, but soon she is too cold.

Tonight is New Year's Eve, which is a family affair. In the kitchen, Valentina is baking. Misha has gone to school to pick up their holiday food packages (small tins of pollock liver, sprats, and the ubiquitous salami sticks). But no one feels like celebrating.

By nine o'clock they set the table: egg salad, potato salad, fish in aspic, meat jelly. They push the table up against Anechka's sofa so that she can stay there. They keep the TV on because otherwise they have little to say. At quarter to midnight, they toast the departing year. Then comes the usual moment of panic as Misha grapples with a bottle of champagne. At midnight they drink to the new and better 1987, and Valentina mutters the obligatory adage about the old sores and scabs that should stay in the past. She's been subdued tonight, and it's never been more evident than now, when good cheer is so badly needed.

"Feeling under the weather, my pet?" Roshdal asks her.

She says, "Just a bit of a headache," and he places his palm over her small, withered hand.

Anechka leans back on the pillows.

"Should we call it a night?" Misha says.

But first they must open the presents. They pile the packages on the sofa next to Anechka. Kat gets a fountain pen, a volume of British poetry, a set of long camisoles to wear under her brace. Misha gives Anechka the bottle of perfume Kat got from Jules's mother. From her handbag Anechka retrieves an assortment of hospital trinkets: an orange fish, a devil with green horns—each creature woven lovingly from used IV tubes.

"You *made* them?" Kat asks.

"No, silly, just a woman from my floor." Every floor of every hospital has a master weaver of this kind.

Kat spies Valentina unwrapping her presents, coming at last to the apron with the rooster appliqué. She looks at it. She doesn't try it on or gush the way she would have in the past. "Thank you," she says flatly. "Much obliged." She folds it and puts it aside like it's nothing.

They clean the table and prepare for the night. The Roshdals take over Kat's bedroom. Misha and Kat camp out beside Anechka's bed.

In the kitchen, while no one is looking, Kat sneaks two more glasses of champagne. *Here's to the new year. Here's to new happiness.* She shrugs and puts away her glass. Never before has she been this unhappy.

IT IS a sunny, oddly quiet morning, so quiet that at first Kat thinks everyone is still asleep. Then she sees that Misha's mattress is gone and Anechka is sitting up in bed, drinking tea.

"What time is it?"

"Eleven. Your dad's gone to Kuzminki."

"And the Roshdals?"

"Packed up and gone home before dawn. Wouldn't even have breakfast."

"Already?" Kat says. "So early?"

"I told them, stay a while, but no, it's the usual: Valya wants to go home. Must do what Valya wants."

"Was she cross? Did she say anything?"

"It's just the way she is, Kat. God forbid she doesn't get Dad's full attention. It's better without her, really. Even the air's better, don't you think?"

Kat breathes in slowly, deeply. She doesn't know about the air (it seems the same), but she is definitely starting to feel better. Like a criminal who's fled punishment, a fugitive who's reached a distant shore. Guilty, and yet undeniably better.

13

No ONE AT SCHOOL KNOWS THE TRUTH ABOUT Anechka. A burst appendix is what everyone is told. No one mentions the play anymore. First, the costumes had to be returned. The playbill, already outdated, came down a week later. "Some people take on more than they can handle," said Margo.

But other teachers are compassionate. "How's your mom?" they ask when they spot Kat in the corridors. So-so, she says, and makes the sort of face that wards off further questions: So-so. Not great. As weeks go by, the teachers seem to get a little more impatient. It's just a burst appendix, for God's sake. How long does it take to recover from that?

And the girls—Anechka's girls—they flutter with concern. They seek Kat out constantly, pass her their folded notes for Anechka. A smiley face scribbled in blue fountain pen. A paper rose. They tell her again and again how lucky she is to have such a marvelous mother, how solemnly and gently Kat must attend to her.

And what can she say in return? They'll never believe it, or understand, this picture of morose, resentful Anechka, who either sleeps or smokes into the ventilation window and calls Kat a snoop when she walks in on her by accident.

"Is something wrong?" Kat asks on weekends, when she's home, and what she means is: Are you bleeding or hurting? Or do you simply want a glass of water? A cup of bouillon?

"You're such an obtuse girl," says Anechka. And when she looks at Kat her eyes are scornful, as if she can't accept that this dull, hapless creature is her daughter.

She has been cleared by the doctors to return to work. Except, it seems, she doesn't want to. She says she can't take being there, among those people, those walls. She finds other doctors who write her the notes she wants. She's got migraines and fibroids, according to these notes. She's anemic. She's bleeding internally. It can't go on like this, Misha warns her. She might lose her job. She says it doesn't matter. The loss, she says. "My loss." They can't begin to comprehend it.

Misha's been trying to cover her classes. He puts up page numbers on the board, which even the most diligent pupils are happy to ignore. Sometimes he tries to cram them in together with his classes. Mostly he assigns a lot of papers, which he later forgets to collect. "The Person Most Dear to Me." "How I Spent my Winter Holidays." Five handwritten pages on the tragedy and spiritual beauty in Turgenev's "Bezhin Lea." Anyone can see it's not working. Misha is floundering under the load of grading, while Anechka stays desolate and absent, sleepwalking through her vacant afternoons.

"She needs more time," he says.

Kat isn't so sure. "Her doctors say she's on the mend."

"Doctors can't see into your soul. She might seem stronger on the outside, but you and I both know that inside she's still in pieces. Sad little pieces barely glued together."

So maybe it's true and Anechka just isn't ready. Kat misses seeing her at school. At home on weekends, Anechka is withdrawn and indifferent. Nothing helps. Not the cups of tea Kat brews, not the messages she brings from school. Anechka hardly reads them. She refuses to come to the phone, so much so that Sveta Vlasenko stops calling altogether. Soon they will all move on. They have regional exams, Komsomol seminars. Those who are graduating have college entrance to prepare for. Some are even seeing tutors, mostly in math, but increasingly in Russian literature and grammar, too. With no Anechka around, they're forced to seek help elsewhere.

THE FIRST substitute appears in the second week of February and lasts three days exactly. She's the school librarian. Incompetent, Kat is happy to report. The gaggle mocks her openly. She speaks softly, too softly to withstand their banter. She confuses participles with gerunds, makes two punctuation errors while writing on the board, and when at the end of the week Kat recounts these missteps for Anechka and Anechka, surprisingly, comes out of her stupor and puts through one well-timed phone call, the poor librarian is history.

"Good girl," says Anechka, and sends Kat to buy them ice cream from the neighborhood kiosk.

Kat mimics the addled librarian: her panicky demeanor, her stuttering, her halting walk. She knows she shouldn't. It's cruel and unseemly. But then she is rewarded by Anechka's laughter—the first real laughter, it seems, since her collapse. "You're such a goof," Anechka says, and hugs her.

"Isn't this a bit extreme?" says Misha, when he catches the two of them whooping it up.

Anechka says, "I'm only looking out for my children."

Yes, but must she be so gleeful? Misha shrugs and departs, lest his concern dampen Anechka's sudden high spirits. It's not wrong to care for one's pupils, and if she cares so much, perhaps she will at last return to teaching.

The next substitute is not unknown to 7A. She is one of their former class matrons, a prim and gently aging woman, who favors ruffled blouses and black knee-length skirts. She is well schooled in the material, and if she makes mistakes, they are not easily discernible. Still, there are strands of old resentment between her and 7A. You can see her tense up when she walks into the classroom—stiffening her shoulders, flexing her spine, anticipating discipline problems. No one is surprised when she resigns.

"That was too easy," complains Anechka, and Kat, not a fighter by nature, chimes in. The two of them need a good challenge. They snuggle on the sofa and watch *Under 16 and*

Older on TV, and Kat must be careful not to jostle Anechka, who is still sore in the stomach area where her stitches used to be. She's always been a little fragile.

THE THIRD substitute is nobody they know. She comes from outside, a lusty and bouncy young woman with fleshy arms and shoulders and healthy pink skin. Her name is Anjelika Semyonovna. Lika, for short. She actually insists they call her Lika.

"Howdy, people," she says upon meeting them, and 7A notes it—they are not as stupid as they seem—this too-informal greeting. She perches on Anechka's desk—which isn't such a bright idea, given her minuscule skirt. That's how she dresses for work: tiny skirts, floppy tops, white stockings, slip-on clogs. Plastic clip-on earrings and lots of plastic bangles, because, she tells them, she's allergic to gold. "How freaking unlucky is that?"

"So," she says. "Anyway. What are you into?" And for the next twenty minutes they talk about what's on TV and the music they listen to. "Disco's so over," she tells them and rolls her eyes a little. "Get with the program, people. The future is punk rock." She has a bootleg of something called the Sex Pistols, which she promises will blow their little heads off.

The gaggle is in love. It's pathetic, really. Give them anything trashy and sparkly, and *finito*—they're yours.

"And did she teach at all?" says Anechka when Kat calls with the news.

Oh yes, Kat sighs. She taught. They did a chapter on isolated appositions.

"Lika," Anechka says slowly, as if tasting the word. Lee-kaa. A challenge? Possibly. Though she doesn't seem concerned.

"You've seen this Lika?" she asks Misha next weekend.

He says he has, in passing.

"And?" Anechka prompts him. She wants to know what he thought.

"Seems like a normal person."

"Ah!" she says. "A normal person. That's very observant of you, Misha." She winks at Kat, which means the game is on. They'd better watch out, because, unlike the other substitutes, this Lika might be treacherous.

LIKA, LIKA, LIKA . . . She's the talk of the school, the toast of their class. She is studied, dissected, from her bottle-bleached hair to her loose, ample breasts. Kat finds her lacking, actually. She's got none of Anechka's loveliness, none of her languid charm. She's not even intelligent.

And yet Lika has found her admirers. Never mind that it's just the gaggle—Shrew, Snake, Little Hog. They cluster around her desk after class, try on her plastic bangles. On Wednesday, when Lika walks 7A to lunch, they squabble over who gets to sit by her.

Jules doesn't mind Lika either. People like Lika apparently excite her—bold, loud, brash, with studs and fingerless gloves and big, tousled rock-and-roll hair.

Kat tells her Lika is tawdry.

Jules says, "Don't be a prude. I think she's kind of cool."

"She's buying us off with her salacious anecdotes."

"Salacious?" repeats Jules. "She's just being open."

"Nobody asked her to be open. She's not a door. She's supposed to teach, not spice up the material with her"—Kat wants to say "exploits," but she sticks with a safer word—"her stories."

"Your mom tells stories too."

But not like this! Never like this! Anechka's stories are appropriate. They are about prose writers and poets of the past, those flaming and gullible souls who suffered under censorship and perished in duels and purges.

Lika, on the contrary, likes to get personal: She's married. Her husband is a rocker, which means either he rides motorcycles or he plays rock and roll. They don't have any children. Lika has a heart murmur and a weird skin condition that can be really gross. She likes sex, and her favorite things in the world are marijuana and chocolate.

Chocolate and *what?* Even the gaggle is appalled. They know about marijuana from Margo. She tells them it fries your brain slowly until you are mentally warped, and the damage is irreversible.

"Baloney," says Lika. "I've smoked tons of pot, and as you can see, my brain is perfect."

"That's up for debate," Kat says under her breath.

"There are lots of drugs out there," Lika continues. "And I've tried most of them. And yeah, some of them can be dangerous." She tells them a long-drawn-out story about heroin addiction among teenagers in her neighborhood: how she and her husband tried to rescue them, how they almost got hurt. She could have been murdered, she says. Honest to God. 7A gapes at her, tries to imagine a pale, murdered Lika, a slash across her throat, her stockings torn.

Class is nearly over, and they've done nothing even remotely resembling literature.

"BE HONEST," Kat says. "Do you like her?"

She and Mironov are in the drama room, ostensibly studying, in reality just wasting time. This quarter they're feeling less pressure. No one is calling for Mironov's expulsion. The faculty is taken up with new concerns. Rumor has it that the new history teacher is having an affair, and their young and much-beloved geography teacher has been seen leaving the school arm in arm with the head of orthopedics.

On these matters, Kat's feeling is, whatever. Who cares what the teachers do in their free time? What gets her, she insists, is the hogwash people like Lika spew in class, in lieu of real education.

"What do you think of her?" she asks Mironov.

"A normal broad, maybe a little cracked—like half of them around here."

To Kat this doesn't seem enough. "Is that the extent of your thoughtful assessment?"

"What the hell more do you want from me, Kat? You want another fight?"

"You've figured it out! At last! You're such a clever boy."

"Uh-huh." He grins. "Keep waiting."

But he's right, she is spoiling for something. In Lika's presence she behaves appallingly—snorts at her lectures, rolls her eyes, pretends not to hear her questions.

"You really don't like me very much," says Lika, and Kat says, "Do I have to?"

Lika has asked her to stay after class.

"I've heard good things about you from the other teachers. They say you're a serious student, intelligent, diligent, willing to help a friend."

"I take it you don't share their enthusiasm."

"I'm a substitute, I'm not your enemy. And I'm not here to replace your mom."

"I know," Kat says, and what she means is, You never *could* replace her.

"Though to be honest, I do enjoy this place. Your class, especially. The girls here, there's something true about them. I feel they understand me."

"So you want to stay, is what you're saying?"

"And that to you is unacceptable? What are you so afraid of, Katya?"

"Kat," she corrects her. Everyone knows her name is Kat.

"They don't like you, your classmates?"

Kat shrugs. "I have my friends."

"Do you? I'm glad to hear that. You strike me as a lonely person."

"You're wrong," Kat says. "You've been misled."

But she fumes for the rest of the day. They don't like her, it's true. They never liked her, even before her parents joined the school. She couldn't understand what caused it. Misha blamed it on the gaggle's jealousy. Anechka thought it was because Kat was a Jew. And maybe Anechka was right. Just like her parents, Kat belonged to a different stratum— distrusted, criticized, restricted, treated like a second-class citizen. They *were* second-class citizens, some of her teachers pointed out. People like them became refuseniks, emigrated, traded their motherland for better realms. There was something unclean about them. They cared too much about money, the common wisdom went. Maybe *that* was what Lika was implying?

"She's trying to manipulate me."

"Or maybe," Jules says, "she's just trying to help."

"Don't be naive," Kat says, wishing she hadn't mentioned the encounter. What did she expect, anyway? From Jules of all people—Jules with her privileged background.

Jules goes off to brush her teeth before nap. When she returns, she's frowning.

"Honestly, Kat, it's getting tiresome. You think the school is full of enemies. Maybe the reason is your parents, or maybe you're paranoid and basically unhappy, and Lika's got it right."

"Lika the oracle," Kat sneers.

"There you go again, being snide."

"Don't you see what we're up against?"

"I don't," Jules says. "Perhaps you can explain it. You act as if your parents are some kind of heroes, saving the innocent and bringing truth to the world. Frankly, I never got it.

They're putting on these little spectacles, tributes to Pushkin and other bagatelles. And that's supposed to be subversive?"

"There're parallels," Kat says. "Internal messages."

"Well, I don't get them."

"You wouldn't," Kat says.

"What's that supposed to mean?" Jules says.

"Nothing." Kat tries to backpedal. "You didn't even come to the rehearsals."

But Jules is too clever to be fooled. "Go to hell," she tells Kat. "Go home to your precious parents."

ANECHKA SAYS, "I think we have her," and for a moment she looks like the head of a gang of brigands, presiding around a fire, dressed in furs and rags. In fact, she's in the kitchen, picking at a pomegranate. There's a large kitchen towel spread across her lap. Her fingertips are stained, her lips scraped raw from the pomegranate pulp. She's been eating a lot of them lately; she says they're good for the blood. Red cells or white cells, something is always off-balance.

There is a lengthy pause, and Kat knows not to interrupt her. It's obvious she is spawning a strategy, pitting advantages against drawbacks, counting pluses and minuses. Can they defeat Lika? You bet they can!

It's taken a substitute to rouse Anechka, but what a brilliant and furious awakening it's been. She's radiant. Kat comes home from school on Saturday and Anechka is not in her nightgown anymore. She's put on a sweater and jeans and even a bit of blue eye shadow. She pats the sofa next to her—"Come sit!"—and Kat, who's just walked in the door, joins her eagerly, not bothering to change her clothes or use the toilet or get a bite to eat. "Okay," Anechka says, "begin." She loves Kat's reports. She waits for them, devours her every word. Her face goes blotchy with excitement. Not entirely healthy, of course, but still, what a difference from the glum, surly, couch-bound form she was only weeks ago. When Kat is done, she asks her if she's hungry, and sometimes there's supper, and other times it's tea and bread with cheese. Later they might talk some more, perhaps about a new article in *Ogonek*—the cult of cruelty among teenagers, the latest exposé of Stalin and his cult of personality. Or they might stay up late to watch new shows on TV.

But maybe they've been too cavalier about this whole situation. She's been such a delicious joke, this big-busted blabbermouth Lika. They've made bets on how long she will last. One week. Two weeks maximum. But Lika isn't leaving—not of her own accord, anyway. She's gained some protectors along the way. The old guard has taken her under their wing. A true Russian girl, Creampuff called her the other day in the canteen.

"I don't understand it," Creampuff was saying. "Why don't we hire more Russian people?"

And the teacher she was speaking to agreed. "The school is swarming with the alien-named element."

Kat was idling by the giant vats of bread. Not spying, mind you—just waiting to ask Creampuff about next week's biology quiz. But she knew they were talking about her parents. Also, about Lefty (Emma Aronovna Levit), who teaches history and civics; about Mariya Zinovievna Fratkina, who teaches math; about the art teacher, Jamilya, who is from Kazakhstan; and even Beatrisa, whose origins—French? Jewish? Polish?—have always been unclear.

"We have to act quickly," says Anechka.

"You're sure you're not overreacting?" Misha says.

"Whose side are you on anyway?"

Whose side indeed? There's always a side. The side of outcasts, the side of the majority. The side of decency. The side of compromise.

Anechka says, "You have to speak to the headmistress."

Kat says, "Can't you call her yourself?"

Anechka shakes her head. "Not anymore. It has to be you, baby." And when she sees Kat hesitating, she adds, "Just tell the truth. Tell her what Lika's been saying. You'll be doing a favor to everyone in the school."

Misha says, "Is Lika really such a danger?"

Anechka won't look in his direction. "Don't listen to your father, baby. Looks like he's so soft-hearted he's ready to give up both our jobs. He refuses to see that these people, they're trying to get rid of us. But you, my pet, you know better. You're my girl. No matter what, we have to stick together."

NEXT TUESDAY, the gaggle shows up for literature and Lika isn't there. They wait ten minutes. It's probably safe to assume the lesson has been canceled. They wait some more, just to be sure, and then Nina Petrenko lets out a happy whoop.

Little Hog says, "Shut up, you retard."

Someone suggests they cut their losses, skip over to the oxygen café. But Little Hog tells them they can't. Someone will see them moving through the hallways. "We can't let Lika down. Understand?"

So they don't go. They stay on their cots and wait—wait by the sea for good weather—and only once the bell rings do they gather up their things and leave.

That day they find out nothing, but the next day Lika's back. She is waiting for them in her acid-washed jacket, which she normally wears outside. They look at her, puzzled: Why don't you sit down, Lika?

She tells them she's been sacked.

"Don't look so surprised. One of you went to the headmistress and denounced me, told her I teach you to take drugs."

Little Hog blurts out, "We didn't."

"Don't insult my intelligence," says Lika. "What I want to know is, who? Who took it upon herself to march in to the headmistress?"

She stares them down, one at a time, though when it comes to Kat, she skips her for some reason.

Kat saw the headmistress on Monday. It took her a while to find the perfect moment and then work up the courage to knock on the door. She's always been shy of the headmistress, a large, severe-looking woman, with close-cropped grey hair and wary, bespectacled eyes. She has no family, apparently, and no close pals among her colleagues. She treats everyone the same. It doesn't matter who you are—a teacher, a student, a parent; if she thinks you presumptuous or ignorant, she won't hesitate to tell you.

She seemed surprised to find Kat in her doorway. Was there something wrong with Anechka? Or maybe Misha sent Kat on an errand? Kat had to tell her it was neither, it was something else.

"Come in then," the headmistress said. She wasn't in the habit of entertaining students. No students came to see her unless they'd been summoned, in which case it was bad news. She had a large office, as large as the whole teachers' lounge upstairs. Kat had to wait on the couch for a while, beneath a loud grandfather clock, while the headmistress put away some paperwork.

"It's about the substitute," Kat said, blanking for a moment on Lika's full name.

The headmistress raised her eyebrows, which, Kat now thinks, might have been a warning, a warning that she failed to heed. But the headmistress wasn't Jewish, and who knew how she felt about Jewish people? Kat had to remind herself of what she was doing: she was saving the school, saving her parents' jobs.

She went on with her story, and the headmistress listened and took notes, and the whole time Kat knew it was wrong, *she* was wrong, knew it by the way the headmistress pursed her mouth and wouldn't even look at her. Kat was doing something secretive, something undignified and vile.

And here is the result: a ruined, raving Lika, standing before the gaggle and tugging at her scarf. "I had heart palpitations," she is saying. "I couldn't sleep all night. I had a hellish skin reaction, so bad I can't show you, you'd throw up."

She sucks in her breath, takes a pause, and now she seems to be looking directly at Kat.

"There's an informer among you. A weak and frightened person who's hurt you all. I used to believe in you, people. But not anymore. As far as I'm concerned, every one of you is an informer."

"Who?" Little Hog demands.

Lika says, "I don't know. It could be any of you. Unless the informer steps forward."

They must know it's Kat. It's a matter of logic. She would feel better if they figured it out and erupted in their cacophony of outrage. Either that, or Lika will out her herself. Because she's no dummy, all the drugs notwithstanding. She doesn't take her eyes off Kat. One, two, three: just tell them!

But Lika isn't telling, because it's a test.

It would be easy to confess, or as Lika says, step forward, tell them that she did it and she has no regrets. She's not a frightened person. Isn't that what Lika is trying to prove— that Kat is afraid? How easy it would be: confess, confess! Except the word "informer" rankles her. There must be other, better-fitting words. She glances at Jules. ("They don't like you," Lika asked her, "do they?")

Lika waits, but no one is talking. There's puffiness under her eyes, and she's wrapped her neck in that big purple scarf to spare them the sight of the welts on her skin. She's only a substitute, after all. No one bothers about a substitute. But somehow she's expecting them to speak to her: We're sorry. Don't go. A few simple words. She still doesn't get it, the way 7A is incapable of anything heartfelt, the way they feel spurned at the drop of a hat, the way they retreat into themselves, turn bitter.

"Your loss," she says to them.

STILL, THEY are affected. They wade through the rest of the day in a blur of jumbled feelings. There are violent outbursts, tears, intermittent threats. Little Hog tries to enlist Margo's help. But Margo says, "We were mistaken."

So there's doubt now, planted by Margo. And maybe— just maybe—some of what Lika said wasn't appropriate. Like the stuff about her rash. And, come to think of it, her skirts were too short, her breasts too uncontained in those floppy blouses. And her language, wasn't it a tad—how should we put it—too relaxed?

"You all claimed to love her!" Little Hog yells, and what can be worse, or more contagious, than Little Hog's uncontrollable rage? Their dorm becomes a battlefield and, as often happens in such situations, Kat gets her share of abuse. "Shut up and die, Kysya," they scream, though Kat hasn't said a word. "You're annoying me!"

In the past Kat would have stayed quiet, waited for the storm to blow off. At least that is what Anechka always urged, saying Kat was too weak to prevail in a conflict, too sensitive to stay the course. She'd start to crack after a day

or so, and it would fall to Anechka to sort out the mess. All
the same, in her place Anechka wouldn't tolerate the gaggle.
She wouldn't mince words or sneak around; she'd tell them
exactly what she thought.

"Lika deserved to get fired," Kat says, and for a moment
it seems that no one heard her. Then, abruptly, Little Hog
sits up.

"You're the one who reported her."

"What if I did?" Kat asks.

Little Hog begins to move toward her, and it must be
this swaggering, gangster-like walk that makes Little Hog
so menacing. "You better speak up, Kysya, cause maybe I
didn't hear you right."

"You heard me," Kat says, not backing up.

Little Hog is closer now, her fists clenched as if for a fight,
but until she swings her arm Kat doesn't believe she might
hurt her.

Just then Jules steps between them. "Enough, you idiots," she says. "Enough!" But it's too late: Little Hog's arm
is already in motion, and Jules has no time to duck, and the
punch catches her square on the nose.

IN THE dorm bathroom, Jules holds clumps of toilet paper to
her face, trying to stem a nosebleed. She wasn't hit that hard,
but her nose is sensitive. She has frequent nosebleeds—when
a snowball gets her, or even when there's a sudden shift in
temperature. She's learned to use them to her advantage, if
she wants to skip a swimming session or hasn't studied for a

test. Except the one she's having now isn't fake. Kat brings her a clean handkerchief and waits as Jules sits on the bathroom floor with her head tilted back and a cold bandage on her nose.

"Sorry," Kat says. "You know it was meant for me."

Jules doesn't answer, just tips her head farther back.

"When you feel better we can go to the oxygen café."

"You must really think I'm stupid," Jules says after a pause. "You think we're all stupid—because we don't sing those dumb guitar songs, or faint at the sound of poetry, or worship your silly self-important parents like they're some sort of little gods. Except they're not that important, Kat. They're not even clever like Lika, who, for my money, was a real rebel and a much better teacher than your mom. She even won over the gaggle, for God's sake. And that's why *you* got rid of her."

"I didn't—" Kat begins.

"Oh please! I don't really care." Jules gets up from the floor.

"Where are you going?"

"The infirmary."

Kat follows instinctively. "Can I come? Are you sick?"

"I'm sick of you," Jules says. "And no, I don't want you there."

IT's NOT easy to get through the rest of the week. No one speaks to Kat, especially not Jules. Not even when they're on canteen duty together. Jules just goes about her business, picking out twisted forks or waiting for the pot of soup. During the evening walks Kat sits on the swing behind the swimming pool, and sometimes Mironov comes to keep her company. "Want me to push you?" he offers, after watching her sit still. "If you want my opinion, I don't think you did anything horrible."

But she doesn't want his opinion, and she's unsure what she did. Did she help the school in some important manner? Rescue her mother's job? Was Lika incompetent or was she a maverick, a rare trailblazing individual?

Anechka, at least, is pleased. On Wednesday, when Kat phoned with the news, she called her a clever girl and a hero. She said they'd celebrate on Saturday, when Kat comes home from school.

Saturday arrives and there are no signs of celebration. They're having supper in the kitchen, a regular supper, potatoes and reheated old steaks. Misha has tucked himself into the tightest corner, and it's strange how such a large person can fit into such a small space.

When the conversation gets around Lika, Misha gets up from his chair. "The two of you, you have destroyed a person."

"You fancied her that much?" Anechka says, but he waves her aside and goes to the living room.

"Never mind him," says Anechka. "Just tell me how it went."

Kat tells all—from the talk she had with the headmistress, to Lika's parting speech, to the gaggle's violent reaction.

Anechka says, "You didn't tell them, did you?"

"Eventually I did," Kat says.

"God, that was stupid. Now the whole school will know and everyone will think it was my work."

"I thought you'd be proud—"

"Proud of what? Of you shooting your mouth off?"

"I was just standing up to them. You've always said to never compromise—"

Earlier that year they were reading "The Song of the Stormy Petrel," a revolutionary poem but also a moral allegory, a tribute to noncomformists: "Only proud stormy petrel soars, fearless and unfettered, high above the greyish waters." Anechka said, "Who among you is such a person? Who is the stormy petrel of this class?" Maybe she thought they'd choose Kat, but they all voted for Little Hog.

Anechka says, "You'll never be a stormy petrel."

"You don't even know me," Kat says.

"I know plenty. Honestly, Kat, what were you thinking? How will I ever go back to work?"

"I thought the point was to rid the school of Lika—"

"The point?" Anechka snaps. "What point?"

She is loud enough that it gets Misha's attention. He returns to the kitchen and asks them what's going on.

"You"—she points at him—"I know you must have planned it. You've been undermining me every step of the way. How long have you been in cahoots with your Lika? Did she come and complain? Did she show up to cry on your shoulder?"

"You don't know what you're saying, Anya."

At first, Kat thinks she must be missing something, a

breach between her parents that happened while she was at school. Then she sees how unhinged Anechka looks: trembling, pupils dilated, face twisted with fury. A picture of someone possessed. She seems to have forgotten Kat's existence.

"I'm not surprised you liked her, really. A normal, healthy woman for a change. I bet she could make you a whole brood of children. Poor Misha, stuck with a defective wife. Defective wife, defective daughter. What was it your mother called us—cripples?"

"Shut up," he whispers. "Not in front of Kat."

"Don't worry," she tells him. "I won't be your burden much longer."

~

IN SECOND PERIOD ON TUESDAY, they recite "Kindness to Horses" by Vladimir Mayakovsky, Misha's favorite. The gaggle, being who they are, make a mockery of the poem: "Horse, you mustn't. Horse, listen!" and they cackle like the mob, the loafers, in the poem itself: "A horse keeled over! It's toppled, the horse!" Misha nods and moves on to the next name on the roster.

He is curt with them, impersonal, assigning grades and saying little else. Even when they butcher his favorite poem on purpose. "A horse has toppled on her rump," and now for some reason Kat is picturing Lika. "Child, we are all, a little bit, horses."

She'd like to believe she is the sort of person who is kind to horses, the person who wouldn't join the gaggle but would kneel in the ice before the wounded beast. Except that lately she isn't sure about anything. "What do you think of me?" she used to ask Misha. She doesn't dare ask him now, afraid of what he thinks.

That evening they take a subway to Perovo, as they now do once a week, to see Anechka at the clinic. She's been sequestered there for a month at least, taking calming pills, doing crafts and yard work as part of her occupational therapy.

They should never have pressured her, that much is obvious. A week after Lika got fired, Anechka actually returned to work. She lasted a week. They should have noticed the cracks in her armor. Instead, they found her on Sunday, prone on the kitchen floor. A small puddle of water next to her, two empty pill packets. The note on a lined sheet of paper read simply: "I can't anymore."

Misha barely looks at Kat now. On weekends he's quiet and tired, hunched up in his warm kitchen corner, while she boils potatoes and hot dogs for the two of them to eat. Later he does grading on the living room sofa, and when he falls asleep, she covers him with his favorite red and green afghan.

Every Tuesday they go to the clinic. They bring Anechka fresh clothes, some magazines she may or may not read. Most other things are not allowed. They don't know if she's getting better. Some days she's withdrawn, tearful, refusing to talk to them or even come out for a walk. Other times she's apathetic, following them dimly across the grounds of the clinic. And yet there are also glimpses of normalcy, vividness, and even traces of her scathing wit. She can be many things, their Anechka: sarcastic, gentle, difficult. Though increasingly one image blurs it all—the shape of her passed out on the kitchen floor.

These days it never leaves Kat, this image, this sepia-colored despair, the hollow ache. It follows her everywhere. She dreams of the long concrete wall painted yellow, the soggy benches strewn along the paths, the grungy angel statues with chipped fingers and faces. How can anyone get better here? she thinks when she wakes up. And how could she have missed it in the first place, the signs of Anechka unraveling?

It takes her and Misha a long time to get to the clinic; the rush-hour trains are crowded and there's no place to sit. They hold onto the handrails and sway to and fro, bumping into each other a little. From the subway station they emerge into the murky Moscow evening—wet sidewalks, pale streetlights, silhouettes of tall apartment buildings. It's surprisingly springlike tonight. Kat's taken off her hat, unbuttoned her warm jacket. They both slow down. It's really not that far.

"Was it my fault?" Kat says to Misha.

He says no, don't be silly, it's not anyone's fault.

"Yes, but you think I was wrong back then, with Lika?"

He is silent for a while before he answers. "There comes a moment, Button, when a person must decide things for herself. What's right and what's wrong. What's honest, what's deceitful. You can't be hanging on to what we think, either me or your mother. Because, first of all, we're not the same person, we often disagree. And second of all, you'll never grow up this way. And you *must* grow up—don't you see?"

She nods, not saying anything.

Misha stops and examines her, slowly. Her untidy, unbuttoned winter jacket; her school pants with their muddy cuffs. The pitiful squiggles of hair that frame her forehead. A gust of sudden wintry air makes her shiver. He takes off his mohair scarf and spools it around her neck. "There. Isn't that better?"

Already they can make out in the distance the start of the long yellow wall.

A moment comes, Kat thinks. A moment came. You're a glitch in a plan, an unfortunate error, and even your parents don't like who you've become. And once this knowledge properly sinks in, nothing else out there can scare you.

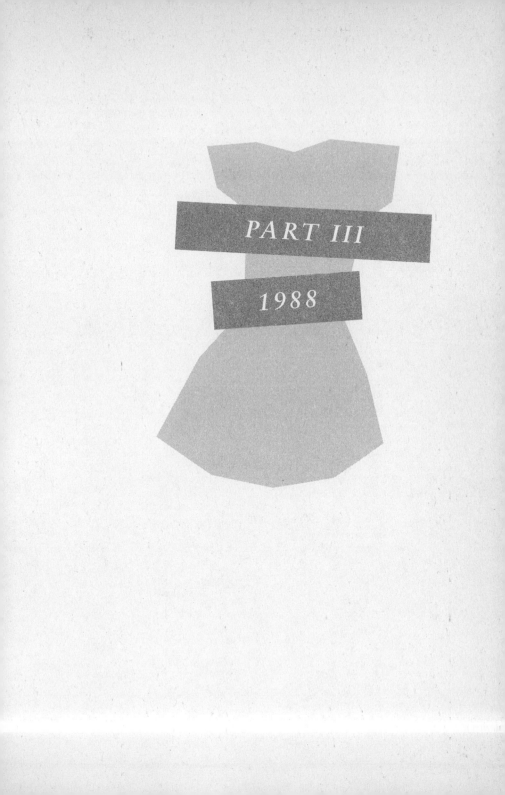

PART III

1988

14

Taganka Square is brisk and tireless, brimming with busy pedestrians, overrun by squealing traffic, tangled in a net of trolley wires, dotted with shops. Streets branch out from it like warm sunrays. Church domes loom just beyond its bounds; a little farther in the distance soar the lacy turrets of a neoclassical high-rise. But the square itself is unassuming, even squat. It's famous for the defunct Taganka prison; for the nearby bird market, where you can buy yourself a pet; and, of course, for the red cube of the Taganka Theater.

On this early January evening, Serge and Kat emerge from the theater entrance. With some effort, they cut across the square—it's really not that easy, with all the crazy traffic and plowed-in sidewalks—and duck under the stone arches of the subway.

"I liked the dude in the Dynamo jersey."

"You're serious?" says Kat.

"Why not? Didn't you like the play?"

Kat says she liked it, the marketplace style of it, the mix-
ing of eras. Football jerseys, bast shoes, leather, furs. She's
less sure about the folk songs and the choir. She says it's too
much folksiness for her.

"But isn't that the point?" Serge argues. "That the play's
about common folk?"

"Picked that up in some study guide, did you?"

He tells her not to snipe at him.

They've seen a matinee of Pushkin's *Boris Godunov*, and
Serge is right, it's not his fault that she's discomfited by folksiness. Why should it be his problem? He, after all, is a simple Russian boy, most likely of peasant stock.

Inside the subway station, she hands him a five-kopek
coin. If she didn't, he'd try to hop over a turnstile, risk
breaking his neck or getting caught. Out of sheer mischief,
mind you.

In truth, she did like the church choir, especially the
final "Eternal Memory" lament. It had an ethereal, chilling
strength, this song of angels. It touched her deeply, and then
it made her weirdly upset. Because, she says, it wasn't meant
for her.

"Don't be stupid," Serge tells her. "Pushkin belongs to
everyone."

Pushkin, perhaps, but not the choir. Lately there's been
much talk of the new patriotic group, Pamyat, which extols
Orthodox Christianity and blames all past atrocities and
present hardships on the Jews. At school, some teachers—
the old guard, primarily—wear crosses atop their turtlenecks and blouses, and one night, not long before the winter

break, Margo said how unnatural it was to have so many Jews on TV—Jew academics, Jew painters, Jew actors.

"Margo is certifiable."

"No kidding," Kat agrees. "Are you coming over for supper?"

They're already at the bottom of the escalator, and Kat can hear the grinding noise of the approaching train.

Serge says, "Are you inviting me?"

The train stops in front of them, the doors swish apart. Kat grabs the sleeve of Serge's jacket and pushes him inside.

"Your folks won't mind?" He always checks, always does this, even though he's spent countless evenings at their place.

"When did they ever mind?" she asks him.

ANECHKA IS fussing by the mirror. She got a new haircut yesterday, and now she's putting on new lipstick (some extravagant purplish shade), touching up her almost spiky hair, capping it with a raspberry-colored beret. She has not a minute to spare. She's running desperately late. "Have you seen my keys?"

"We just came in," Kat says.

"Don't be so sulky, baby. I need your bus pass, by the way."

"It's a youth one," Kat tells her.

"So what? I'm still a youth." She pecks Kat on the cheek and pockets her bus pass. Her perfume smells tropical, expensive—tart flowers, oil, wood. She goes through her checklist: keys, money, cigarettes, something to read on the subway. "Heat the soup, or whatever. Feed your father. Be good."

Kat gets nervous when Anechka is so manic. Is she on the verge of another breakdown or simply in a happy mood? After what happened last year, Kat would rather not take any chances.

Only after Anechka is gone does Misha poke his head out of the kitchen. "Aha, reinforcements!" he greets Kat and Serge.

"Where's she off to?" Kat asks.

"Some school thing." He throws up his hands. "She's like a hurricane, your mother. A cyclone." He's trying to be nonchalant, jocular even, but judging by the fact that he's been hiding in the kitchen, the two of them just had another spat.

Since September, Anechka's been teaching at a fancy humanities lyceum, where the students study Latin and art history and don't wear uniforms. It's housed in an old-style mansion, somewhere near Karl Marx Square. Kat hasn't been there yet. Anechka won't take her; she says she must get acclimated before she starts dragging in guests. It's not a free-for-all like other schools; it's quiet and exclusive, with pupils that are practically handpicked.

In Kat's opinion, Anechka seems acclimated already. She's collected up another coterie of students, and she's there until late every day. On weekends she takes her boys and girls to films, museums, or theater premieres. If Misha objects, she tells him that it's part of her responsibilities. If he doesn't believe her, she's got her contract here—he's welcome to see for himself.

He says he's just thinking about her health, about her energy levels.

"I'm perfectly healthy," she says. "Healthy and happy. We can't be like Siamese twins forever, attached at the hip." She tells him that they both need space to grow and develop.

Misha is uneasy with this state of affairs. He's unkempt and slack, showing up at school in the same dilapidated sweater, neglecting political seminars and grading, doing crosswords instead. Only when Serge is around does he light up a little.

Tonight he's glad to have their company. He actually makes an effort. "We're going to improvise ourselves some supper. What's on the agenda, hmm? Some potatoes, some herring. And what's that in a jar? A bit of salad? Not bad, my friends, not bad."

They excavate whatever they can find, pile it all on the scratched kitchen table. Plates for the salad, strips of news-paper for the herring. Kat brews a pot of tea.

"How was *Godunov*, you lucky beasts?"

Kat busies herself cutting bread.

The production had been supposed to open in 1982, but it got vetoed. This year, the banished director of the Taganka theater came back from abroad for ten days. Ten days to revive his masterpiece. It sounds insane, but they did it. Except that it doesn't seem that risky now. So much has come to light in recent years: banned novels, underground rock bands, magazine exposés, persecuted scientists, Stalin's camps, Red terror and White terror. Even Lenin is no longer considered a saint. A staging of a historical Pushkin play, no matter how innovative, can't possibly compete with the onslaught of the news.

Luckily Serge loved the play. He tells Misha about its unorthodox direction, the penetrating characters, the marketplace arrangement of the stage, the crutch as the symbol of tsarist tyranny. He has really blossomed under Misha's tutelage. The two of them continue with their tutoring, even when Misha is down in the dumps. They have long-drawn-out conversations regarding drama, comedy, and history. Autocratic regimes and the future of democracy. The Moscow Arts Theater and its recent split.

Kat still proofreads Serge's papers for spelling, but he needs no more assistance with content. He has ideas in spades, and, in fact, there are times when Kat herself draws a blank and is tempted to ask him for suggestions. It's as if they've traded places. She's grown directionless, lackluster, apathetic about her studies—though her grades, so far, are holding up. Left alone in the apartment, she blasts the tapes of new rock bands that Jules supplies her with, reveling in the glum aggression of Alisa ("We're together!"), the breathless absurdity of Nautilus ("Our kin is an uncanny something"), the star-crossed despair of Kino ("I'm going, close the door behind me").

After they finish their impromptu supper, they move into the living room. Kat turns on the nine o'clock news. Misha digs through his papers for an *Ogonek* article he long ago promised Serge.

"Did you give any more thought to what we talked about?" he asks matter-of-factly.

Serge doesn't respond; only the line of his jaw seems to tighten and his eyes get a stubborn, steely look. Misha's been on his case about surgery. All the doctors are urging Serge to have it—not only for the cosmetic benefits, but to decrease the chance of pain in the future, to lessen the pressure on his lungs. They say the curvatures are crushing his ribcage.

The girls from their class have been going under the knife since last year, and many teachers think it's a disgrace. They blame the trend on the attending doctor, who's writing a book on the so-called Krasnoyarsk method. The Krasnoyarsk surgery begins with two incisions, one at the base of the spine, the other at the top. A steel rod is threaded along, attached to the spine with hooks. At least it's not the slaughter it once was, back when they split the whole back open.

For the ambitious doctor, the gaggle must have been easy prey—despised, neglected, with blundering and heedless parents who didn't need much persuading. Three girls got shipped to Krasnoyarsk last May; in September, another four followed. Even those who dislike the gaggle are calling it a massacre and a scandal. The girls come back after the long months of recovery—spent flat on their backs, in a cast—and most report serious discomfort. Lena Romanova has had recurring inflammation. Kira Mikadze's gone for a repeat procedure—something's slipping inside her, a ratchet or a clamp—which means more pain, more scars, more months of missed schoolwork.

Serge is a different case, though. He's got the most severe scoliosis in their class, and even Professor Fabri has told him to think hard about his future. But Serge doesn't listen to doctors. He's done his own research, and on the basis of it he has decided that he's better off without this surgery. The risk of nerve damage alone, he says, is five percent. As for the pain, he can manage.

He won't admit it, but Kat knows that he's already got some pain. He can't be upright for long stretches—in crowded subway trains, in line in the canteen. He pauses in the middle of a sentence, his face gets white and tense. She's seen him sneak handfuls of aspirin, which don't seem to work very well.

After the nine o'clock news, they walk Serge to the bus stop. Tomorrow's Monday, the start of a new quarter, which none of them looks forward to.

Kat is hoping that the subject of surgery has been exhausted, but Misha brings it up again. "I feel as though you're gambling with your life, Serge."

"We all die, Mikhail Aronovich. A brick might crack my noggin tomorrow. A car might squash me like a crab."

"God forbid," Misha gasps. "Of course, you can't prevent all accidents. Still, you can try to be more cautious."

Serge lights a cigarette, and Misha frowns and looks away.

"It's like he has a death wish," he later complains. "Such

a lucid mind, such talent, and yet he's intent on destroying himself."

They've put Serge on the bus, and now they're ambling home. Misha keeps glancing backward. It's too early for her, Kat wants to say. He hates the idea of Anechka returning so late, crossing the vast snow-covered grounds by herself, walking along the poorly lit paths. Now that Serge is gone, Misha has sagged again, withdrawn into his worries.

But he never says anything. He never confronts Anechka, or even admits they're drifting apart. He nags her sometimes, which is his roundabout way of showing displeasure, saying he's worried that she works too many hours and doesn't eat or rest enough. Even to Kat he won't confide his true misgivings, and she feels that to challenge him would be too cruel, or impolite. And so it continues: the two of them walk home in silence, absorbed in their respective troubling thoughts, each feeling too shy to discomfit the other.

KAT SWIVELS her head—left to right, right to left—like a wind-up toy, like a Pinocchio. It's a new mannerism, something she does unconsciously. Jules has to point it out to her: "You've got your peripheral vision, you know." But Kat can't help it. For the first time in years, her neck feels so wonderfully loose.

She's been free of the brace since December, and she is still learning the movements of her body, how to arrange it, how to put it forward. "A beautiful figure," Professor Fabri said at the consultation a few months ago, but Kat knew the score—she was flawed. Passing a storefront, she'd catch her reflection in profile: the weak, sunken shoulders, the limp posture (despite the many hours of exercise), the bump protruding on the right. She'd never wear open-backed sundresses or saunter in bikinis on the beach. She won't be a mannequin girl, the way Professor Fabri so often promised.

Yet, she is free. Completely free. Every motion feels fluid and novel. Jules has also been released from her confinement, though for her it's hardly a big deal. She's never been very disciplined about her brace or worn it off campus. This is their final year. A year from now, they'll be attending normal high schools, wearing blue skirt-vest-and-jacket uniforms, routinely using makeup. The sooner the better, Jules says. To her, this school is like a bad nightmare, one she'd just as soon forget.

For Kat, though, it's more of a mixed bag. Good memories, bad memories. A big chunk of her childhood is here, her adolescent crushes, her first love. The drama club. Her parents. Here's Kat, age seven, representing Turkmenistan in the Friendship of the People pageant, in a red jersey dress and Tartar skullcap. Here she is in third grade, on an outing to the House of Culture with her class, the day she tripped at the bottom of the stairs, bloodied both her knees and skinned her arm. Fifth grade, and she is learning the Sirtaki circle dance. Sixth grade, and it's the opening night of their best play, *The Shadow,* and she is standing in the wings in her villager's garb.

She knows every hallway here, every chair, every scratch,

every bit of graffiti in the bathroom stalls—"Igor K. is a goat." "Bella plus Alex equals Love." She's been captured by this place. She's destined to be one of those who are forever coming back.

It's no mystery that there are such students. They get discharged, but they can't stay away. Some return in a dignified manner, for the alumni gatherings or discos or drama club rehearsals. Others rush in without warning, arrive abruptly, teary-eyed, practically flinging themselves at their favorite teacher or matron. "I can't be out there. I miss you guys." They pine for their lost buddies, the ease and coziness of communal life, the security of the school's boundaries. They may never adjust to being outside.

Sveta Vlasenko returned at the start of the year, after trying for the Pedagogic Institute and flunking the entrance exams. She now works at the school as their senior Pioneer counselor. She says it's a useful experience; it might even get her extra points next summer when she applies to the Institute again.

Kat likes to visit Sveta in her office, a narrow room just off the main walkway, filled with red banners, drums, and bugles. A long conference table runs along the center, though it rarely gets any use. It seems like such a dreary job: attending meetings, staging drill-and-song days, supervising the school's Pioneer board, overseeing the Komsomol panel.

"When are you joining Komsomol?" asks Sveta.

Kat tells her there's no point. Margo won't endorse her or write her a character reference.

"There are ways to work around your Margo. What do

you think is going to happen when you show up at some lyceum and they see that you're not in Komsomol?"

"I'm not going to Anechka's lyceum."

Sveta balks, looks down at her fingernails. Over the winter holidays she's chopped her hair to shoulder-length, which makes her look plainer and older. She's grown thinner, more rigid in her movements. There are dark circles under her eyes. She says she has insomnia. Last month she said goodbye to Vlad. He'd failed to get into the Medical Institute, fell short by one point, and now he's been drafted to serve in the navy. "Three years," Sveta groans. That's how long she has to wait for him.

Sveta is glad to have Kat's company. The elementary school teachers in block five across the campus are the only ones close to her age, and they steer clear of Sveta. Kat's probably not an ideal companion, but she can listen well. When Sveta's done talking about herself, she asks her about the holidays: what she did, where she went. How's Misha? Is he any better? Does he have any plans for the drama club? (The drama club hasn't met once since the beginning of the year.)

She never asks about Anechka, won't even mention her name. If Kat brings her up for any reason, Sveta is careful to change the subject. Anechka has forsaken her, severed their friendship, though Sveta did nothing to warrant this break. It's not just you, Kat wants to say. She can see it pains Sveta. The girl could use a word of kindness, a gesture of support, especially now that everything's turned so wrong and she's gone from being a Botticelli-like creature to an average college-age girl with a shoulder-length bob and mild, pleasant features.

Instead, they talk about Misha, who, Sveta says, had better snap out of his funk. The old guard is quietly stirring the pot. The bosses are unhappy. There were some outbursts at the last union meeting, which Misha neglected to attend. Creampuff reminded everyone that Misha was getting paid extra. "For what, I ask you. For the dormant drama club?" Margo made it known she'd always found him "unsavory": "All that supposed devotion to the children. Not worth a broken dime."

"He's sinking and he doesn't realize it, Kitten."

Kat says, "I tried to speak to him." But how do you speak to a person who's heartsick and overworked, who still runs twice a week to check up on his mother in Kuzminki? He's got to understand how tenuous his position is. The drama club has already lost its room. It's now the home of the school's Wartime Glory museum.

"We have to do something to rescue him," says Sveta. She'll try to round up some folks, trusted old-timers from the previous years. Alex, Nikita, Ritka. "He doesn't need to know what we're planning." She flips through her calendar, each day delineated, dressed up in multicolored ink. "We'll meet at our normal time, next Wednesday."

SERGE VOWS to be at the meeting, and though he was never one of the drama club regulars, Kat has to admit that his presence might help. He's been a good influence on Misha.

He says, "Your dad should come as well."

"We have to think it through first," Kat explains. "We don't want to overwhelm him."

"We do!" Serge disagrees. "Stagger him! Overwhelm him! Give him clamoring crowds and stuff. He's got to see that it's not some mundane obligation he must fulfill for a check mark. He needs a kick in the pants, some inspiration."

"How come *you've* said nothing to him all this time?"

Serge says it's because he's an imbecile, a dumbass.

But when they gather in Sveta's room next Wednesday, they're both relieved that Misha wasn't told. There are no crowds, clamoring or otherwise. Just Kat, Serge, and Sveta. Sveta says she tried to get their old gang, but they're all so preposterously busy with college.

"So," says Serge, "what do we do instead?"

"Maybe we talk to him?" says Sveta. "Tell him the school's not the same without the drama club. I work with the kids, I can see it in their faces, the lack of beauty and artistic outlets."

Serge rolls his eyes. "Pathetic."

"You got a better idea?" she snaps.

"I say we start without him," says Serge. "Get a script, cast the actors—"

Sveta laughs before he's even finished. "You want to run the drama club yourself?"

"Misha will step in when he's ready, when he hears about our play."

"A play?" Kat says, suddenly wary. She can't do it again,

can't take a repeat of last year. The last time she stepped on stage was at the dress rehearsal, the night Anechka collapsed, but even before that, she'd realized that her theater dreams were a delusion.

Sveta says a play would be too challenging. "It's best to start with something modest. An evening of music and poetry, maybe?"

"Modest my ass," Serge says under his breath.

"To hell with this false modesty," a voice booms in the back, and they all jump a little and Kat's heart does a leap. In the door stands Nikita, looking exactly as he did last winter, exactly as she pictured him week after week, in his dark denim jacket with its matted sheepskin collar. She had tried to convince herself she didn't like him anymore, that her crush on him was childish, unreal. For a while she even believed it, or at least she had more crucial concerns: Anechka almost killed herself that spring and despite Misha's claims to the contrary, Kat knew it was at least in part her fault. She was too guilt-stricken, too ashamed to think about him; but halfway through the summer things started to get back to normal and her memories of him returned.

"You said you couldn't make it." Sveta gets up and walks toward Nikita. She tries to appear displeased, even though her eyes fill with happiness and her whole face turns a lovely shade of pink.

And Kat's own face feels like it's stretching in a dopey grin. How easily her heart and mind deceive her. Her cheeks burn and she's glad that she put on some makeup, that she's wearing a decent sweater, and that two weeks ago she let Jules cut her bangs.

Nikita shakes Serge's hand, then takes a seat between Kat and the still pouting Sveta. "Cheer up, ladies and gentlemen. Of course, we'll do a play." He says the old guard has become completely brazen, while everybody panders to their whims. "The times have changed," he says, sounding a bit like Misha. "We've got to hit them where it hurts, show them what we're made of."

They kick around and debate some titles, mostly the latest perestroika prose they could adapt: *Life and Fate. Children of the Arbat. The New Appointment. White Robes.* Nikita says he'd like to write something original.

"But can you handle it," asks Sveta, "with your institute business?"

Nikita laughs. "I'm a man of many gifts."

They make a plan to meet again next Wednesday.

Kat follows Nikita out, and he is halfway down the stairs when she speaks. "What's going on with your institute?"

He pauses, turns, a little startled. He's looking at her, and his eyes twinkle with amusement, which makes her want to disappear on the spot. "You've grown up, Kitten. You're different."

For a moment they study each other, his laughter giving way to something serious and soft, and she's struck, once again, by how familiar he looks, a long-lost relative or soulmate, and she is sure he must feel it too.

"Sorry," he says. "I didn't mean to mock you."

"No harm done," she responds.

As for the institute, he tells her it's nothing. A minor inconvenience. A knot in an otherwise smooth line.

"That's good, I suppose."

"I'll see you in a week, Kat. Same place, same time." Before he leaves, he smiles at her.

15

"GET UP, GET UP, GET UP!" THAT'S HOW THE mornings start—with the music teacher bellowing in her overworked contralto, the sound of her heavy-booted footsteps, and then the abrupt burst of light. Kat stiffens as the voice draws near. "Get up, get up, get up. I'm leaving the floor in ten minutes precisely." That's what she does, the music teacher, to make some extra money: shows up before the crack of dawn to wake their floor, to herd them outside for morning exercises.

"Smolkina, do you need an extra invitation?"

There! She's made it, and now she won't leave them alone.

"I'm on duty," mutters Jules, burrowing deep under the blanket. But the rest of the girls groan and stir. Grudgingly, with effort, they draw themselves up. It's not as easy as it used to be, now that so many of them are weighted down with casts and metal. They are slow, so slow it must be maddening, pulling on their clothes, nursing their aching bones, making their shuffling way toward the bathrooms. Pain has made them dull, subdued their anger. No one gets in Kat's face anymore.

Kat's also on dorm duty this morning, so she doesn't need to hurry. Once everybody else is gone, she and Jules rise, get washed and dressed. Only then do they set about cleaning—tidy all the beds, go over the windowsills with a wet cloth. Slowly, leisurely, they drag their brooms over the pale squares of linoleum. Jules sings: "Don't Take Your Leave of Me, My Darling," and later, "The Reeds Were Whispering, the Trees Were Drooping." She's good at old romantic songs, her voice sonorous, spirited, with a strong undercurrent of hurt, and Kat, not for the first time, wonders why she won't train for a music career.

Jules says it's a stupid idea. "To be a music teacher like that cow we've got?"

Kat asks why not consider the stage, and Jules quickly says, "Not talented enough." Besides, she's got her heart set on diplomacy and international relations. She even has a high school picked, one with the specialized English curriculum. Though she claims her language skills have dwindled lately and she is worried she won't pass the entrance interview.

"Can your grandfather tutor me?" she asks. "My folks, of course, will pay him."

"He won't take your money," Kat tells her, but the more she thinks about it, the more she likes this plan. She's not that keen on facing Valentina, but she's missed her grandfather. She didn't see him much last summer, opting to stay in the city instead, pretending she was needed there. In fact, she was nothing but a hindrance, asking superfluous questions and getting in everyone's way as her parents attempted in vain to piece their lives together. It was then, at the end of that long, confusing summer, that she found herself without a destination or a goal.

Unlike her, Jules has gotten more tenacious. She's already mapped out her future, and the English school is merely a stop along the way.

She says, "Why don't you try it too?"

"Me and diplomats' children? Get real, Jules."

"Then what about your mom's lyceum?"

"And study under Anechka's surveillance? I think I've had enough of that," Kat says—though in truth it's Anechka who would probably discourage the arrangement. She takes her students to museums and theaters and never invites Kat along. Nor does she bring them home like she used to. She says it's because of the distance. Her new students, without exception, are bright, ambitious boys and girls. They have no time to fritter away on subway trains.

Privately Kat believes the reason must be her and Misha. Damaged, dispirited, they won't make the right impression, won't cast an aura of success. Whatever fiction of their life Anechka is trying to create, they won't fit her descriptions. And so, like half-mad ancient relatives, they must be kept hidden away.

Kat doesn't like to think about the future. She figures she'll just go to a local school next year, and who knows where after that. Most likely engineering. The Institute of Auto Industry, of Steel and its Alloys, of Oil and Gas. If she's lucky, by the third year of college she'll be married. It doesn't really matter where she goes or what stupid career she attempts. Whatever she does, she is unlikely to impress her parents.

Her parents welcome the idea of English lessons, though, and the Roshdals are also overjoyed. English is good. English is practical, the lingua franca of the world, useful even if you choose to study engineering. It is assumed that Kat will learn alongside Jules. Alexander Roshdal starts comparing curriculums, stockpiling tutoring materials, planning weekly sessions for the girls. And Kat plays along, acts as though she is also intent on bettering her English.

THEY GATHER on Sunday while it's still dark, meet under the blue Zodiac clock at Kazansky Terminal. Jules and Kat arrive separately, both in thick woolen sweaters, light jackets, ski boots, and woolen tights. Serge is already waiting. He's stomping in place and smoking fitfully, trying to fend off the cold. "A drink right now would be good," he says, and seeing Kat's eyebrows jerk, he quickly adds, "A hot one."

As always, it was Misha who suggested they take Serge along. Better than letting him languish in his lawless neighborhood or with his drunkard parent. At least, he said, in Kratovo there's fresh forest air and good food.

The trains are mostly empty at this early hour on Sunday. Kat, Serge, and Jules clamber aboard, settle on the hard wooden benches. Their carriage is unheated, and they squirm in the cold and huddle closer together. They doze, or stare dimly out of the window. Stations flash by. The train rattles along. Serge is reading *Doctor Zhivago*.

They've had two more meetings with Sveta, and Kat went to the first of the two, the one where Serge revealed his harebrained idea to stage *Doctor Zhivago*. Nikita turned up late that Wednesday. He stumbled in at half past eight, weatherbeaten, unwell, looking as though he'd been roaming the streets for hours. "The dean's office again?" Sveta asked him.

"They tell me I can try again on Monday—but only if I finish my three remaining labs. I said, who's going to give me all that lab time?"

They know his story by now, how he flunked his first winter exams—though "flunk" is not the word. He simply didn't take them. Something had happened to him in the summer. Instead of the Institute of History and Archives, he took his papers to the Institute of Railway Works, and in his happy-go-lucky fashion got in with hardly any studying. Then, halfway through the term, he stopped showing up to labs and lectures, missed so many assessments that by the time winter exams rolled up, he wasn't permitted to take them.

At the meeting they discussed *Doctor Zhivago*. Nikita seemed uncertain, disenchanted, but Sveta embraced the idea. She said she loved that book. It was about the Civil War and the Revolution, but most of all it was about passion, and Sveta, predictably, expected to play one of the two romantic leads. She actually said to Nikita as much—"You'll be Zhivago, and I'll be your Lara!"—as if he and Vlad were interchangeable.

The whole meeting was a fiasco. They only had about half an hour, not enough time to move forward or make any specific plans. Nikita didn't speak to Kat, and she had no time to seek him out. Though what could she possibly say to him? To take better care of himself? He coughed a lot that night. His cough was something terrible.

This week Nikita has bronchitis, and Kat isn't sure he'll ever return. Sveta and Serge met without him on Wednesday. Kat couldn't bring herself to go. Without Nikita there, their whole plan seemed preposterous and wrong.

Serge, of course, is still fully committed. He is sifting through *Doctor Zhivago*, taking notes, talking incessantly about saving Misha's job, about bolstering his confidence.

Kat says, "He's not a child, Serge."

"Grown people need help too once in a while." He shivers, and Kat thinks he really should get a better coat.

Jules, as usual, stays out of these discussions. It's her general principle—to not get involved. Good intentions, she reminds them enigmatically, have a way of turning out wrong. She stares out the window and breathes on her knuckles. "What's wrong with this train? Why is it so goddamn cold?"

By the time they arrive at the dacha in Kratovo, they are frozen to the point of numbness. But tea is already set out for them on the glassed-in, weatherproof veranda, the radiators ticking rhythmically, expelling puffs of hissing steam. Kat's grandfather reclines in his favorite rocker, an afghan thrown over his knees. Out on the storm porch rest Kat's and Jules's skis, which he has rubbed with special wax this morning.

"The snow's too sticky," he warns them and flinches a little, because the dampness in the air wrenches his hip and bad leg.

Valentina brings pastries and bread on a tray, small saucers of jam—cherry and raspberry. She fusses endlessly, pours their tea, pushes choice slices of cake toward each of them. She can't get over how cold they look, how thin. She rubs Jules's shoulders, gets Serge a dry pair of socks. She heaps on them this strange maternal tenderness, and only with Kat is she painfully formal.

Kat herself doesn't quite know where she stands with Valentina. Since last year, there has been little in the way of contact, just a dutiful phone call now and then, when Anechka can force herself to make one, and when she does she only speaks to Roshdal. A few obligatory questions about Roshdal's health, strained promises that everyone is well, that life is uneventful, normal, that she is not about to try to kill herself again. She never asks about Valentina, never concedes her existence or utters her name. She's too busy to talk anyway, she really must go, but here's Kat instead, the family's proxy, who can spit up more pleasantries and even visit on weekends.

A high-pitched yelp escapes from somewhere in the back, and Valentina goes to fetch the puppy, the chocolate miniature poodle named Bublic. Kat thinks the Roshdals have both gone a little loopy over the puppy: they spoil him rotten, feed him the most expensive tidbits, let him chew on the chair legs and even pee on Roshdal's leather couch. They call him their joy and their love.

And Kat has to admit that Valentina does look joyful. In the last year, she's softened, grown thicker in the waist and shoulders, lost some of her nervous, girlish verve. You wouldn't expect it, but it suits her. She comes back cradling the impatient Bublic and says she'll take him for a walk.

"Don't be too long," says Alexander Roshdal. "And button up your coat—the weather's foul."

She kisses the top of his head.

"She's like a child," he complains, once she is gone. "Completely heedless. Not even a pair of mittens or a hat."

After tea, they start their lesson. First come vocabulary drills. Then Jules and Kat take turns reading aloud from *Jane Eyre*, translating every paragraph and noting the unknown words, which Roshdal won't let them look up until later. They do some grammar exercises and practice sample dialogues. They finish off with a series of *Moscow News* articles. They're given three minutes per article, to scan it and grasp the central point, and then they have to summarize it. No help, no dictionary. Three minutes are so piteously short. But Roshdal says the exercise is useful—it makes their minds more nimble, their language acquisition more intuitive.

Serge takes no part in this schooling. He wanders off in the direction of Alexander Roshdal's study, and after a while returns with a book. Beckett, or Ibsen, or Brecht. A thick tome of Shakespeare's plays. These days he mostly goes for drama, the same books Kat herself used to devour. They probably still have her pencil marks. Now she eyes them with embarrassment.

Well then, no use sitting around. When the lesson is over, she and Jules go off to ski—there's a wooded area not far from Roshdals' dacha—while Serge and Alexander Roshdal stay in and drink more tea. It's only their second time in Kratovo and Kat is amazed by how well these two get on. Perhaps it's their physical ailments. They often ache on the same days, their bodies vulnerable to the whims of weather.

At two o'clock they all sit down to dinner—pea soup, some meat concoction in clay pots—and then, dazed by the warmth, they slip into a drowsy reverie. Roshdal expounds on the failings of perestroika prose. Kat wants to interject— she liked those novels—but her head has gotten fuzzy and slow. She leans back in her chair, eyes half-closed. Roshdal and Serge are talking about Brodsky's Nobel Prize. Jules shows Valentina a sewing pattern in the latest *Burda Moden*. The next thing Kat knows, it's evening, it's somehow gotten dark. She stretches and catches Jules's eye: It's time to go. Before they do, Valentina presses on them small jars of fruit and jam.

"Ah, what a life," Serge says, back on the train. He hands his jar to Kat because, he says, why waste the good stuff? He doesn't explain why he can't take it home himself.

"You know, you've got the best grandma."

"She's not my grandmother," Kat says.

Back in the city, Jules catches the subway to Taganka, and once she leaves, Serge tags along with Kat. He says it is for her protection—the least he can do is make sure she's safe—

and she, of course, doesn't point out that given his physical state, there's little he could do to ward off an attacker.

"So," Kat begins, "what did you two discuss today?" She's slightly irked by the quick bond that's developed between Serge and Roshdal, and has an urge to mock their chats. "*Julius Caesar*, was it?" Gone are the times when she and Roshdal were that close.

Maybe her teasing is excessive, but if so, Serge doesn't take the bait. He shakes his head. "Your grandpa, he showed me this thing. Said not to tell you, but goddamn it!" The object in question was a flyer, a nasty piece of work. "There was a cross and also some slogans. 'Get rid of Jews. Keep our nation pure.' Only instead of 'Jews' it said, you know—"

"Yids."

"He said these flyers, one day they just appeared. The one he showed me was pinned to their front door. You know what this means, Kat? Someone got over that fence of theirs. Your grandpa, he tries to act all calm, but really, I think he's scared."

"It could be kids pulling a prank."

"I don't think so, Kat. He said it's been going on since last summer. Not the flyers, but you know, the talk. 'Don't rent your summer houses to Jews, or they might burn down.' A house around the corner got destroyed. No one knows what started the fire. Then there was that old lady who was clubbed to death last fall, though I guess it was her family that did it."

She wants to dismiss it as gossip, empty talk that pension-

ers delight in while waiting outside the local store. But she
knows about the clubbed-to-death old lady, and suddenly all
she can think of is how easy it must be to breach a country
fence or door, how exposed you are in Kratovo.

"Your grandma's been taking it really bad," Serge goes
on. "That's why they got themselves that puppy."

"She's not even Jewish," Kat mutters.

He looks at her like she's being dumb. "Who cares what
she is. Honestly, Kat, are you heartless or clueless? I mean,
if you and I were . . . If somebody were threatening your
life . . ."

"Fine, maybe I'm heartless." They stop before her building entrance. Her eyes are smarting from the insult, and in
another second she will bolt. "I'm a heartless and horrible
person. A monster!"

He catches the sleeve of her jacket and won't let her go.
"Shut up, Kat. You're not. You're a decent person; it's just
sometimes you get so full of spite. I don't know what happened between you and your grandma, but she—Valentina—
she's kind. Maybe you don't realize it, but most folk aren't. I
mean, I should know, I've felt it on my hide. Not everyone's
this kind, not even real grandparents."

He stops, and for a while they stay quiet, her sleeve gripped
in his fingers, so it's almost like they're holding hands.

"You're scared?" he says.

"For them, not for myself. Here it's not so scary." She
nods at the rows of lighted windows, the grid of her apartment block. Nine floors, four sections, 144 identical apartment doors. It makes her feel safe, this anonymity. "Now

the atom bomb, that used to give me terrors. I'd look out the window and picture this horrific flash—"

"The mushroom cloud," Serge says, with relish. "Used to scare me shitless. Now I just think: Bring it on!"

"They won't, not anymore."

"I know. I'm just saying."

They stand like this a while longer, holding on to each other just outside the entryway. Inside, the elevator clangs, and Kat pulls back her hand. Reality asscrts itself: it's night, it's Sunday. Anechka's out at the opera. Misha is waiting upstairs and driving himself mad.

"Are you coming up?" she asks.

Serge looks hesitant. "It's late."

"Please come," she says. "Just for a short time."

EVERYONE LEAVES the school eventually, and Kat will have to leave as well, and though for years it was all she dreamed of, lately she's been flinching from the thought of it. She's not used to being out there. She doesn't like to be alone, on buses, trains, or even on a short walk to the bread store. Her brace is gone, but she can't shake the feeling that people are still staring.

This year—her last year—she doesn't mind the school at all. The schedule that used to feel so oppressive, the jumble of classes and medical procedures, now seems soothing, well controlled. The gaggle doesn't bother her, and Jules is here with her. Jules, who eventually forgave her.

At night, she and Jules walk up and down the campus

alleys, bored senseless with the never-changing scenery, but also remarkably content. Kat frets about Nikita, about his health and whether she'll see him again.

"Just call him," Jules says. She doesn't understand Kat's hesitancy.

"For one thing, I don't have his number—"

"And for another thing?" Jules says.

Kat shakes her head. "Forget it."

They round the corner, and Kat catches a glimpse of the familiar blue denim jacket, the stooping shoulders raised against the cold. It can't be, she thinks. It's not Wednesday. But yes, she sees, it *is* Nikita. He's leaning against the entrance gates and smoking, studying a frozen patch of earth.

"What's he doing?"

"Beats me," Kat says. "Waiting for Sveta maybe?"

"Or else for you," Jules says.

"You really think—"

"Go talk to him," Jules says. "I'm heading inside anyway. I think I've lost all feeling in my fingers."

It's not far, just a few dozen meters. Kat feels like she is soaring, though she tries to pace herself.

"Hey," she says, out of breath.

"Hey, kiddo."

In her head, she goes through a score of awkward greetings, all of which amount to "Why are you here today?"

He says, "Couldn't think what to do with myself. You ever feel like that?" and she says yes, though in truth she almost never has this sort of freedom. Most of her days are scheduled down to the minute, decided by somebody else. And yet, she knows what it's like to be restless in spirit.

"You want to talk?" she says.

He nods and turns against the wind to light a cigarette.

She leads him to one of the distant recesses on campus, where no one will spot them in the descending dark. He's finally seen her. He needs her.

HE SITS hunched on the swing, his face blurred in the limp evening light. Every few minutes he bursts into a spasm of coughing.

"I still want to write it," he tells Kat, who's standing before him and slightly to the side. "Even if no one stages it." They are talking about a play he has in mind, a historical play, because he's a historian at heart. "It's the last thing I have in me. The *only* thing."

"And college?"

"They're done with me there. Can't say I blame them."

"How did it happen? I mean, Railway Works? It's not what you'd been planning."

"Ah, yes." He laughs bitterly. "Of course. The idiot's dream, the Institute of History and Archives. I almost did apply, you know. Brought in all the paperwork. There was this nice girl in the admissions office. She took one look at my passport, another at my stupid mug, and said, 'It's none of my business, but you seem like a sweet boy, so I might as well tell you. I'd hate to see a boy like you get burned. We have no quotas for the likes of you.'"

"The likes of you?" Kat says, not understanding.

"Maksakov is my mother's name. My father's last name is Gelgor."

"You're Jewish?" she says. "Does Misha know?"

Nikita shrugs. "He can't keep track of everybody. Plus, I was so damned cocky, I didn't want anybody's advice."

He coughs again, the sound wet and painful, and she presses her fingers to his back, feeling the roughness of his jacket, the labored rattle of his breath. It's the first time she's touched him and it makes her light-headed.

"What now?" she says.

"The army, naturally."

"But you can't, Nikita. Please! You won't."

"Vlad trooped off like a good boy, and I'm no worse and no better."

"He had connections, though. Just ask Sveta. He got assigned to a good place."

"Nope, nothing here, no special connections. I bet for me it's the infantry. Infantry all the way. 'Forgive the foot sol-diers,' " he croons the famous Okudzhava song, " 'for being so thoughtless, foolhardy, and rash.' " He grins and looks her in the eyes, and she is split in half with pain and hope, unable to hold on to him or to let the moment pass. " 'Don't trust the foot soldiers . . .' "

16

"DON'T REPEAT MY MISTAKE," SAYS NIKITA. "DON'T set your heart on something and then give it up. I see it in you, Kat, this bright artistic spark, this sensitivity. You must have got it from your parents."

He shows up randomly. They don't make plans or dates, though he usually knows her schedule. They meet, as if by accident, in the secluded corner with the oak tree. Together they escape into the park. He comes when he's feeling unsettled. He says most likely he's already been expelled. He talks and she listens. Their talks are meandering, endless.

He asks how come she is able to do this: go off into the park with him. "Won't somebody miss you?"

She shakes her head. "No one will." These days Margo acts as though Kat doesn't exist; she's abdicated all responsibility.

And Kat—she's like a dog who's broken free of the leash. She wears eyeliner every day, along with mascara and lipstick. She teases her hair and pulls it high into a messy ponytail. She dresses in skirts, in Jules's fitted sweaters. Her coat is unzipped, her head uncovered, her scarf loose around her throat.

"What about your Serge? Where is he?"

"He isn't mine," she bristles.

"You become responsible, forever, for what you have tamed."

Saint-Exupéry! She'd known and loved *Le Petit Prince* for years, but then Nikita told her to read his other works. *Terre des Hommes. Vol de Nuit.* The stories of pilots, strong, fearless, and doomed. Even more doomed than Nikita.

Night after night they wander through this unkempt and vacant park, plunging knee-deep in the thawing snow, striking at the scraggly stalks of dead yellow grass. He walks fast. When he sees that she's fallen behind, he stops and waits for her. Like now, for example: her foot's gone through a patch of nasty ice. He helps her extricate herself, his steadying arm around her shoulders, her heart getting frantic, speeding up. It's you, she thinks. You've tamed me.

And Serge—what of him? He must have grown bored with their unfinished project, frustrated with their lack of dedication to the cause, the broken plans, the canceled meetings. Don't they care about Misha at all?

"He's right," Nikita says. "Every night I tell myself I'm going to write." He doesn't mean the *Doctor Zhivago* adaptation, but rather something of his own. Something honest and raw that will change everything. "And then, good grief, I don't know what happens. My brain goes sluggish, the wheels, the cogs, it all goes to hell."

"You're still ill," Kat says. "You had bronchitis recently."

"Maybe that's it." Nikita leans against a tree.

"What you need is a break." Kat stands before him. Her hands graze the tops of his shoulders; his hands slip quietly inside the pockets of her coat.

"A break," he agrees, tugging her closer. "Just don't get too excited, Kat. I'm a lost man, you know. Besides, things aren't easy for folks like you and me."

"I know," she says, her face upturned, as she rises on tiptoe.

KAT IS unfocused, feverish, forgetting her assignments, daydreaming through the hours allotted for homework. She barely squeaks through a history quiz, and later in algebra she's slapped with an "unsatisfactory." She nods when Beatrisa tells her to collect herself. The big exams are coming up. Kat says she understands. But all she can think of is seeing Nikita again, the heartbeat she felt through his sweater, the hard tang of tobacco on his lips. She finds herself smiling in odd situations and randomly touching her face. This must be what love really is, this ceaseless, pulsing madness.

Apart from Jules, no one knows, and frankly, it's not difficult to keep her new entanglement a secret. Misha stays most nights at Zoya Moiseevna's—because, he says, she's getting worse—and Kat tries not to think about what is becoming of their family.

Last Saturday they waited for Anechka all evening, waited until after twelve o'clock. Kat was reading, Misha grading, though neither could focus for long. Both listened for the clatter of the elevator, tensing every so often at the approaching noise. Anechka had gone to a play again. She was due back some hours ago.

Shortly after twelve Misha put on his coat. He said he'd wait for Anechka at the bus stop. Kat asked to come along, but he said no, she must stay by the phone. "In case she calls."

Of course, she didn't call. She came home in a taxi, while Misha kept on waiting—first at the bus stop, then outside the subway station—until the last train came and went. By the time he got home, Anechka was in bed. That night he slept on the floor of Kat's bedroom.

Jules is the first to suggest it: "She could be having an affair," she blurts out, as if it were the most natural thing. And maybe for Anechka it is.

Kat gapes at her. "You think?"

"Anything's possible, my child. People are nutty when it comes to love."

Kat isn't completely naïve: she has considered it, though fleetingly, before cringing and banishing the thought.

"I'm sure it's to do with her lyceum. She's so secretive about it."

"Just don't try to fix it," Jules warns, and Kat nods, not quite listening.

Next Monday, instead of going to school, she takes the subway to the Revolution Square stop, where she pauses momentarily between the sculpture of a girl with a pneumatic rifle and another of a border-guard lad with a bronze dog. She had the lyceum's address, but apart from that, she

realized, she didn't know very much. Not Anechka's schedule, not even which grades she was teaching that year.

The lyceum, a three-story mansion, stands in a quiet
cul-de-sac. Many years ago, it must have been somebody's
home. You can picture a family—something out of a Tolstoy
novel—young girls in pantaloons and longish dresses escaping to the garden outside. A handsome iron fence surrounds
the property.

Kat lurks outside the fence, some distance from the
entrance. After a while, it gets unnerving (she might be too
conspicuous), and she ducks into a doorway across the
street. For the first half hour, the schoolyard stays empty.
Then a young man—a teacher? a student?—comes out to
have a smoke. He must be a teacher, she decides; a student wouldn't smoke so openly. He is boyish, dark-haired,
dressed in a knitted vest, white shirt, grey slacks. His face
is narrow. He loiters on the school porch, glancing back at
the front door repeatedly as if waiting for someone—a colleague, a lover, a friend. Kat pictures her mother emerging
and joining him. They may exchange a glance, a cigarette.
Will their involvement be obvious? Visible? The image in
Kat's mind is so vivid, she's certain that it's going to happen.
But the man—who, on second thought, is too slight and tentative and no match for Misha—puts out his cigarette and
goes back inside.

Kat waits at least one more period, and then, when she
is ready to give up, Anechka indeed appears. She perches
on the steps without her coat, smoking and shivering, tugging the edge of her skirt over her bony knees. When did

she start dressing like this, in tight pencil skirts and frilly blouses and heels? She seems so dainty, so breakable, lost in a dreamy, wistful state, a bird that has escaped captivity. All she wants is a safe, neutral place, a place where she's just Anechka. Not a mother or daughter or spouse or mental patient. She is still young. She's hardly lived. That's the reason, Kat thinks. That's why she's been so secretive. The lyceum is her refuge, hers alone, and if Kat cares for her, she must go away and find her own refuge.

SHE MEETS Nikita at Mayakovsky Square, across from the famous statue of the poet. He pulls off her school bag and slings it over his own shoulder—two bags, his and hers, swinging along. "Where to?" he asks, taking her hand. She beams at him, carefree and gleeful. Their first stop is usually the record shop down the street. Apart from that, they're unconcerned with the direction. They might continue down Garden Avenue, wend their way through the Boulevard Ring, linger around Pushkin Square, where they'll splurge on a cup of hot chocolate. They've been spending the dregs of Nikita's last stipend—on movie or museum tickets, meat pastries, ice cream treats in waffle cups.

To be with him, Kat misses half her classes. Some days she skips classes altogether, returning to school in the evening, around homework time. She is changed, unrecognizable, buzzed on her own disobedience, and most of all, she is in love. Not that anyone shares her happiness. Even Jules, who is hardly a stickler for discipline, decides to give her a hard time. She says Kat is asking for trouble—everyone has noticed her absences, and if it weren't for her father's situation, the teachers would have spoken to the principal by now.

Trouble. Kat sighs. But they have so little time! No one knows when Nikita might get drafted. Besides, what's a couple of missed classes in the grand scheme of their unfurling lives? There are more important things than trigonometry and algebra.

"Namely?" says Jules.

"Namely, love."

Jules says, "What's gotten into you?"

Serge doesn't get it either. "Where were you?" he asks whenever Kat returns after a string of absences.

She winks at him and tells him it's a secret.

The secret can be the Moscow River embankment. On a cold day, it can be the Lenin Library or the Pushkin Museum of Fine Arts. It can be Arbat Street or Gorky Avenue, a park in Ostankino, a cemetery at the New Maidens' Monastery— the resting place of tsars and luminaries, where she and Nikita discover by accident the grave of the famous physicist Landau. "A Jewish physicist," explains Nikita. "He even won a Nobel Prize."

He keeps bringing up Jewish scientists, celebrities. The old actress Faina Ranevskaya, the historian Natan Eidelman, the bard Alexander Galich, the writer–dissident Yuli Daniel. It wasn't easy for them, to be sure. Some, like Galich, were forced to leave the country; others, like the poet Mandelstam, perished in Stalin's times. And yet, despite their ethnic handicap, or possibly because of it, they made their mark. Nikita says he didn't use to care, didn't make a distinction between his Jewish and non-Jewish friends. But now, since the fiasco at the institute, he feels that only a Jewish friend can understand what he's been through. "Like you, Kat," he says. "We're cut from the same bolt of cloth, me and you."

And he is right: they fit together so neatly, her head in the crook of his shoulder, his arm wrapped tight around her waist. They make out at the movies, in random doorways, on countless boulevard benches. They are typical homeless Moscow lovers, with no place to go and no future.

WHETHER OR NOT Kat's teachers are concerned, they don't speak to Misha about her. Maybe they think it would be fruitless (can he really discipline his daughter when he's barely getting by himself?), or maybe it's a measure of how low he's fallen. His colleagues avoid him as though his misfortunes might spread and infect them like a disease.

Whatever the reason, Kat is powerless to help him. When she does see her parents together—on weekends—it's like they're strangers already. They keep to their separate corners, take care of their private tasks, make individual servings of kasha or hot dogs. Or bread and butter sandwiches, if everything else fails. Though they do continue to combine their laundry.

When the Roshdals ask Kat how things are going at home, she isn't sure what to say. Roshdal says, "Tell your mother to call me," and Valentina looks away. Why do they bother to ask, Kat thinks, if they already know?

She and Jules have stopped going skiing. Whatever snow is left now lies in dirty, shriveled piles. After their English lesson, they stay inside by the woodstove. Reading or studying or dozing, or drinking cups of tea, while Serge plays dominoes with Alexander Roshdal.

One Sunday the Roshdals have a visitor, a friend of Valentina's who has barely escaped the violence in Sumgait. She is a tall, majestic-looking woman, with an aquiline nose and great mane of silvery hair. A guest of honor, she sits in Roshdal's rocking chair, her face impassive, perfectly composed. Her name is Gayanoush. All day she tells them stories.

They know little about this regional conflict; the TV has barely mentioned the recent unrest. And as for the city of Sumgait, they'd be hard-pressed to find it on the map. She tells them about the violence: the Azeri rallies in Lenin Square, the calls to kill Armenians, the drinks and narcotics served freely to the mobs.

The mobs combed through apartment buildings, looking for windows with no lights. They seemed to know where to go; they'd come prepared. "All these years we've lived side by side. Azeri, Russians, Armenians . . . And now if it weren't for the family next door, we wouldn't be alive. A good Azeri family. But how did *they* know what was coming?"

Of the slaughter itself, she says little. There were knives. There were axes. There was blood in the courtyards. They waited, but no help came. Three days later, when it ended, she packed up just a few belongings and left her home behind. She's now staying in Moscow with her eldest daughter. But it's her son that is the problem, a hothead and only nineteen. He ran off when they were on their way to the airport, ran off to join the rebels in Nagorno-Karabakh. There has been no news from him since.

She starts weeping softly and Valentina holds her.

She says, "You're so lucky, Valechka. Lucky you didn't have kids."

Valentina puts a blanket over Gayanoush's shoulders— "Hush, my darling. Come have a bit of rest. It's not over yet, you must preserve your strength"—and leads her off toward the bedroom.

An hour later, the woman has regained her composure. She says she is sorry, she hasn't had much sleep. At dinner, she and Valentina delve into lighter topics. They are both World War II veterans, former comrades in arms. They reminisce about their front-line past ("Valechka was always so popular!"), hum songs from their favorite *Sevastopol Waltz*, recall old bits of gossip. "Remember Shurik? What a joker! Two children, three grandchildren, lost his wife. Guess who sent me a card for my birthday?" They try to sidestep any perilous topics, anything that might suggest the recent tragedy and take them back.

But Kat can't stop thinking about the Sumgait pogrom, and on the subway ride home she keeps bringing it up—how for days the media was silent and the paramedics and police didn't respond. The whole thing, it seems, was planned. The mobs had lists of Armenians; their phones had been shut down in advance. She now doubts the safety of apartment living.

"But Sumgait's so much smaller than Moscow," Serge reasons. "And the tensions there are, you know, more acute."

"I wonder if our neighbors would hide us. They seem like nice people, but really, we hardly know them. We usually just nod and say hello."

Serge says, "It won't happen."

"And what if it does?"

Her voice falters and she looks away, embarrassed. He touches her hand, which is trembling. She didn't realize it was.

"I'll hide you," he tells her.

WHEN KAT comes home that evening, no one is there. Misha is probably at Zoya Moiseevna's and if so, he's likely to stay overnight. Zoya Moiseevna has grown grubby, shaggy-haired. She's like a child now, irrational, contrary, refusing to eat or be fed. She sits at the table, her mouth clamped tight. "Just try a spoonful," Misha begs her. She shakes her head. Or even worse, she takes it—only to spit it in his face. Alone, she raids the kitchen cabinets, eats sugar or hard candy.

Kat hardly ever visits anymore. Not because of the horrible rank smell that permeates the whole apartment, but because being with Misha drives her mad. She can't understand or excuse his inaction. He won't take his mother to the doctor, and he won't speak to Anechka, and his job situation is a mess. The drama club is doing nothing; stacks of untouched compositions gather dust on his desk; he's failed to submit lesson plans, assign important chapters, give dictations.

Kat dials Zoya Moiseevna's apartment and when Misha picks up, she doesn't ask if he is coming back.

"Do you know where Mom is?" she says.

"Probably working."

"Have you checked your watch lately? It's a quarter past eleven."

"I'm sure she'll turn up eventually."

"When did you see her last?" Kat says, and he says, "I don't know."

She stays up all night waiting, checking the phone every hour to make sure it's got a dial tone. She leaves the lights on everywhere, even in the toilet and the bathroom. She waits even after it's clear that Anechka has stopped coming home.

In the morning, Kat goes back to the lyceum. Since it's Monday, she knows that Anechka will be at work. She watches for her, as before, from the doorway across the street. She'll ask her, point blank, whether she's given up on them, whether she's having an affair, whether this means that she and Misha will divorce. She'll ask her if she's heard about the flyers in Kratovo and the unrest in Sumgait. She'll tell her everything about Misha's problems, how some teachers look away when he approaches and then disparage him behind his back, how the old guard says he's fizzled out and defaulted on his duties. And it's not just the teachers. Kat herself has heard two students from 9C complaining. "He looks unwashed, like he's on a drunken binge," said one of them, a blonde, bespectacled girl. "I thought Jews didn't drink?" the other one said in response.

The scorn in the girl's voice was unmistakable, the implication couldn't be clearer: Jews were unclean. Jews were vermin. They degraded Russian people, turned Russian children into alcoholics, spread drug addiction, AIDS, and rock and roll. Kat's heard it all—from TV, from the gaggle, and even from some of the teachers. There are those who, like Creampuff or Margo, delight in bringing these tidbits to school—pamphlets, hearsay, articles from *Young Guard* and *Our Contemporary*. Any public figure they found objectionable had, according to them, a secret Jewish last name. Margo even ventured that the Jews had sat out World War II. Her mother, she claimed, had seen it with her own eyes, perfectly healthy young men hiding out in Uglich, evacuated. It was Russians, she said, who won the war.

Kat found it easy to deal with people like Margo. You knew where you stood with them, you knew who they were. It was the others, the circumspect ones, that were tricky. The ones who kept quiet or talked of "our Russian nation," of going back to their faith and their roots. What did they mean by that exactly? What did they think of Kat and Misha? You had to rely on your instincts, your powers of observation, pay heed to the slightest inflection, the smallest of smirks. You never trusted anyone completely.

Was it like that for Anechka at her elite lyceum? Kat thought probably not. Why else would she leave Kat and Misha behind so decisively, so eagerly?

Kat waits all day. Soon after two o'clock, the school

begins to empty out. A dirty orange Lada pulls up outside the fence. It's not an eye-catching or fancy car; it blends in so well with the scenery that Kat almost misses it at first. The man at the wheel is reading a newspaper. Someone's parent perhaps? He seems impatient. Anechka said the students here were handpicked and many had important parents. The man is dressed in a leather jacket; he's bald and has a bullish boxer's build. He seems like the type, though his car is too grimy for him to be anyone special.

This is when Anechka appears, in her long coat and high boots and that atrocious raspberry beret. She squints around for a second, and then, before Kat can react, she practically flies across the schoolyard. The man leans over to unlock the car door and she slips in, matter-of-factly, like she's done it a million times. They kiss in a quick, practiced way. They kiss! Her mother and the bald guy in the Lada car.

The man guns the engine and they are gone in a small cloud of exhaust, gone before Kat can scream or memorize the license plate. The license plate! She'll laugh about it later, though at the time it seems like the only thing to do. What was she going to do with it? Rush to the local police station? Report an abduction? Explain that her mother couldn't mean it, couldn't kiss a bald stranger unless she'd been bewitched? Brainwashed? How dumb she will feel, how gullible, when she recalls standing there in the street trying to make out the dirty orange car, as if finding it could salvage anything.

17

ON A WET AND CHILLY SATURDAY, KAT MEETS Nikita at their usual place. Her shoulder bag holds a few books, some clothes, and a toothbrush. She hands it to him and says, "I need a place to stay."

Nikita says, "What happened?"

She says she and her parents had a disagreement, though she won't divulge any details. She's too ashamed and furious to tell him what she saw on Monday: her mother in flagrante, the orange Lada car.

"One disagreement?"

Kat says one is enough. "If you can't put me up, I'll go somewhere else." She can go to Jules, or stay in Kratovo, or sleep at a train station with the best of vagabonds. What she can't do is go home. She's got no home anymore. After everything Anechka has put them through, now this final betrayal. And what is Kat supposed to do? Play along? Be a dutiful daughter? Pretend she saw nothing?

Nikita takes her to a drab three-story building not far from the Barricades station. "It's not where I *really* live," he says, as he unlocks the door on the top floor. "My brother rents a room here, but right now he's not using it."

The place has an awkward arrangement: a poorly lit hallway, a string of strange adjoining rooms, a kitchen with nothing but a stove and sink.

"Does anybody live here?"

Nikita says, "Some students. It used to be a dorm, I think."

His brother's room is stuck haphazardly behind the kitchen. Inside lies an old, stained mattress. No tables or chairs or lamps or potted plants. No books. Not even a small radio.

Nikita smiles apologetically. "It's dreadful."

Kat slowly takes off her scarf and coat. "It's dry," she tells him, "and it's warm." She cautiously sits down on the mattress.

She knows, in general outline, what happens between men and women. She's looked at the sex manuals in Jules's home: the hand-drawn pictures of bearded, naked males and sluggish, wide-hipped female bodies. They seemed crude, those drawings, purposefully unflattering, as if meant to discourage you from having sex. Sex, they seemed to say, was for married, unattractive couples.

Nikita moves around anxiously. "Are you thirsty?" he asks. "Are you comfortable? Do you want something to eat?" He peeks into the kitchen, which, by the looks of it, hasn't seen food in weeks.

Kat tells him she's okay. "Come sit with me." She pats the mattress.

After some hesitation, he joins her. It's not very cozy or restful—they might as well sit on the floor. She stretches out on her back. He settles down next to her. They lie side by side, gazing up at the ceiling, unsure how to be, how to act.

"Imagine if your parents saw us."

"Don't think of them," Kat says, and pulls herself up on one elbow.

They lose track of time for a while, their bodies jammed against each other, their lips becoming rubbery and sore. They do manage to keep most of their clothes on, though he's shed his sweater and her blouse is now unbuttoned. The room grows dim and they barely notice; only later do they find out that the light in the room doesn't work. She loves how easily she can entrance him: a knee pushed just so, a certain tilt or shift in pressure, and his whole body goes crazy in response. He has to excuse himself a couple times— to get a sip of water, to use the bathroom.

"Are you tired?" he asks when he returns. She kisses his throat, says no. She leans into him, simply to test once more this new and thrilling power. Nice girls don't do this. Nice girls stay home—but she is not a nice girl. She's a wicked, wretched creature, no better than the trashy girls at school who get drunk with the local boys and then strip naked in the bushes.

"Wait, Kat. We mustn't." He sits up abruptly. "It would be like taking advantage of you. What if tomorrow I'm

gone? I'm a transient person right now. You've read what the
army is like in our country, with all the violence and hazing.
I might not come back in one piece."

"Can they send you to Afghanistan?"

"They can do anything."

She tucks her face into his shoulder, crestfallen, ashamed
of her eagerness, while he absentmindedly strokes her hair.
She's just like her mother, a wild, selfish woman.

That night they sleep next to each other in their clothes,
except Kat finds that she can't sleep. She's been like this all
week, nodding off around midnight only to wake up an hour
later, churning with heartache and frustration, thinking of
confronting Anechka, plotting what she might say. The
words spin themselves in endless arguments.

In the morning, she and Nikita have a makeshift breakfast of tea and bread with dried-up jam, and later in the
afternoon they go out to look for groceries.

"I don't mind you staying," says Nikita, as they walk
back with their bags. "But aren't you too young to run away
from home?"

"Home?" she says. "What's that?" Then she tells him of
Anechka's bald suitor and Misha's refusal to see that anything is wrong.

"Good grief," says Nikita. "Are you sure?" Not that he
doubts her story, but Anechka and Misha—how can they be
with anybody else? They are these perfect, ethereal beings,
the stuff of poetry and legend. Orpheus and Eurydice.
Marie and Pierre Curie. If their love is untenable, what hope
is there for anybody else? Poor old Misha, he says. Poor Kat.

At the end of the block, he pauses by a pay phone. "Call him, Kat. He's going to worry."

"I bet he hasn't even noticed that I'm gone."

She tries to tell him that her parents aren't perfect, that for all their talk of sacrifice and honor, they can be weak and self-absorbed. Nikita remains unconvinced. "I still feel you should call them."

Outside the apartment they stop. There's music blaring through the door and they glance at each other, unsure whether they should enter, except that they have no other place to go. Inside there's a party—twenty people or more—judging by the music on the stereo, the steady din inside the rooms, the twang of a guitar, the dull clink of bottles.

Before Kat and Nikita can escape into his room, they're intercepted by the host, a tall, emaciated-looking boy with weird hair, shaved in the back, long and bleached in the front. He's got an earring in each ear, one in his nose. His smile is so intense it actually might bespeak insanity.

"Nikita, my friend, good to see you! How's your brother doing? He's such a character, your bro. And who is this lovely young lady? You must join us, you wonderful people. We've got some drinks and grub."

They attempt to decline, but the host is insistent, almost dismayed at their reluctance to join in, and it's true they haven't eaten much today, and what they've got in their bags is just hot dogs, potatoes, and milk.

In the large central room the lights are off and there's dancing. Two rooms over, a small crowd has gathered around a modest dinner table. There are some empty vodka bottles and a couple that are still half-full. Some bread and sardines. A cracked dish with the dregs of a potato salad.

"Howdy," says a hulking lad dressed in a sailor's shirt, who seems to be the instigator here. Their host has dissolved as suddenly as he appeared, and they're left at the mercy of these folks. The sailor boy tells them to sit. "Better to be cramped but with no sore feelings." He orders the rest to make room. They crowd onto a battered couch: Nikita, Kat, the sailor, a country bumpkin boy with a guitar, a surly girl with streaked and bristly hair.

The sailor, Kat thinks, is kind of handsome (though definitely not her type), dark-haired, square-jawed, green-eyed. He's like an actor in a movie—a Red Army commissar or the skipper of a mutinous ship—though his features are a tad too heavy. He speaks in a slurry, lisping way, and Kat can't tell if it's a real speech impediment or whether he just does it to be silly.

He pours her vodka in a faceted glass, before passing the bottle to Nikita. "Drink," he says. "Drink up. Booze is our riches." He is looking at her with approval, at her miniskirt (Jules's), her low-cut lilac sweater (Anechka's), her legs in sheer nylon hose; and though he's nobody and she's got Nikita, his admiration pleases her.

She hasn't eaten anything since breakfast, but she picks up her glass gamely and takes a midsize gulp. The horridness, the burn of it, knocks out her breath for a few seconds, but soon the warmth begins to spread inside her chest, and suddenly her problems begin to seem fuzzy and distant. So what if her mother is having an affair? So do hundreds of women and men. She doesn't need her mother anyway. She's not a baby.

Nikita says to go easy. She smiles in a dopey, already drunken way—not that she's drunk, she can't be yet.

"She's a pro," says the sailor, "a real Russian girl who knows her liquor."

Kat takes another, smaller, sip.

"What college do you go to?" she asks.

The sailor grins. "The Institute of Alcoholic Engineers." The surly girl bares her teeth (is she the sailor's girlfriend?) and the country bumpkin nods like he agrees.

Kat is squeezed on the couch, Nikita's arm around her shoulders, her knee bumping the sailor's knee. Without the drink, it would be awkward. She takes careful swigs of her vodka—like swallowing fire, but worth it—and laughs at the sailor's dumb jokes. When she hears a rock song she knows, a manic underground song she's only heard a couple times before, she tells him it's her favorite.

"Mine too," he says. "Let's dance." He pulls her to the dark room with the stereo. She looks back to Nikita, who just shrugs. Doesn't he want to have some fun, to be one of these drunk, uncomplicated people?

The song is boisterous and fast. Kat abandons herself to the music, swivels her hips, extends her arms, and it seems like for once in her life she can be normal.

The next song comes and it's a slow one, and now the sailor clutches her too close. He twists her at the waist in crude, exaggerated motions, grinding his hips into hers. She tries to draw back, but he won't release her. "You're such a fox," he mumbles. "What's that kid doing with a foxy thing like you?"

"Let go of me," she says. He acts as if he doesn't hear her.

He runs his hands over her back, and he must sense its weirdness, because all of a sudden he loosens his grip.

She wriggles free and rushes to Nikita. She says, "I'm such an idiot." He holds her, lets her whisper her apologies into the warm skin of his neck, that spot where the skin meets the rough yarn of his sweater, the faint trace of cough drops, aftershave, and sweat. Without him she's nothing, a drunk girl at a party, motherless, homeless, easy and physically flawed.

"Take me to bed," she says. "Make love to me."

INSTEAD OF going to school that week, Kat stays at the apartment. On a couple of mornings she sneaks home, to shower and pack fresh clothes, then dashes back to their small room. She lets herself in with a key Nikita gave her. Most days the apartment is empty; only she and Nikita are there. Nikita makes their dinner—eggs, hot dogs, fried potatoes. He asks her if she's hungry. "Starving," she says. They eat cross-legged on the floor, a pot or frying pan steaming between them, and later they move to the mattress, to nap, talk, or make love. He jots down notes for his fledgling historical play, which features both Stalin and Peter the Great. Or he reads Natan Eidelman, his favorite Jewish historian, who seems to have defied all odds.

"Did you know he went to Moscow State University?"

Kat says that that was the fifties, a totally different time.

"He stuck to his guns," says Nikita, "while I, like a coward, backed down before giving it a try. And now look where my caution has got me. The exact place I was so eager to avoid."

"Yes, but you haven't been drafted yet—"

He says, "It's going to happen."

"Maybe they'll somehow miss you, or give you a deferral of some sort, and then when summer comes you'll go for the History and Archives."

"Oh, you!" he says, hugging her. "You're such a dreamer." And yet he must need her assurance, the strength of her devotion and her love. No matter what happens, she knows she will stay with him.

They talk about Sumgait and Kratovo and what it means to be a Jew, to live in a world so hostile and random. "What I've learned," says Nikita, "is that you can't betray your conscience. Better to take a risk and crash, go to prison or into the army, than lie low like a reptile all your life."

Reptiles, Kat thinks, and then she thinks of Anechka and Misha. She used to believe they were heroes, dissidents, risking their lives every day. But were they really? They never left a trace or signed any important letters, and when they published anything, in small samizdat magazines, they always used fake names. Was it such a big risk to copy manuscripts or watch a demonstration from across the street? True, they spread the word among their students, they had those illicit gatherings where they played Okudzhava and Galich songs and read Solzhenitsyn's works aloud. There was danger in that, she supposed. A slight danger. A student could have blurted out the truth to someone and then they would have lost their jobs. But they stopped the gatherings around the time Kat got sick. It was all in the past, in the seventies.

"Don't be unfair," says Nikita. "They're human, they did what they could. Most people in their place did nothing." It seems that he still worships them a little, still trusts in their bohemian, freewheeling ways, unwilling to accept that it's a sham or a magic trick, at best—a beautiful illusion.

Some nights Nikita goes out to the phone booth, since the apartment has no phone, and then one night he goes home. His parents, he says, want to speak to him. He tells Kat to be careful, to lock the door and stay inside their room. She hates being there without him.

"Playing house?" Jules asks when Kat calls her on Saturday. "How long are you planning to live in that dump?"

"It's not a dump. We both happen to like it."

"We?" Jules says, in her sarcastic voice. "I thought he was getting drafted. Just do me a favor and don't get knocked up."

"We're being careful," Kat says, though she doesn't really know if they are or not. She just takes it for granted that Nikita's doing *something*, and if they fail then so be it. She pictures it sometimes, becoming pregnant with his child. Working by day, studying by night, living in squalor while Nikita's in the army. It seems like something from a movie, a dignified if taxing life.

She does return to school the following Monday, because Nikita says she must. There's no sense in her getting kicked out of eighth grade, in both of them becoming failures. She misses him terribly, though he comes to see her twice that week. She wonders what he does without her. Does he stay in their room or with his parents? Read, study, or work on his play? Or does he give in to despair?

School is torture, everyone a stranger shooting Kat sneering, mean looks, though Jules insists she just imagines it. "You missed a week of school—it's not that weird. They probably think you had flu." But Kat knows better. Never before has she felt like such a misfit. She can't conceive of speaking to these people, trusting them enough to tell them something true. It's like she and Nikita have their own language. Even Jules wouldn't get it, the sort of things the two of them discuss. Whenever Kat mentions being Jewish, Jules turns dismissive, brusque, as if she finds the fact embarrassing.

All week Kat keeps avoiding Misha, fleeing his classroom after literature and grammar, hiding in crowded hallways, even ducking into the bathroom when she sees him advancing her way. It goes on like this for a few days, until they bump into each other at the canteen entrance, Kat leaving, Misha going in.

"Are you all right then?" he says, stumbling, not daring to look her in the eyes.

"Couldn't be better," she answers.

"You want to maybe talk about it?"

"About what?"

He shakes his head. "You know, life."

"Life's shooting up like a fountain," she says, being a jerk. But it's all she can think of at the moment: song lyrics, adages, clichés. "Life is not a picnic." "Life is not a bowl of cherries." "Don't feel down, pal—your life is still ahead of you." "If you live with wolves, you have to howl like one."

Of course, he has to know that she left home and that she missed a week of school. And yet, once again, he does nothing. How like Misha to avoid the slightest conflict, to descend into utter passivity, to suppress, even obliterate himself. She could step in front of a bus tomorrow and he'd make no move to save her.

"How's Anechka?" she asks him pointedly.

"There's nothing wrong with her," he says.

"Is that so? You spoke to her? You know where she's staying?"

Misha says, "Stop it." He raises his hand as if trying to defend himself.

"She left," Kat says, "and you—you *let* her go!" But Misha won't listen; he just walks away.

Jules says she is wasting her energy. She should be thinking of her future. It's just a few months until their graduation, and Kat's been acting stupid and so far made no plans. On the way to Kratovo that Sunday, Jules makes a list of schools Kat should apply to: two English schools, one with a strong humanities curriculum, plus Anechka's lyceum, which she adds despite Kat's protests. Local schools, Jules says, are for plebs and nobodies, and Kat is way too smart to go there. Nor can she stay at their current school, because that would be hell.

Kat didn't want to go to Kratovo this morning. She'd missed the last two Sundays and it seemed easier to skip this one as well. She woke up on Nikita's mattress, her forehead pressed against his back, and thought, why can't they stay like this all day? But soon enough he stirred and said he had to meet his brother—he'd promised to help him with something, a move, a room, a broken-down car—and that he'd see Kat in the evening, after it was done.

So now she's stuck on this train, and Jules keeps nattering on about Kat's lack of motivation, while Serge gazes out the window, as if he can't be bothered with either of them. He's been disapproving about Kat's absences, incensed that she'd behave in such a reckless way, and as for Jules's plans, he probably thinks them a fantasy. She fully expects him to ask what's wrong with their current school, why it's good enough for him but so detestable fo Kat. She wouldn't know how to answer.

"There's this school I heard about," he says, still focused on the passing scenery. "Part of the Gnesinsky or something."

"Acting?" Jules asks. "Kat has no interest in acting."

Serge says, "I thought she might. But what do I know? I'm your village idiot, your holy fool."

"Touchy," Jules observes. "Fine, I'll add it."

"Gnesinsky or something," she scribbles at the bottom of the list, reading it aloud as though to pacify him.

Kat thinks how easy it must be for the pair of them to give advice. To live in a world with no limits, where no one will squint at your passport. To become a diplomat, journalist, historian—or even an actress, if you're so inclined—

because, as the famous song goes, all roads are open to our youth! Unless you're a Jew, of course. In which case you find yourself just like Nikita, standing in the admissions office and being told about quotas.

It occurs to Kat now how much she must have changed. She's a different person—a better person, to be sure, but also wearier and older. In just a few months, her world has grown simple: it's her and Nikita and no one else. So what does it matter what school she might attend next year, or if she's going to stay in school at all? They'll take it day by day. They'll figure it out together.

It's clear, though, that for Jules school is important, so maybe it's not that surprising when later that afternoon, she turns to speak to Alexander Roshdal.

"I'm so grateful, Alexander Pavlovich. My parents, too— they say I've made tremendous progress. But you see, I've only got two months before my interview, and the school is simply too competitive. They've been doing geography in English. Next year it's modern history and math. So my father's made arrangements with another tutor. I hope this doesn't upset you." She trails off, looks down at her plate.

"Thank you, Jules," Roshdal says. "I appreciate your candor. Of course you must do what is best for your work."

"You're quitting just like that?" Kat says. She's hurt that Jules didn't think to tell her. But now she sees that it's Valentina who's the most upset. She seems unsettled, almost frantic, looking from Jules to Kat to Serge, as if afraid she's missing something. "Jules," she says, "darling, you won't be coming next weekend?"

"I'm sorry," Jules says, "I'll really miss my time with you."

"What about the rest of you, children? Surely you're coming back."

"They're always welcome here, Valechka. I think they know that."

Serge jumps in to say that they'll see them both next Sunday.

But how can he promise that? Doesn't he know that they won't be coming back? Or they might—for a birthday or berry-picking in the summer, but not like they used to and not every weekend. Life has already scattered them to their respective corners.

She's about to say she can't make it when Serge catches her eye. Don't do it, he seems to be asking her. Don't tell them yet.

Kat drops her head and mutters that she has to check her schedule—school has gotten so busy, what with the upcoming exams.

Serge rolls his eyes theatrically. "That's Kat for you. Always fretting about her grades."

"Grades are important," Roshdal says. "Maybe next week you both should take a break and study."

"We'll see about that," Serge says, and what a perfect little scene they've just enacted. The three of them, they ought to be on stage. Valentina leans back in her chair, relieved. What good children they are, Serge and Kat. What good actors.

JULES CATCHES the subway to Taganka, leaving the two of them together on the platform. Serge probably expects to go with Kat, to shadow her home like he always does. She could have thought of an excuse, but she's too tired now. Tired of faking it. Tired of hopping on and off trains. All she wants is to climb into bed. Except there isn't even a bed where she's going, just the old saggy mattress that makes her back cramp.

"I'm not going home."

"Where *are* you going?" Serge says.

"Nowhere," she says. "It's personal."

"Really, Kat. What are you doing? You don't even look like yourself."

"I'll take that as a compliment."

"It's not a compliment," he says. "You look haggard, like some consumptive woman. Like Bones on a bad day."

"Shut up, Serge. That's a horrid thing to say."

"It's like you're not the same." He touches her elbow briefly. "You used to be, you know, *driven*. You used to read that acting book."

"That was ages ago. All girls dream of becoming actresses, all boys, astronauts and firefighters. It's something we all outgrow."

"I never wanted to be a firefighter. A taxi driver, maybe, but just for a short spell."

"I'm being serious," Kat says.

"Okay, but what about your father? He's been so sad and lonely lately—"

"Why don't you ask him to adopt you then?"

She regrets it the moment it's out. Something changes in Serge: he stands taller, his face becomes more angular. He gives her a sharp, chilly look. "I'm good with what I've got. I never asked for charity."

"That's not what I meant—" Kat begins, but he's already gone. She runs after him, but he's dissolved into a crowd of passengers, amidst steep staircases and intricate walkways. A slight, quick-moving boy in a thin coat, who learned years ago how to vanish.

18

NIKITA DISAPPEARS AT THE END OF APRIL. ONE
Saturday Kat shows up at the apartment and he's
already gone. Except she doesn't realize he's gone. She thinks
he's out getting groceries for them or staying the night with
his parents. Or maybe he's straightening things out at the
institute, filing a last-minute appeal. Maybe his brother is
helping him. Normally he tells her in advance, or leaves a
note, if he's spending the night elsewhere, but tonight she
can't find anything. She stays up as late as she can manage
before sliding the door latch closed, and even in her sleep
she listens for his footsteps on the stairs.

Next day the apartment is empty again. Kat goes to the
phone booth and rings his home number, but no one picks
up. She walks to the subway and waits outside the entrance.
All she's eaten today is an apple and she's got no money
to buy food. She knows he wouldn't just abandon her, so
it must be something urgent, something bad. An illness or,
God forbid, an accident. Or maybe he's been drafted? Maybe

that's how it happens, with no grace period or note. She tries to call twice more, but the phone rings and rings and there's no answer. She doesn't know how to reach Nikita's brother, or even where his parents work.

Doubt creeps in; it always does when Kat's alone. What if Nikita really is gone? What if he never returns? Without him, her life seems long and meaningless, full of bad choices, precarious turns. She thought that he would help her. He'd tell her whether she should go to high school or maybe learn some useful trade. He'd introduce her to his parents and she would stay with them when he was drafted.

Next week at school, she continues to wait. At first she thinks he might come for her, and she waits every night outside the front gates. She cuts class twice to check on the apartment, but each time the room is exactly as she left it, no sign of him being there. On Thursday, she even asks Sveta about him.

"Nikita?" Sveta says. "The last time I saw him was three weeks ago. We went to a concert at the Gorbunov House of Culture."

Kat thinks that Sveta might be lying, or possibly she has her weeks confused. Because three weeks ago Nikita was with Kat. Three weeks ago they were already lovers.

"He's fine, Kat. The thing you need to understand is, he's a sweetheart but completely unreliable. Look what a mess he's made of his life."

"You don't get it," Kat says. "You don't know what it's like—"

"Ah, Kitten." Sveta smiles. "You've got a crush on him."

ON FRIDAY morning, Misha asks Kat to see him after classes. He's especially serious this morning and Kat worries that something must be wrong: Zoya Moiseevna has taken a turn for the worse, or Anechka is in some kind of trouble.

"I know you think I've been a bumbling idiot, but, Button, let me tell you, this can't go on anymore. You can't miss school for days or cut half your classes. I had an hour-long talk with the headmistress. I had to tell her you were helping with your grandma, that she was in a critical state. I had to *lie* for you, Button. Do you know what that felt like?"

"You didn't have to," she tells him, but secretly she is relieved he did. "Don't worry, I won't miss school again. Are we done? Is this it? Because I don't want to be late—"

"Wait," he says. "You really think we haven't noticed? It has to stop, Button. You've got to come home."

"I can't," she says. "My life is elsewhere."

"It's not a good life for a schoolgirl."

"Is that all I am to you?" she says. "A schoolgirl?" She grabs her bag and walks toward the door.

"There's a lot of talk," says Misha. "I have a pretty good idea who you're staying with. I never thought he would do such a low thing, but I guess one never knows."

"That's right," Kat says. "You don't know. Because you never pay attention. Your students, they just come and go. You convince them they're special and that you care, and then you turn around and forget about them. I bet you're not even aware what Nikita's been going through. Well, for your information, he's got more honor and integrity than you and Mom combined. Plus, unlike you, he loves me——"

"How can you be so unfair! Your mom and I don't love you? After all these years? After everything we've done and sacrificed?"

"You got a cushy job because of me," Kat says. "You sacrificed exactly nothing."

SATURDAY COMES and Kat returns to Nikita's apartment. She's got all of her notebooks and textbooks and a baggie of bread she stole from the canteen. She meant what she said to Misha: she plans not to skip any more classes and she might as well study while she waits for Nikita this weekend.

She stops on the landing when she hears the sounds of a party, and for a moment she's unsure what to do. She could go away, but what if Nikita's inside? Her hands shake as she unlocks the door. "Quiet," she whispers. "Be quiet." She takes off her boots before crossing the threshold and slips through the kitchen in socks. Only once she's latched the door to her room can she at last breathe out. She hopes that no one heard her. The latch offers little protection against the lumbering, boozy college boys; the door itself is a minor obstacle.

It's six o'clock, the room is shrouded in semi-darkness, and the light, once again, fails to work. Kat squats in the corner on the mattress, her body shaking and her stomach tightening whenever someone steps into the kitchen or stands too close to her door.

An hour later, or maybe two hours, someone raps on the door and then tugs at it. At first she thinks it's Nikita, but the voice, though male, isn't his. "Anyone there? Come party with us."

"A friend of yours?" another voice inquires.

"This dude, I haven't seen him in a while. His little brother stays here sometimes, and also this chick—"

"Yeah, right, I remember the chick. She was wild."

"She had something wrong with her, though."

"A crooked little cat caught a crooked little mouse."

"Just get another shot or two in her—"

"Drink enough and it don't matter what they look like."

"Wait till your girl hears about it."

"Yeah well, that's the thing with my girl."

They kick at the door, though halfheartedly, and when it doesn't budge, they go away.

The party goes on until three in the morning, but even after it gets quiet, Kat can't sleep. A crooked little cat, she thinks. A crooked little mouse. It didn't matter with Nikita. He never said a thing about her body; he knew what to expect. His own back was also crooked, though maybe not in the same way. Maybe for boys it's different. No one seems to care whether a boy happens to slouch. In fact, being a little slouched is kind of hip.

He made her forget she was faulty. She forgot as she rode the train to meet him. She forgot as she walked to the store. She forgot as the two of them roamed the streets of Moscow.

Now, left alone, she's forced to remember, and it's horrible, humiliating, worse than it ever felt before.

In the morning, when it's light enough to see, she picks up her things and stuffs them in her shoulder bag. Just like the night before, she tiptoes through the kitchen, hoping that everyone is still asleep. She slips outside and walks toward the subway. It's Sunday and her parents may be home, but right now it doesn't matter.

WHEN SHE sees Sveta Vlasenko in the canteen next week, her first instinct is to look away, pretend she hasn't noticed her. Sveta always seems to be there when Kat is at her lowest, as if to taunt her with her beauty, her bits of wisdom, and her teasing voice. But Sveta has spotted Kat and now she's coming toward her.

"You're busy?" she asks her.

Kat tells her that she is.

"I thought you'd like to see Nikita—"

"See him where?" Kat says. "Is he okay?"

"Relax, you lovesick child. He's in the hospital, but he's fine. It's just to keep him out of the army." Sveta explains that Nikita's been placed in a psych ward, that he might stay there a while. "What he needs is a strong diagnosis to disqualify him. Like schizophrenia, for example. It's called a white pass."

"Will it work?"

"I don't know. It might. Anyway, he said to tell you. He said you can visit if you like."

If I like? Kat is too dazed to think coherently.

"It's not a psychiatric hospital," says Sveta, mistaking Kat's pause for a sign of unease. "Look, I told him it's a bad idea. He's not the right guy for you, Kitten. He's too impulsive and unstable. Too frantic to know what he wants. I mean, I've seen the two of you together. The whole school has seen you; it's buzzing with all sorts of stupid talk. I'm sure he enjoys your company, but to him, first and foremost, you're Misha and Anechka's daughter. Not that you're not attractive, Kitten. It's just that I know his type."

Kat doesn't correct her. She bites her tongue and writes down the address and directions, the visiting hours, the number of the shuttle that goes back and forth between the hospital and the subway station.

"If you want," Sveta says, "we can go together. I'm free tonight after five o'clock."

"I'm going now," Kat says. Because, she thinks, Nikita's waiting.

THE HOSPITAL is linked to the Ministry of Civil Aviation, which means that no simple person can access a facility like this. Which, in turn, means that Nikita's parents must have connections. The evening is balmy, and some of the patients are strolling or sitting on benches. You can always tell the patients by their standard-issue stripy robes. A sad and familiar sight. Kat's been to too many hospitals lately.

A group of men in similar-styled robes are smoking on the front porch. They see Kat and smile at one another.

"Good evening, young lady," one says. Despite their advantages, they're not the crème de la crème. They are regular middle-aged family men: they nurse their hernias, gastritis; do annual stints at this hospital; go to sanatoriums for a short spell—to flirt with waitresses and have affairs with junior associates, who've also come to mend their health. They are the type that Anechka has taken up with.

The psych ward is poorly lit, very quiet. Kat slowly walks down the hall, checking each door until she finds the right one. She knocks and thinks she hears a response, a burble of embarrassed voices, a cough that seems familiar, Nikita's cough.

It's strange to see Nikita in one of these striped robes. Unshaven and dressed as a patient, he is diminished, oddly unremarkable. He's holding a guitar across his lap.

There's a girl seated beside him on the bed. She's childlike, tiny. Her feet, in ugly Keds, are dangling. She is dressed in a yellow sweater and jeans.

"What a terrific surprise," says Nikita. "Kat, you're such a good egg. I didn't expect you today. Please forgive me my shabby appearance. They don't give us smoking jackets here."

The girl next to him giggles. "Or even proper pants."

"Can you scrounge some tea for us, Zinochka?"

"I'll see what I can do," Zinochka says, and goes out into the hallway.

"Who is she?" Kat says.

"Just a friend from the institute. You'd love her, Kat— she's absolutely great. She organized a protest after they expelled me. Of course, you know, it didn't help—which brings me to *this* charming place."

"I've been waiting for you. All this time I've been at our apartment."

"It's not ours, Kat. It's not even properly mine. I'm sorry I couldn't warn you. This whole thing's been a bit of a minefield."

He won't look at her now. When he catches her stare, he blushes, rubs his unshaven cheeks.

"What's going to happen to us now?"

"Nothing," he says. "You go back home, and I stay here awhile. We've been careful, kiddo. We've been reasonably happy. But we both knew it wasn't meant to last. I told you from the start: I'm a lost man. With or without the army."

Zinochka comes back with an electric kettle, gets cups from Nikita's nightstand. It dawns on Kat that she herself has brought nothing—no fruit, or flowers, or cake—though thanks to the resourceful Zinochka they have a plate of stale oatmeal cookies. The prodigious, magical Zinochka, who knows all the nurses and who is clearly familiar with the layout of this room. She takes her place beside Nikita.

"Play something for us, Zinochka."

She takes the guitar from him. "What should I sing?"

"Oh, I don't know," he says. "Sing my favorite."

And so she does, she sings—of cuckoo clocks and storms and furious ninth waves—her voice crystalline, understated. She is older than Kat, more mature and capable, less prickly, and possibly prettier, though not in Sveta's blatant way. Her posture is effortless, excellent. Perhaps she's what Nikita needs—a confident, steadfast girl, who can guide him and keep him from going up in flames.

"Is she Jewish?" Kat will ask when Nikita calls to check on her months later. He'll say, "She doesn't need to be."

And maybe this is what it's like to love: to abnegate yourself, to give up almost willingly, to stomp on your own stupid heart. Before Kat departs, she places the apartment key under Nikita's pillow.

19

IN THE COLD WALKWAY OUTSIDE WHAT USED TO be their drama room, Kat stares at an issue of the journal *Yunost*. "Hear me out," says Serge. "I really think I've found something. Only two major characters, and best of all, it's short." It's the first time they've spoken since their fight a month ago.

"What are you talking about?"

He says, "Just read it first. It won't take you half an hour."

"Fine," she says, "I'll read it. At some point." She rolls up the journal and stuffs it in her shoulder bag.

"Come on, read it now," says Serge.

"You're kidding? Right now? What if I'm busy?"

"But you're not."

He is right, she has nowhere to go anymore. No one to see on the sly during evening walks, no secretive trips on the subway. She stays at school and follows the schedule, and then on Saturday she goes home.

"All right," she says to Serge reluctantly. "I'll read it now

MANNEQUIN GIRL 325

if you want. But don't just stand here and breathe down my neck."

She waits until he leaves, then slowly flips to the story he told her about. She doesn't expect much, but she is grinning before reaching the end of the first page. It's a good thing she sent Serge away. The story is about them: a boy, a girl, a school play. She—gawky, not entirely attractive, possessed of literary zeal. He—a small-time hoodlum with bad grades, always a step from expulsion. For the *Boris Godunov* production, she is cast as Grigory the impostor, he as Pimen the monk. She's outraged because hers is a male part; he didn't want a part at all.

Serge returns at the end of the hour. "Did you like it?" he says, and she says yes. She's thinking of the *Boris Godunov* they saw that winter at Taganka, how they argued as they plodded home from the theater, how they always seem to disagree these days.

"I'm sorry," she says, "for what I said back then."

He waves her off. "I overreacted." What he's concerned with is the play. They can rehearse and stage it before the summer break. Perform it and show the whole world that the drama club hasn't been dormant. "It's you, Kat," he says. "That girl. She's your character."

"But Serge, I don't want it," she says. She's been exhausted lately, gutted. She can barely muster the energy to speak in class.

"No," he insists. "Don't decide anything yet. Just wait and, you know, think about it."

"But it's too late," she tells him, in a tired voice. "I know you want to help Misha, but he's broken down, just like me. He'll never agree—"

"Maybe he will."

"Why are you being so stubborn?"

"Because of you," he says. "Because last year you were all about acting. You shouldn't have to sacrifice your dreams."

"Oh, dreams!" She lifts her hands up to the sky, in the manner of a tragic character. "I am a seagull—no—no, I am an actress."

He stops her. "Maybe to you it's a joke, but not to me. Let me prove it to you. Come with me to Kratovo on Sunday."

How perfectly simple and clean is his world, with its noble pursuits and boundless belief in people's goodness. But people are not like that at all. They are slippery, fallible, fickle—even if they say all the right words. Words that are peanut shells. Words that are tinsel. What's worse is that they don't even see it: they continue to think themselves self-less and virtuous, above all commonplace concerns, and just as you convince yourself you're one of them, they chuck you out like a broken toy.

THE FACT that Kat came home wasn't treated as anything remarkable. No one hugged her, or scolded her, or said I told you so. Maybe her parents knew what had happened with Nikita. Maybe they thought it was inevitable. She was grateful for their tact, if that's what it was.

Now she comes home from school on Saturday, and Misha, and sometimes even Anechka, are there. Anechka works, and Misha cleans and does the laundry. Sometimes they make supper together, sometimes they watch TV, and on those nights it's easy to believe that things are returning to normal.

But the very next morning Anechka might be gone, and there are some weekends when she doesn't appear at all and Misha just acts like it's par for the course. He sits on the edge of Kat's bed in the evening and reads to her chapters from *Anna Karenina*—those proverbial unhappy families—as if attempting to persuade himself that what Anechka has done is understandable and natural and maybe not his fault.

Kat is also thinking about *Anna Karenina*.

"You think I'm ruined now? Tainted?"

Misha tucks in the edge of Kat's blanket. "We're human beings, Button. We botch things a lot. But in the end we bounce back, get better."

Kat doesn't feel better. She gets panicky whenever she's not at home or at school. She keeps seeing those college boys from the Barricades apartment, in the back of a bus or in line at a grocery. She knows it can't be them: they don't belong in her neighborhood; they wouldn't know how to find her. But she can't shake the sensation that they're following her. One time she thinks she sees Nikita outside the subway.

She still has no plans for after graduation, and maybe— just maybe—she doesn't have to graduate. She could stay at their current school for ninth and tenth grade. She asks Misha what he thinks of this, but he tells her the school is scaling back the top two grades. Most of the students are done with their treatments by then, so it's best to let them go—in the interest of savings. It takes a lot of money to keep and feed these students, not to mention to pay extra staff. Next year they might be down to just two classes.

In the past Misha could have simply asked the principal and the headmistress, and Kat would have been guaranteed a spot. They wouldn't say no to a faculty member. But now his own standing is precarious, and it's likely his contract will be dropped. And Kat herself is not the model pupil she once was, what with the talk that still abounds about her. Still, Misha tells her, he'll give it a shot. But she must help him in return.

"Sure," she says, "but how?" and she has a bad feeling even before she hears his answer.

WHEN KAT enters his classroom on Monday afternoon, the first person she sees is Serge. Misha comes in minutes later. He is chipper and confident, sashaying down the central aisle, a stack of typed sheets under his arm. He hands a few pages to Kat. "Read these aloud, will you?"

"What's this?" she says, thumbing through the pages, though one glance is enough. It is the story Serge discovered.

"I don't think it's a good idea," she begins, but already, almost despite herself, she's rising. As if driven by force of habit, she walks to the front of the class.

"My ineptness had become evident by the time I turned thirteen," she starts, and she wants to cry it's so true—her ineptness, her poor choices, her bad posture. She reads all the way through the opening soliloquy, and when it's over she stops and waits for someone else to speak.

"Here's what we'll do," says Misha. "Kat will play the girl, Serge will play the boy, and I'll ask Sveta Vlasenko to play the teacher."

Now it's Serge's turn to argue. "I'm not stage material."

"Learn your lines," Misha tells him. "We'll be starting rehearsals next week."

"Don't you want me to, you know, audition first?"

Misha pretends he doesn't hear him.

"I guess if you don't need me anymore—"

"Serge," Misha calls, when he is almost at the door. "I meant to say, thank you."

"No problem, Mikhail Aronovich. I hope I wasn't butting in too much."

"On the contrary, my friend. On the contrary."

"What's this about?" Kat asks Misha, when they're left in the classroom alone. She's still confused: A play? A role? She stares at the pages. "When did you turn this thing into a script?"

"I didn't. Your partner in crime did it all. Your grandfather helped him a little, but mostly it's Serge's handiwork. I must say, he surprised me this morning. Really gave me a piece of his mind, said that I'd never encouraged you and never given you a chance—"

"Serge has no business getting in the middle of this. I don't need anyone's encouragements."

Misha continues, "I daresay he's right. He said you used

to dream of becoming an actress. How could I have missed this fact?"

"It wasn't serious," Kat says. "It was a phase."

"And now look at you, so dispirited. No wonder you're afraid to leave this school."

Damn Serge, Kat thinks. She could kill him. "Does he think he's my savior? Does he think it's his mission in life? To rescue old men and poor maidens?"

"Old men." Misha smiles. "I think that's true. That's what he does, our Serge, our guardian angel."

REHEARSALS ARE EASY, surprisingly easy. It must be because Kat and Serge play themselves. At the start their characters are hostile, in the typical way of all dutiful schoolgirls and hooligan schoolboys. Then, halfway through the script, the two begin to change—Serge's character especially. He becomes obsessed with his role as a monk, with *Boris Godunov*, with history and theater in general.

Only the final scene gives them trouble. According to the story, fifteen years have passed. Kat's character and Serge's character are now adults. She is a journalist. He is an innovative theater director. They meet by accident and reminisce about their wayward high school past, and only at the very end, as Kat's character is boarding her bus, does he tell her that he was in love with her.

Around this point, they both clam up and can't evoke the proper feeling. To make them less self-conscious, Misha suggests they tweak the lines. "Didn't you know," says Serge's character, "that you . . . that I . . . You were the reason I agreed to play the part." And Kat's character says, "Why didn't you say so?"—but it's too late, the doors are closing, the bus is carrying her away into her separate and settled life.

Jules often comes to sit in on rehearsals. She says it's because she's got nothing else to do. Asked if she likes the play, she says it's cute. "You know, you and Serge. It's touching, almost."

For once, Kat and Serge get along—both during and outside of rehearsals. It would be a total, flawless harmony if only he'd stop pestering her about theater school. Or rather: Secondary School No. 25, with its in-depth study of the aesthetically–artistic disciplines. It is located on Kislovsky Lane, a stone's throw from Pushkin Square. Auditions are on June 10. Candidates must prepare a poem, a song, a dramatic monologue, and a fable. Kat learns this from the three typewritten pages Serge managed to unpin from the front office of the school. "One of these days you'll get busted," she tells him.

Talk of theater school gives Kat heart palpitations. She tells Serge that she's thinking of staying at their current school.

"Stupid," he says.

"Why not?" she says. "You're staying."

"I need to. I have no other choice."

"Maybe I need to too? Maybe I'm not ready yet—"

"You're ready," he says. "You're just scared. Which means

you have to get over yourself. To stay here would be a waste, and you can't waste your talent."

"What talent?" she asks him, though she knows what he'll say. "I've never been that good at acting, or, for that matter, at anything else. I'm just average and that's okay. Because somebody's got to be average."

20

S ERGE IS RUNNING. IT'S STRANGE, BECAUSE SHE hardly ever sees him running. He can be fast, even elusive, moving in easy, catlike steps—but never in this obvious and clumsy way. It's when he runs that you really notice how badly deformed his body is, how deeply he's damaged.

At first she doesn't see him. She's in the canteen with the rest of their class, idling through a meager lunch, and she only looks up when Jules prods her. Still, she's not alarmed, only surprised.

He stands across from her, tries to control his wheezing. It's not much of a secret anymore that he and she are close. Enough people have spotted them together or heard he's doing something with the drama club, and they all know about last year's tutoring. Despite that, he and Kat keep their distance in public, or at the very least try. Yet here he is in front of her, winded and gasping, the rows of witnesses be damned.

"What is it?" she whispers. There's something in his face

that sends chills down her spine. Jules must also feel it, because she clasps Kat's hand.

He tries to speak, though he's still gulping air, and somehow Kat already knows that it's going to be a name. Not Anechka, she thinks. Not Misha, please. She watches his lips, as if in slow motion, attempt to form a word.

And then he says it: "Valentina."

IN THE initial seconds she finds the word meaningless. A collection of sounds, of disparate notes. Four syllables that somehow add up to "Va-len-ti-na." Moments later come the smell of lavender, the summer dress with flowers, the linen jacket with a bright red pin, the afternoon she took Kat to the Children's Railroad in Kratovo. A person: Valentina. Her basket, her apron, her wink. A stub of carrot lipstick on the bathroom vanity.

They're walking dimly to the bus stop, Serge guiding Kat like she's a wayward sheep.

"Where are we going?"

"Home," he tells her.

She hasn't yet asked him how it happened. He tells her while they're waiting for the bus: Valentina and Roshdal were out, not far from their house, taking the puppy for a walk. At first, Roshdal thought Valentina must have stumbled. He tried to support her, to keep her upright; but her weight, the way he felt it, was that of an unconscious person. She never recovered, never came to, left no parting smile or words. The doctor said it was either an aneurysm or a stroke. A quiet, near-instant death. "We all should be so lucky."

Later Kat will wonder how Serge managed to learn so much, though by then it won't really matter. He takes her up to her apartment and then immediately goes back to school. Kat's parents and Roshdal are home, and it's total chaos. The phone rings constantly. Both Anechka and Misha pace. They start doing one thing—try to locate a certain document, for instance—only to drop it halfway through, become absorbed in something else.

Only Roshdal stays motionless. When not on the phone, he sits slumped in a chair, his expression embarrassed, perplexed.

"I'm sorry," Kat says, and hugs him tenderly.

He smiles at her, a crooked, shaky smile. "Thank you, my pet. Such a misfortune. We'd just been having breakfast. And then ten minutes later she was no more. My mind refuses to accept it."

The phone rings again, and he says, "Darling, can you get it?"

Most of the phone calls are from relatives, relatives Kat hardly knows or hasn't met. A few of Valentina's female friends call, and also, some of the Roshdals' neighbors.

By suppertime they are exhausted. They turn off the ringer and drink to Valentina's poor soul. "How could she go so quickly?" wonders Roshdal. "No pain, not even dizziness."

"The death of the virtuous," says Misha.

Anechka stares at her fork. All day she's had this blunt, determined look as she went about her business. Making tea, or answering the phone, or covering the mirrors with blankets. She went through their family albums and found a photo of Valentina that Roshdal always liked. Later she puts it in a black frame.

After supper she makes a bed for Roshdal and gives him some pills from her stash. The two of them talk quietly in Kat's room.

Kat awakes on a folding bed in the thick of the night. Something's woken her up—a disturbance, a sound. She peers at her parents' sofa, but can't see a thing in the dark. The springs of the folding bed whine as she sits up. And then she hears it again, the noise of running water in the bathroom. On tiptoe she crosses the hallway. She leans her head against the bathroom door and listens to the water gushing down, and underneath it, hard and brutal sobs, the sound of Anechka crying.

ON THE day of the funeral, Kat keeps smelling lavender. It's with her in the morning; it follows her on the subway, on the bus that she, Serge, and Misha take to Vostryakovo cemetery, while Anechka and Roshdal arrive in a cab. It's there in the narrow, muddy, barely passable pathways.

A lot of people turn up for the funeral—Roshdal's old colleagues, Valentina's friends, a slew of distant relatives. Jules comes with flowers like everybody else. Anechka holds Valentina's photo, and Roshdal a small pillow with Valentina's medals from the war. His hand shakes as he leans upon his cane.

Kat stands a few feet away from them. Jules whispers that she has to leave early, to get to her weekly English tutoring; she won't be joining them for the funeral repast. But Serge won't step away from Kat. He's there by her side when the coffin is lowered and Roshdal drops the first handful of dirt and when, despite his most valiant efforts, his face contorts and he starts weeping.

They all come back to the apartment. The table is already set. There's an empty place setting reserved for Valentina: a glass of water and a slice of bread. The mourners talk about her.

"It's the flyers that killed her," says Roshdal. "The rumors, the threats. And like a dumb old fool, I told her not to worry."

Anechka nudges him gently. "What else could you do?"

"I should have taken her to Israel. She'd have lived to be a hundred years old."

"She was fragile," says Gayanoush, the friend who escaped the Sumgait pogroms. "On the surface she seemed strong, always busy, always tending to everyone else. But underneath it, she was frayed. She never completely healed after that war wound."

Kat never knew Valentina was wounded, or that, as Gayanoush now mentions, she couldn't have children of her own. "She wanted a family so much," says Gayanoush. "Her first husband, they only lived together for one year before he passed away. You know, he was our captain. After that, she just assumed she'd be alone forever. A girl like our Valechka, imagine that!"

Still, Gayanoush says, it was years before Valentina met Roshdal. "How happy she was after she married him, how proud of Anechka's successes, and then once Kat was born it's all she'd talk about anymore. She finally had it, her family."

Anechka leans her head on Roshdal's shoulder. She has been doing things like this for days: staying close to him at all times, patting his hand, kissing his cheek, clutching his arm, hugging him at random moments. For hours she sits next to his chair, searching for something to say. A light-hearted anecdote? A half-forgotten memory? She is his daughter; she should know how to comfort him. But she doesn't, apparently. She is tense and tongue-tied. She has him to herself at last, but now it means nothing. The years of hostilities have strangled something tenuous between them, the ease they used to share, the necessary trust. He now seems distracted in her presence.

Around ten the guests start to disperse, though for a long time they linger in the hallway, holding and kissing one another and promising to stay in touch.

"How will you manage?" Gayanoush asks Roshdal. "You can't live there in the country all alone, in that enormous house." She has already offered to adopt the puppy, but Roshdal said he'd like to keep it.

"Serge will stay with me for the summer, as soon as he's

done with his exams. And maybe Kat will come from time to time to keep us old goats company."

Unlike Kat, Serge never stopped visiting. He's been coming to Kratovo every weekend. He saw Valentina last Sunday. Kat still pictures their last visit together, the way Valentina kept fidgeting and fretting, how she begged them to come back. Back then Kat didn't think her visits really mattered. Even now it seems she wasn't that important there, not in the way Serge and Jules were. She'll never know whether Valentina forgave her.

THE GUESTS have left. Roshdal has gone to bed. Misha has gone to check on Zoya Moiseevna—though Kat wishes he'd waited until the next day. She and Anechka are in the kitchen. Kat's doing the dishes while Anechka sits on the cool linoleum, her back against the fridge.

"Just you and me. It's been a while, baby."

"How are you holding up?" Kat says.

Anechka shakes her head. "All this time I thought I hated her, but now it's like I'm orphaned once again. I was sixteen when I first met her, not that much older than you. I can't believe I'll never see her again. I keep thinking it's not really happening: it's not she who's dead, it's someone else, and she's just stepped out for a second to check on a roast or a cake."

"I keep smelling lavender," Kat says.

"Her lotion. That's because I've put it on."

"Oh, that explains it. I thought I was going crazy."

They both laugh, in a demented sort of way. Kat stashes the last plate in the cupboard.

Anechka stretches. "God, it's really been forever."

"Have you come back for good?" Kat asks.

"Oh baby, it's not so easy. Me and your dad, we were kids when we first got together—"

"I've seen you," Kat interrupts. "With that man in the car. Outside the lyceum. I came because I had to speak to you, it's not like I was snooping—"

"How could you?" Anechka bursts out; then, catching herself and settling down, she adds, "I'm sure you were confused."

"I know what you look like, Mom."

They turn away, both trying to occupy themselves with dumb minutiae, Kat wiping the counters, Anechka rooting for a smoke.

"Who is he?"

"Please, Kat, not now! He's just someone. A man, okay? A normal man. Not a villain or anything. When you're eighteen you think you know everything. You fall in love and think that it's forever. Then it's ten years later, and you have both completely changed, and when you look at your husband you can't even remember what it was you liked about him. He nags you and you snap at him, and you don't get each other at all, and when he speaks you feel like you're being strangled."

She stops, and Kat, too, remains silent. Her mother and father. Her self-absorbed, beautiful rebels. Her Orpheus and Eurydice. Marie and Pierre Curie.

"Does it mean you don't love him?"

"I don't know what it means. I just knew that I'd die if I stayed here."

Kat says, "But what about me?"

"You have nothing to do with this, baby. None of it is your fault."

"What do you think of me?" Kat asks her. She's asked Misha before, many times—it's almost like a running joke between them—and yet she has never dared to ask Anechka, guessing that at best she'd be dismissed. Do you love me or hate me? Am I clever or dull? Am I ugly and are you ashamed of me?

"You're a bit like me, and a bit like your father. It's when I look at you, Kat, that I remember what the two of us used to be like. And that's the hardest part, baby, that guilt, and knowing how much we've squandered. It makes me want to throw myself under a car. But I can't go back, you understand? Because whatever life we used to have, it's over now."

"What if you change your mind?" Kat tries. She sits on the floor next to Anechka, and Anechka hugs her and cries into her hair.

ANECHKA SAYS she'll come. The new play will have only one performance, on the last day of school, May 25. It's just one act and calls for a simple set and costumes: two cassocks, two desks, a bench, a book, a crutch. It's nothing like their old, lavish productions, though they've padded it with a montage, a few earnest poems and heartwarming songs on the topic of "our dear school."

Kat is dreading the day of the performance. Each time at rehearsal she forces herself to emote, while underneath she feels nothing. It's bad enough that the school is full of gossip; now she'll have to stand before them all, unguarded, exposed to their derision. What she wants is to blend in and disappear, come down with something awful that would keep her home for weeks. "I don't think I can do it," she tells Jules. "I don't want anyone to look at me."

The two of them sit amidst flowerbeds, at the most central point of the campus. It's May 24, and the play is tomorrow. But today is the school's anniversary, the day when former students come back. They start arriving shortly after nap time, a stream of dressed-up girls, some elegant and staggeringly healthy, others stumpy or hobbling or visibly misshapen. Kat's been to enough of these reunions to know how the conversations go. The teachers will ask them how they're faring, and the girls will talk about their families or jobs and say that their backs often hurt and they wish they'd kept up with their therapy. Still, each one carries herself with a certain sense of boldness, and each one has a story to tell—a child or two, a marriage that's thriving or collapsing, a flourishing career, ailing parents who need help. Even the youngest of the lot, the ones who are still in high school, seem to be living full and busy lives.

"A year from now this could be us," Jules says.

Kat says, "I think I might be staying." She's been afraid to tell her, afraid of how Jules will react, though now it seems she's heard the news already.

"I know you think it's stupid," she hurries to add, "but honestly, Jules, I'll be all right. Plus I'll have Serge to keep me company."

"Provided he's here next year."

"Where else would he go?" Kat asks.

Jules stares off into the distance. "He's going in for surgery next year. He and your dad made a deal."

"A deal," Kat repeats.

Jules says, "It's simple, really. Serge agrees to surgery if Misha agrees to do the play."

"But why—" Kat begins.

"Oh please. Don't pretend you don't get it. It's exactly the sort of thing he'd do. He's totally besotted with your family. With you, in particular. Don't look so shocked—it couldn't be clearer. Besides, it's not a bad thing. Your dad might actually keep his job, and the surgery, well, you know how much Serge needs it."

"But what about complications?" Kat's thinking of infections, damaged nerves, the horrible months of recovery, the pain that has flattened the gaggle and sapped their very souls. And Serge? He will have no one to see him through this agony.

"Just do the goddamn play," Jules says.

"Are you upset?"

Jules turns away, says she's got something in her eye and that she needs a minute. The unflappable, sensible Jules, who once swore she'd never show her feelings, is wiping her face with the cuff of her sleeve. "You two," she says. "Such idiots."

FOR HER first scene Kat is dressed like a regular schoolgirl, in a brown dress and matching pinafore, not unlike the ones her parents purchased for her almost nine years ago. The uniforms have changed for high school girls, so this is Kat's last chance to look like she once was supposed to. White ribbons, white knee socks, white lacy collar. Her hair in two braids.

It's just minutes before the performance, and she is sitting out on the landing, hunched over, her head between her knees.

"Got the jitters?" Serge asks when he comes outside and finds her there.

She says she's just feeling light-headed, that's all.

He sits on the step above her, and she sees that he's also nervous. He's breathing with effort and shivering. "I shouldn't be on stage," he says. "I mean, look at me, Kat. I'm a freaking hunchback. I should be playing Quasimodo. Rigoletto. A court jester maybe, or someone out of Dickens, some poor deformed little chap."

She can't believe what he's saying. A troubled, broken boy, a barely-scraping-by student who last year almost got expelled, he's about to star in a new play, the play he himself has adapted from a story. How can he doubt this triumph, this almost inconceivable success?

She says, "It doesn't matter what you look like. That's the whole thing with acting: you can convince the audience of anything. That you're short or tall, a child, or even a woman. I know you can do it, Serge. I've seen you in rehearsals. We go up there and make all those jerks shut up."

"What if they laugh?"

"They better laugh. It's mostly comedy."

"I'm scared," he tells her.

Kat says, "I know. Me too."

She grips his hand, and that's how they enter the assembly hall, both petrified with stage fright, yet soothed and even bolstered by the knowledge that they're doing this out of gratitude and love, and that they are together, if only for a short time.

THE ASSEMBLY HALL is packed. All the students and teachers are there, plus some matrons, a few doctors, and other members of the staff. Misha sits in the third row, and next to him is Anechka, who has returned to the school for the first time. He is hopeful, boyish, clean-shaven, his hair neatly cut, and it's tempting to think that not all is lost between them, that he might win her over somehow, that they might reinvent themselves, become lovers, or outlaws, or champions of the disadvantaged.

And then the lights are switched and Kat forgets about them. She steps onto the stage for her soliloquy and waits for Serge to join her there—her charge, her former nemesis, her friend. She marvels at him as they go through their paces. Her own part is paltry in comparison. Her job is simply to embody her character's misguided hopes and flagging self-esteem, while he must totally transform himself—from a lackluster, troubled student to an undiscovered genius.

He does. And when it's over, the play gets a standing ovation.

Professor Fabri makes his way to the stage. He presents Kat with a bunch of roses and gives her a kiss on the cheek. "Our mannequin girl," he calls her, "if ever there was one." His hands smell of the same good soap as they did nine years ago.

Her parents come over. Anechka says, "You were great." And Misha hugs both Kat and Serge and says, "You've really taught me something, you devils."

Jules rushes toward them calling, "Thespians!" She is happy because it's the last day of school. The future is now. The future is theirs. Tomorrow she's throwing a party and she says that she'll kill them if they dare to not show up.

A handful of teachers hover around Serge, saying how good he was, how proud he's made them. They say that they believed in his abilities. They knew that he had it in him. In this flurry of praise Serge's face stays strangely unresponsive. He answers them in grunts and monosyllables, marking time in an ungainly way, and slinks outside at the first opportunity.

Kat means to go look for him, but the assembly hall has almost emptied and then her parents ask her to stay behind.

"You did good," Anechka says.

"Better than good," Misha adds. "Serge told me about

theater school. Your mom and I had a chance to discuss it, and we think you should try for it, even though it might be a long shot."

"Based on what we've seen today, you've got the potential," says Anechka.

"Yes, and your mom can help you practice for the audition. She's almost a professional, your mom."

"And if you don't get in, you'll come to my lyceum."

It suddenly looks so easy. They're giving her a road map, a plan. Here it is, they seem to be saying. Here's everything you ever wanted: our faith in you, our love. All yours for the taking. They haven't given up on her. No, just the opposite. They want her to go out and shine. A mannequin girl, said Professor Fabri. So brilliant. So exceptional.

Except, Kat knows, it won't happen. Because being exceptional is nothing but a trap. It makes you obsessed with your own significance, and also, it riddles you with doubt. You do harsh things when you believe yourself one of a kind. You push away those who love you and sneer at those you deem not good enough. She's seen it up close. She's done it herself all her life—believing that she had some sort of promise.

She's had a chance to think about her future—she lay awake all night—and now she tells Anechka and Misha exactly what she has in mind. She'll go to a local school, one where nobody knows her. She'll start alone, from scratch, with nobody to please and nobody's path to follow. She'll have to discover what she's good at and what it is she likes. Math, geography, history—who knows? She'll read a lot and study hard, and try to be a kinder person—

"But they're so pedestrian," Anechka blurts out, meaning the local schools around where they live.

Kat doesn't tell her that she doesn't mind pedestrian, that pedestrian is what she needs right now, that she herself, she knows, is only a regular schoolgirl but that doesn't upset her in the least. She has no more wish to stand out, to be either a mannequin girl or a freak. She wants to be normal, unnoticeable, average.

She doesn't explain this to Anechka, though—because Anechka would never understand. Instead she says, "I'll make it work somehow."

"I think you're being rash," says Anechka, still disappointed by Kat's choice.

But Misha, who gets it, says, "No. She's being rational."

FROM THE window of Misha's classroom, Kat looks at her parents. The two of them stand in the yard, having a silent conversation there, and for a while it seems like they're okay. They might be discussing what's for supper or who's getting the groceries today, except they stand facing each other and there's an awkward space between them. Now Misha is speaking and Anechka is listening, adjusting the strap of her bag. Kat wills for him to reach for her, take her hand, touch her shoulder, lean in and brush away her hair— anything that would erase that space. But he doesn't. He keeps it. He says something else and Anechka nods in agreement, and you can see from the way she's gathering herself that she's about to turn away from Misha. One moment and he's missed it, because now she's leaving and he, in turn, sits down on the steps.

"You can't change them," says Serge, and Kat says no, she can't.

"Come on," he says. "I'll walk you out."

"I know about the surgery," she tells him as they stroll through the campus.

"Yeah, well, it's just something."

She says, "It's going to help."

"A grave is what cures the cripple. But sure, I'll get to miss some school. Next year will be rotten without you or Jules or Misha."

"Maybe Misha will stay?"

"Nope," Serge says, "he won't. So you better keep in touch and visit."

For a moment it seems they are back in their play, in the farewell scene at the bus stop, and she's afraid of what he's going to say.

"You're the best guy I know," she tells him preemptively.

He says, "I get it. No sweat." He takes her hand and looks at it, as though he might tell her fortune. "I just don't want to lose you."

"You won't ever lose me," she says.

They are walking again, holding hands for the second time today. Beside the elementary school block, a group of first graders are playing. "Bride and groom," someone is chanting, though not about them. On the last day of school everything is allowed. The girls are playing hopscotch, tag, elastics. They are restricted to the small paved square where they do morning calisthenics, the rough empty lot at the back of the block, and the short distance to the entrance gates. Not that it troubles them. Today everything is allowed—as long as they remain within these gates.

Serge stops and says, "It's time," and Kat lets go, reluctantly, though she knows he will stay and watch her take these final steps. "I'll see you," she says.

Alone she turns and walks toward the outside.

ACKNOWLEDGMENTS

I WOULD LIKE TO THANK everyone at W. W. Norton, especially my editor, Jill Bialosky. My deepest gratitude to my agent, David McCormick, who helped every step of the way.

I am grateful to the Rona Jaffe Foundation for their recognition and generous support.

A special thank you to my colleagues in the English Department at the University of Connecticut for their support and encouragement and, most of all, to my friend and mentor, V. Penelope Pelizzon. Thank you to Darcie Dennigan. Thank you to Suzy Staubach and the UConn Co-op Bookstore.

Thank you to Thomas Yagoda and *Dossier* journal for publishing a short story adapted from an earlier draft of this novel.

Thank you to my wonderful writers group: Rebecca Morgan Frank, Jane Roper, Jessica Murphy Moo, and Jami Brandli.

Even though we rarely see one another in person these days, you remain my most trusted readers and I am grateful for your wisdom and help.

Thank you to the Vertefeuille family, and especially to Laurie and Steve Vertefeuille and Samantha Huhn, for your friendship, love, and all the tremendous help and care. We'd be lost without you.

Thank you to my family. And most of all, thank you to my husband, Ian Fraser, for always believing in me. I am so lucky to have you in my life.